Praise for

MW00640113

"*The North Woods* is both a ~~terrify~~ ~~g~~ heartfelt story about coming home from war... Hoover throws his nat in the ring with that other Maine horror author, and not only holds his own, but brings something entirely new to the genre. This story made me feel like I would gladly face eldritch horrors in the Maine woods if it meant I could go on one more patrol with the boys."

–Kacy Tellessen, Eugene Sledge Award winning author of
Freaks of a Feather: A Marine Grunt's Memoir

"*The North Woods* reads like a Stephen King novel that went to war. Hoover writes with the infantryman's sardonic wit — a mixture of wisdom and dark humor only found in fighting holes and smoke pits."

–Mac Caltrider, journalist for *Coffee or Die Magazine*
and founder of *Pipes & Pages*

"It's a book that has made me feel fear unlike anything I've read since I read *Cujo* at 8 years old. It captures every aspect of classic horror that we all fell in love with while still bringing the sweet breath of fresh air that is originality. The beginning half will leave you guessing if it's reality or supernatural 'til it is just bluntly shoved down your throat in a terrifying heap. This is by design; there are no accidents... I have no doubt in my mind that this novel will one day be considered a classic and talked about in niche circles about the author's early days and his style. Don't miss the train. Go walk into *The North Woods*."

–William Bolyard, author of *Sober Man's Thoughts*

"Who are we when stripped of the armor of our self belief? What happens when a man must look into his own eyes and confront the stark truths within? Heroes are born of confronting the reality of their human frailty; of walking into night dark caves to be measured against the monsters within. In entering Douglass Hoover's *The North Woods* three flawed warriors, men far beyond their prime, are forced to face that reality. It's a horror story far more familiar than many of us wish to acknowledge, and one with which we must all reckon."

–Russell Worth Parker,
LtCol, USMC (Ret)

"[Hoover] yet again flawlessly weaves a dark and thrilling character-driven adventure with suspenseful and mythic elements woven throughout... I love this book, it is at once an exciting character-driven horror novel and a deep conversation about life, evil, and redemption. And perhaps more importantly than anything, it's a window into the very real struggles of combat veterans even after they come home."

–Christopher Packard, author of
Mythical Creatures of Maine

"It kept me up all night and haunted my dreams for many after. This isn't your typical horror story of incompetent characters that leaves you shouting at the page. It's the story of apex predators backed into a dark corner and forced to fight their way out. Be careful diving into these pages, especially if you frequent the woods."

–Joseph Donnelly

The NORTH WOODS

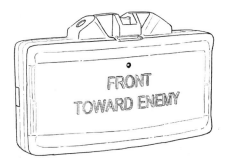

FRONT
TOWARD ENEMY

Douglass Hoover

www.strippeddogforge.com

Published by
BlackPit Publishing
www.blackpitpublishing.com

Copyright © 2023 Douglass Hoover
All rights reserved

ISBN 978-0-9994074-2-4

Printed in the USA

www.strippeddogforge.com

For all those still fighting the good fight.

"Droll thing life is — that mysterious arrangement of merciless logic for a futile purpose. The most you can hope from it is some knowledge of yourself — that comes too late — a crop of inextinguishable regrets."

– Joseph Conrad, *Heart of Darkness*

Prologue

IT WAS their third week in country when Bauer got hit.

The IED was small — a simple yellow jug of ammonium nitrate buried on the side of some nameless Afghan road. It did little more than take off the MRAP's front wheel, barely damaging the tan steel of the up-armored beast and giving the boys inside a good, hard, brain-jiggling shake.

Bauer joked about the event afterward. He put on like it was hilarious — the thought of a pair of dirty, man-dress wearing scoundrels scurrying through the night, risking life and limb and aerial bombardment to emplace a bomb that would end up hardly fazing him. For weeks he went on about luck and invincibility, and how the next one *might* go so far as to take off a windshield wiper. After those jokes got old, he turned to sewing long tales during midnight posts of his father's narrow escapes in Vietnam. He would fill the hooch with booming proclamations of God's love of the Bauer men, how the Lord was preserving his physical form so that he might return home and breed with all of his hapless squad mates' sisters and mothers. It was fun at the time, and it gave his fellow Marines some small ounce of levity in their otherwise bleak existence.

It wasn't until Wyatt looked back, years later, that he saw the jokes for the coping mechanism that they were.

Bauer was absolutely terrified.

A brush with death can do strange things to a man. None of those boys were new to the game at that point. Most already had at least one combat tour under their belt. They'd all seen the twisted wreckages of armored vehicles, torn to sharp metal ribbons by bombs just a hair meaner than the one that had struck Bauer's truck. They'd seen the hunks of flesh and bone and sinew tossed haphazardly over a fifty-meter spread. Burnt, tattooed skin and torn red muscle caked in a fine film of moondust. Bauer knew as well as any of them that the only thing that stood between him and death that day had been sheer luck. He knew that if one miniscule factor had been different, his friends might have been able to scoop what was left of him into a Ziplock bag.

So, he'd joke about his God-given armor, and they'd laugh with him because they all found it so damn funny. All of them except Bauer.

Thirteen weeks after the IED hit his truck, Bauer died of a brain aneurysm.

He and Wyatt were sitting together in the smoke pit, musing over half-fictitious stories of the girls they'd been with back home. Bauer was midway through a crass word when his voice just cut off. There was no buildup, no dramatic flair or memorable last words. Hell, Wyatt wasn't even looking at him when it happened. Later, Wyatt would only remember staring off at the ugly Hesco walls that bordered the remote patrol base as he heard the all-too-heavy *thump* — Bauer's lifeless corpse impacting the dirt at his feet.

They found out later that Bauer's death was listed as natural causes. Their command, whose concern seemed to center more around statistics than reality, had been adamant about that. It looked better for them than admitting that the burst blood vessel in his brain was likely a result of the suddenly-not-so-funny IED. Given, it was a small IED, yet apparently it had been *just* powerful enough to violently damage a young man's brain and end his life only sixteen days out from his twenty-first birthday.

There was no awarding of a Purple Heart, no name scrolled across the bottom of the evening news, no placard at the battalion office. While Bauer was honored upon their return to the states, there was a painfully deliberate lack of the phrase *Killed In Action* when his name was referenced by those of significant rank. For them, he was just a case of bad luck. A poor kid from West Virginia who must have smoked one too many cigarettes and had a genetic predisposition for falling over dead on a Tuesday.

To Wyatt and the squad of men who'd actually fought beside Bauer, it was different. To them his death meant something; he *was* a casualty of war, even if the Lieutenant Colonels and Sergeant Majors refused to acknowledge it. His brothers knew the truth, and furthermore, they knew it was their duty to honor that truth — to honor him.

Thus, they made the solemn commitment that every year on the anniversary of Bauer's death, the remaining squad of thirteen would gather at the small hilltop cemetery in rural West Virginia to pay tribute to their lost brother.

On the first anniversary, they all showed. Some, Wyatt included, were freshly released from their military bonds, while the rest took what little leave they had to make the journey. Over the course of the next year, they lost Johnson to a motorcycle accident, and Costello shot himself on a beach in Jersey. Mortimer and Gonzales both had kids, and Hill found out he had a rare form of lung cancer. They all kept in touch though, and they were all there for each funeral, including Hill's.

On the second anniversary of Bauer's death, the ten who remained made their appearance in front of that humble granite gravestone on a cool morning in early October. By then, all but one of them had finished out their contracts with Uncle Sam. They were free men, for what it was worth. The only man still living under the stern thumb of the military was Crossman, their squad leader. A strange young man who seemed destined to live out his life with a rank on his sleeve.

By the third anniversary of Bauer's death, only six men showed. They'd lost another to suicide, and the rest had moved on across the country or simply lost touch. They'd all taken their own routes, spread out further and further from that violent shared experience that was their time in Afghanistan.

By the fourth anniversary of Bauer's death, four men showed up at his grave. Wyatt was again one of them. Thomas "Siggy" Sigmund, who Wyatt once considered to be his best friend, was another. There was their oversized Corpsman, Fred Chapman, a grizzly of a Navy medic who they all loved and still simply called "Doc." Then there was Crossman.

That was the first time Wyatt noticed that Siggy was faltering. Despite their closeness back in the day, they hadn't been the best about keeping in touch. Siggy looked a week behind on sleep, and the aura of spastic energy that normally animated him seemed to have died to a dull murmur. Still, he insisted everything was fine. It was just a bad week was all. Wyatt and the others chose to believe him, probably because it was easier.

The next year, Siggy had track marks and thin arms. Crossman was deployed. As always, Doc was there — plumper and with less hair on his head and more on his face, and just as much a jolly giant as ever. Doc and Wyatt tried to talk to Siggy. They tried to intervene and help in what ways they could, but he would just laugh and make excuses, and at one point he disappeared to have a cigarette and simply didn't come back. Wyatt and Doc committed to do better, but as always, life got in the way.

That was the year Wyatt finally finished his master's degree. He'd been burning through school at a breakneck pace, obsessively consuming his GI Bill and doing whatever he could to keep the momentum high. It was always the quiet lulls that got him into trouble back then, so he kept busy.

After graduating, he was offered a job at a small research school in a sleepy town in New Hampshire, and he took it. That October, there was a three-day conference he was expected to attend in Seattle, the final day of which fell on Bauer's death anniversary. He meant to leave early, to catch a redeye and meet with the boys atop that sad knoll, but he met a woman at the conference who managed to convince him to stay. Maybe he truly thought they had something, though they never talked again after their three-day romance concluded. In hindsight, he suspected his passion at the time was little more than an excuse to avoid something that he had grown to dread.

He felt guilty missing that year.

Less so the next.

After that, he just drifted further away from those long lost memories of youthful violence. The fact was that he had begun to feel that he had moved on. That he had done the impossible and actually digested all of that chaos and horror and confusion and scaly dried blood that had been festering deep in his belly for so long. That he had made enough forward progress and put enough life between himself and those sprawling poppy fields that his soul had finally been cleansed of the grimy black diesel-and-shit soot of war.

Obviously, this wasn't true. All of that was still inside him, smoldering and rotting beneath an ever-increasing avalanche of academia, barbells, expensive whiskey, and cheap dates. But as long as Wyatt couldn't see it, it couldn't hurt him. He could move on. He could forget.

And he did forget. Mostly.

However, if there was one thing in the world that threatened to unearth that stagnant pool of burning bile buried deep inside, it was that hilltop cemetery on a dead-end road in West Virginia and the broken, greasy-haired old friend chain smoking atop it.

Some part of him knew that.

So, he never went back.

Part One
The Reunion

1

Wyatt

THE PHONE call came well past midnight. The rattle of rain against the antique windows threatened to drown out the gentle buzz of the cellphone. If Wyatt hadn't already been half awake, he likely would have missed it.

The woman splayed out on the bed next to him mumbled something as he pulled away. He didn't catch her words — his focus caught on the throbbing of his temples and the pasty dryness of his mouth. The sparsely furnished room swayed in the darkness as he sat up and clawed for the phone. When he finally found it, lodged between an empty beer bottle and a copy of *Theogony*, a number that he didn't recognize seared into his drunken, sleep-blurred eyes.

He had no idea why he answered it. He never answered numbers he didn't know.

"Hello?"

The other end was staticky. Or it could have been rain; he couldn't tell. There was a long moment of silence, broken only by a wet cough.

"Who is this?" Wyatt didn't bother to hide his annoyance.

"Hey, man," a voice seeped through the speaker. It took Wyatt a moment to place it.

"Siggy?"

"What's good, man?" Thomas Sigmund's voice was barely understandable. He sounded drunk, and then some.

"Everything alright?"

"It's groovy, man, just fuckin'…" There was a dry chuckle, and the voice trailed off into an unintelligible mumble.

This fucking guy. Wyatt resisted the temptation to throw the phone across the room. Leave it to Siggy to be fucked up beyond comprehension on a weekday, drunk-dialing old contacts.

"How drunk are you?" Wyatt asked, swallowing the bitterness. He was painfully aware that a good portion of the frustration he felt was with himself. The meeting that would decide his future as an associate professor at this college — perhaps even the course of his career as a whole — was in a few hours. Yet here he was, already sporting the hearty beginning of what was sure to be one hell of a hangover.

Siggy didn't answer.

"Look, Siggy, I've got a big meeting in the morning, and I'm already hitting the hangover stage myself, so maybe we can do this another time—"

"I'm sorry, man."

Wyatt felt a sudden shame as a dull red warning light ignited in the back of his brain. He didn't know what set it off — the words themselves, or the single weak sob that punctuated them.

"Hold on, man," Wyatt said. "I'm… I'm being a dick. You just caught me half asleep, that's all. What's going on with you?"

There was another long pause. When Siggy's words finally came, they oozed out of his mouth like old motor oil. "I just wanted to call and tell you, I'm sorry. I… I just can't… anymore. I'm sorry."

Like a strike of lightning, Wyatt was wide awake, speaking rapidly. "Where are you?"

Silence.

"Siggy, where the fuck are you right now?"

"I'm here."

"Where is here?"

No response.

"Where is here?" Wyatt was nearly shouting. The girl beside him laid a concerned hand on his back, drawing a flinch. He shot out of the bed and crossed to the next room, swiftly shutting the door behind him and trying to control the rising panic in his own voice. "Siggy, tell me where you are. What are you going to do?"

"It's already done, man. I… I made a mistake." The words all melted together into one long syllable.

"Where the fuck are you? Answer me, motherfucker!"

"I wanted… say goodbye…"

"Just tell me where you are and I can get there." Wyatt's throat was starting to close up. He choked on his next words. "Please don't fucking do this. Please, please tell me where you are."

"I'm here…"

"Where the fuck is here?"

"*Here.*" The singular word was crisp and forceful, then the phone line clicked dead.

As suddenly as it had all started, Wyatt was alone.

He smashed his thumb into the phone number that still hung on the screen. The phone rang twice, then played a generic voicemail message. He frantically tried again. This time it didn't ring at all.

The patter of rain filled the damp kitchen air as his mind reeled.

Where the fuck did Siggy live? The last time Wyatt had talked to him was years before, and even then, he couldn't recall what town or even area in Michigan Siggy claimed to be holed up in. He didn't have Siggy's parents' numbers, and he had no idea who else might be able to—

Doc.

Wyatt's hands were shaking as he scrolled through his contacts. He hadn't spoken to Doc in just as long, and he had no idea what stupid nickname he would be in his phone as.

It wasn't under *Doc.*

Was it under *Fred Chapman*?

No.

What stupid fucking name had he—

"Is everything okay?" the girl's voice came from the doorway.

"Go back to bed," he snapped, a little too hard. Her name was Aubrey. She was a nice girl, a TA in the English department who he'd just started seeing. She retreated silently beyond the darkness of the doorway. He knew she was only concerned for his well-being. But at that moment he didn't care.

The Silver Bullet.

The contact caught his eye as he passed it. He scrolled back quickly and hit the call icon. The phone rang and rang, and no one picked up. The horrible realization began to seep in; Doc could have changed his number since they last spoke. But before the sixth ring, the call connected.

"Hello?" Doc's voice was heavy with sleep.

"Doc, get on your feet."

There was the distinct shuffle of covers, then his voice came back, still groggy but also tinged with worry. "What happened?"

"Siggy called me, I think he's going to—" Wyatt stuttered over what word to use. "—to kill himself, Doc. I think he's going to fucking kill himself."

"Jesus Christ, where is he?" Doc's phone went to speaker and Wyatt could hear him tearing through his room, presumably yanking on whatever clothing was at hand.

"I have no idea. He wouldn't tell me and now he won't answer his goddamn phone. He was fucked up and he just kept saying 'here'."

"'Here'? Like where you are?"

"No, just the word 'here.' Like I was supposed to know where he—"

"West Virginia." Doc spouted the words at the exact same time that it hit Wyatt. He spun to the calendar tacked to the kitchen wall. The room was dark, but he could see the last date crossed off in the faint blue glow of the oven clock: October 4th.

The tenth anniversary of Bauer's death.

"Did you go?" Wyatt asked.

"I couldn't get the vacation days— Fuck, I'm calling the police, you keep trying him."

The phone once again went dead. Wyatt pressed the nameless number, silently praying that Siggy would pick up. No luck. This time it just rang and rang. Eight rings before the voicemail. He tried again and again, losing count after the fifth failed attempt.

There was an old, half-empty pack of cigarettes stashed in a coffee can at the top of one of the kitchen cabinets. He hadn't smoked in three years, and he hadn't smoked sober in twice that long. He dug out the crumbling menthols and drew the stale smoke deep into his lungs, filling the kitchen with the acrid aroma of old tobacco.

He considered jumping in the car, tearing down 95 from the small New Hampshire college town toward that distant hilltop halfway down the coast. But that was a fool's errand. It was a twelve-hour drive without traffic, and whatever came next needed to be done in minutes.

He tried the number again.

Nothing.

He scoured his brain for some clue, some memory of those old days that he had repressed, anything that might offer an opportunity for him to help or intervene or do anything at all. But there was nothing, and no one answered the phone.

One cigarette turned into a second, interrupted with a slug of vodka to clear the congealed gunk of sleep from his mouth.

Eight hundred miles stretched between Wyatt and the horrors that filled his mind. A slideshow played in his head, each heartbreaking image backdropped with that wooded hilltop cemetery and punctuated by the steady ring of Siggy's unanswered phone. The images recycled, growing more detailed, each one expanding into narratives as something inside screamed furiously at him: *Why the fuck weren't you there?*

If he'd been there, none of this would be happening.

Even at just 30 years of age, Wyatt had felt he'd run the gambit on unfortunate life experiences. In that moment, however, he realized for the first time the true horror of being powerless.

2

Doc

FRED "DOC" Chapman stared at the bourbon in front of him. Fat beads of sweat clung to the glass, every now and then losing their grip and dribbling lazily down to the kitchen table. The ice was nearly gone. Only a few thin flakes floated in the amber liquid, undisturbed in the ten or so minutes since Doc had poured the cheap liquor over them.

A gentle breeze drifted through the window over the sink, bringing with it the wafting scent of the whiskey. Doc considered the glass, then the old clock hanging between the cupboards.

10:00AM.

He could hear the chug of a neighbor's lawn mower outside. Farther out, barely audible above the small engine, came the high-pitched peal of children's laughter. It sounded almost like Jeb, his youngest. But it wasn't. Jeb was a hundred miles away, along with the rest of his children and his soon-to-be ex-wife.

Doc gritted his teeth and stood, seizing the glass and marching swiftly over to the sink. He made to pour it out but found himself hesitating.

At the last second, he lifted the glass to his mouth, tilted his head back, and emptied it in one swallow — ice and all.

He didn't bother to grab more ice from the freezer before sitting back down at the table. He filled the glass a quarter way and downed that too. When he finally opened the small black book that lay on the table before him, he'd already begun to feel the warmth rushing through his veins.

The first name he came across in the list of messily scribbled contacts was Victor Suarez. He dialed the number and, as the phone began to ring, realized he had no idea what to say. The line clicked and a voice he didn't recognize answered.

"Who is this?"

"It's Fred Chapman. Is this Suarez?"

"Ain't no fucking Suarez here."

The line went dead.

The second number he called was for Mick Ryan. A series of tones sounded, then a mechanized voice informed him that the number he was trying to reach was unavailable at this time. The same happened on the third number.

He took another drink, then skipped through the pages, searching for one name in particular. He found it and punched in the number beside it.

"Hello?"

"Hey, is this still Greg Flynn's number?"

"Yeah. Who is this?"

"It's Fred Chapman, man. How've you been?"

"Who?"

"Fred Chapman— you know, *Doc* Chapman."

"Holy shit, Doc! What's up man? God, it's been ages, You still down in Georgia?"

"Oh yeah. You know me: bulldog 'til I die." Doc chuckled.

"What's good, man? Everything alright?"

There was a charged trepidation in Flynn's voice. Doc recognized it all too well; it was seldom that calls like this didn't bring bad news.

"Yeah. Well… No. Not really. Do you remember Thomas Sigmund?"

"You serious? Of course, I remember Siggy. Something wrong with him?"

"Yeah, he— I mean, he's alive. He, uh, something happened though."

"What?"

"An overdose. It was last night, at Bauer's grave. He's still in the hospital now. They say they're going to release him in the next couple days to make room for more COVID patients."

"Jesus Christ. That's terrible. I'm, uh… I'm sorry to hear that, dude. Do they know if it was on purpose?"

"Honestly, I don't know. I want to say yeah, but…"

"The doctors, I mean."

"What was that?"

"The doctors, you know, the ones treating him. Do they think it was on purpose?"

"Well, I haven't talked to his doctors, but—"

"I just mean that, like, you know. Last time I saw Siggy he was already pretty strung out. If he OD'd, it doesn't necessarily mean that it was on purpose."

"He called Wyatt during. The way he was talking, I'd say it was an attempt."

"Oh, okay, man. Sure thing. That's terrible. Really, really terrible."

"Yeah." Doc paused, charging himself up to ask the question. Already, Flynn's voice was edged with a patronizing tone. He'd always been an outsider in their squad, a rich Masshole who seemed to be doing his time in the Corps just to appease his prick father. The next question hurt to ask. "Anyway, he's getting out of the hospital in a couple days, and Wyatt and I were thinking we should get some guys together and take him somewhere away from all the hustle and bustle for a little bit. You know, get him detoxed and make sure he's doing better… and I was thinking— I mean, I remembered that your family has that summer house on the Cape that we visited that one time, and—"

"Yeah, hold on a minute, Doc, would you?"

Doc ground his teeth, then filled his mouth with whiskey, worried that some frustrated comment might slip out otherwise. Flynn was still a prick. In only a minute Doc had already been able to assess that. It also didn't help that Wyatt was involved. Wyatt had gone out of his way to have Flynn reassigned to headquarters platoon halfway through their final deployment. There was no love lost between those two. No love lost between Flynn and anyone of their crew, really. But Flynn was a *rich* prick, and at that moment, in the midst of a pandemic that had shut down virtually all access to travel lodgings, that was worth something.

"Oh shit," Flynn came back suddenly. "I'm sorry, man, I've got to go. My goddamn kid is being a little shit. I swear he's going to kill himself one of these days— fuck, I'm sorry, dude. I shouldn't've said that. Anyway, I appreciate you letting me know about Siggy. If there's anything I can do, just let me know."

"There is. That's what I'm trying to—" Doc managed to get out, but he was suddenly speaking to a dial tone. "...trying to say, you fucking dickhead."

Next was Mortimer, then Fitzgerald. Neither picked up. He left messages but doubted if the numbers he called were even still theirs. Lastly, at the bottom of the list, was Crossman's number, underscored and with a scribbled email address. Like so many others, the phone went to voicemail. He rattled off the gist of the situation before hanging up, then pulled his laptop to him from across the table.

Crossman was the only one who had stayed in the Marine Corps. In the past, he had communicated almost entirely over email — a necessity of being regularly deployed outside of the United States. The Google email address he had left with Doc was meant exclusively for staying in touch with his Marines. With a few short keystrokes, Doc summarized the past evening's events and posed his dilemma. He didn't know what Crossman could offer, if he was willing to help, or if he was even stateside. But Doc's options were getting thin.

He hit send, then took a final sip of bourbon. He was about to push the laptop away when the browser dinged.

> Autoreply from: crossman03xx@gmail.com
> If you get this, I'm up at my cabin in the North Woods.
> Shoot me some snail mail at the PO Box below, or, if this
> is one of the boys, feel free to stop in.

Below that, there was a PO Box address, as well as a list of directions outlining the backcountry roads that led to the remote Maine cabin.

3

Wyatt

TWO DAYS later, Wyatt was driving northbound on I-95. The highway was relatively clear, given that it was a weekday afternoon. Still, the relative absence of traffic somehow surprised him. Somewhere, probably many miles south of him on that same interstate, Wyatt knew Doc was making the same journey, Siggy no doubt packed into his passenger seat, puffing away at an endless stream of Newports.

Unless, of course, Siggy had changed. That was a thought that had lived in Wyatt's head more than usual lately. It had been years since his last encounter with either of them, and even that was only for a few hours. Wyatt knew that he himself had grown into a completely different man since the last time the three of them had *truly* spent time together. Who knew? Maybe Siggy had given up the cancer sticks, replaced them with a fruity vape pen or a fat dip, or even quit by taking up a mild gum obsession, the same way Wyatt had.

He doubted that though. Siggy had more than earned his nickname through the years. Every memory Wyatt conjured of the man featured a smoldering butt hanging from Siggy's thin, sunbaked lips. Plus, it seemed that someone concerned enough for their health to endure the displeasure of quitting nicotine might also have laid off the heroin...

There it was again. The bitterness. He fought against it, but it was a hard habit to bury.

What the hell had happened to his old friend? Siggy had always been such a force of life, a bright goddamn beacon of fun in even the bleakest of times. The last time Wyatt had seen him — strung out, pale, and thin as a lamppost — seemed an insult to the friend he once knew.

You're partially to blame, a voice in his head whispered. *It happened on your watch.*

Wyatt dismissed the invasive thoughts. He'd been through that dialogue too many times in the three days since Siggy's broken call. He'd processed and processed, second guessed his own conclusions and blamed himself again and again. In the end, Cain's prophetic question rang loudest in his mind: *Am I my brother's keeper?*

Yes, he supposed he was. But what if his brother refused to be kept?

It wasn't long before the gentle British voice of Wyatt's GPS guided him to pull his truck off of I-95 and onto the gently sloping Maine roads. He cranked up the radio, beating the steering wheel in concert with Stan Rogers as the shopping centers that bordered the highway gave way to quaint country towns and their picturesque main streets. As he made his way north, the trees faded from bright green and dappled orange of early fall into an explosion of reds and yellows. He passed through micro-suburbs where children chased each other on freshly mown lawns and rolling green pastures with their postcard herds of black-and-white cows. Then, gradually, the towns gave way to an endless sea of looming pines, broken only by the occasional roadside house or trailer or sprawling megafarm.

The sun was brimming the treetops when one particular sight caught his attention. A weather-beaten double-wide stood beside the road. In the yard, a faded kid's pool was crushed under a rusted-out truck that had clearly slipped off its corroded jack. A ring of overgrown rubbish and scrap metal encircled the small lot like stagnant asteroids caught in orbit. Two people sat on the trailer's stoop — a thin young man in an oil-stained wife-beater and a hefty woman clad head to toe in a faded sweatsuit. Though haggard, neither looked over twenty five. They watched with blank stares as Wyatt's shiny new truck passed them. It was as if the glimmer off the hood was enough to catch their eyes, but not enough to trigger their minds. Wyatt looked back over his shoulder as he passed. He couldn't help it. For some reason they enraptured him. A true modern American Gothic — burnt out, young, and hopeless.

It wasn't long after that Wyatt spotted a worn general store with a pair of gas pumps sitting outside. He was at a quarter tank, plenty to make the final leg of the journey, but he'd always been the type to play it safe. Pulling off into the gravel parking lot, he eased his truck up to the antique pumps. A damp cardboard sign hung above the pumps: PUMP B4 U PAY scrawled in sharpie. They were old school; steel boxes with faded white ticker counters and the pitted metal handles you had to flip in order to engage the sale. It took a few seconds longer than he would've liked to admit to figure out how to get the gas to flow. Once the pump finally cut off with a heavy *chunk*, though, he meandered into the humble building.

The general store had a cave-like atmosphere. The scent of stale beer and old smoke was nearly overwhelming. His shoes stuck to the uneven tiles as he wandered through the short aisles, grabbing jerky and a bottle of soda water on his way. The cashier was an unremarkable woman — middle aged with kind eyes and plump cheeks. When she saw him eyeing the large plexiglass case of ammunition behind the counter, she smiled wide, revealing only a handful of mustard-colored teeth.

Meth mouth, Wyatt thought, the images from Tiger King flooding his mind.

"I seen you from out of state. You up here hunting?" she asked.

He returned the smile. "No, just here to see an old friend."

He paid for the gas and the snacks, then asked as an afterthought, "Do you know Foxhorn Plantation?"

"I do. If that's where you're headed, then you've still got a leg to go."

"Yeah, my GPS says it's another hour or so—"

"GPS? Hope you've got a real map on you if you're headed up that way." She reached behind the counter and pulled out a Maine road atlas. "Your phone's gonna shit out before you even get close."

Wyatt knew that she was likely just trying to make a sale to a passing yuppy, but he bought the atlas anyway. Just in case.

A figure stood beside the hood of his truck in the parking lot. He was an older man, a scraggly beard covering his face and an ill-fitting plaid shirt failing to conceal the bottom of his gut. He ran his fingers over the GMC's hood, seeming to admire it.

"Can I help you?" Wyatt demanded as he approached, his voice dropping half an octave lower than it had been with the cashier.

The man glanced over dismissively, then did a double take before raising his eyebrows. This was a normal occurrence in Wyatt's life. He was not a small person. Standing at six-foot-four and well over two hundred fifty pounds, his years in the gym had left him with the broad outline of an NFL linebacker.

The man took a step back, then muttered "nice truck" with a clear hint of disdain. Even so, he cut a wide berth as they passed each other. Wyatt watched him pass and enter the store, then heard the echo of the cashier's greeting. "Oh, hey Johnny."

The interaction left a bad taste in Wyatt's mouth. He knew he was entering a different world. The North Maine Woods was as rural as rural gets, and the shiny new truck marked him clearly as an outsider. He might as well be a foreigner, as far as some might be concerned. His own fitted flannel shirt, fresh jeans, and unmarred hiking boots doubtlessly did little to detract from that perception; a walking target with a money sign for a bullseye.

Even before starting the ignition, Wyatt checked his glove box. The matte grey of a stubby .38 revolver stared back at him.

Just in case.

The last leg of the journey proved the cashier right. His phone lost service with forty five minutes of winding dirt roads left ahead, and he was forced to consult the small fold-out atlas repeatedly. More than once he had to convince himself that he had not become hopelessly lost. Finally, just as the endless forests around him were basked in nothing more than a dusky glow, he made the final turn down a long dirt driveway. His headlights caught the glint of windows ahead.

The cabin was modest, maybe four hundred square feet by Wyatt's initial estimate. It was built in the exact style he'd expected: thick lateral logs laid atop each other like the Lincoln Log toys he'd grown up playing with. Unlike the bright wooden sticks, though, the wood of this cabin was dark and worn. It sat in the middle of a small clearing in the otherwise impenetrable woods, the home of a frontiersman lost in time.

He didn't particularly like to admit it, but as the last remnants of light faded, the shadowy cabin cast quite an ominous visage.

A stubby porch hung off the front of the cabin, and a beat up grey truck was parked just off to the side. Based on the darkness beyond the windows, though, Wyatt doubted Crossman was home to greet him. He hesitated to turn off the truck, thinking to call Crossman to make sure this was the right place. Then he remembered the phone lodged in his cupholder was little more use than a flashlight this far beyond its service area.

The northern air carried the crisp bite of fall as he cracked the truck door. From somewhere beyond the cabin came the unmistakable gurgle of rushing water, barely audible above the symphony of crickets. Beyond that and the whispers of the wind through the leaves, the evening was silent. Wyatt considered pocketing the small revolver, but immediately threw away the idea. *Don't be a pussy.*

"Crossman!" Wyatt called, hoping some light would flip on beyond the darkened panes, but after a few moments, the cabin remained still.

Fuck. Come on, man.

He pushed away the creeping unease and trudged up to the front door. The damp boards of the porch sagged under his weight. After knocking several times, he tried the handle, and it turned freely in his hand. The door let out a creak as it eased open.

"Hey, Crossman, if you're in here don't shoot me. It's Wyatt."

His voice faded into the mildewy darkness, but nothing came back. He fumbled along the wall for a light switch. Giving up, he clicked on the flashlight on his phone. The beam of light illuminated the wall beside him, and his heart skipped at the bear that stared down at him from its wooden mount, yellow fangs reflecting back at him in a snarling grimace.

"Jesus Christ, Crossman," Wyatt muttered, shaking off the tiny edge of adrenaline.

Panning the light around the room, he found himself standing amidst what he could only describe as a complete and utter clusterfuck. A window on the opposite side of the room was shattered. A thin tree branch hung through it, and from its angle, he figured that the better portion of the tree it belonged to lay propped against the side of the cabin. A sea of loose papers were scattered across the room, some soaked with the rainwater that still pooled under the broken window, the others scattered around the floor, presumably from the wind. A single sparse bed sat in the corner, opposite a kitchenette and an antique writing desk, over which hung a lopsided map that had folded down over itself. The walls were coated in every woodsman-like accoutrement Wyatt could imagine; a series of hiking packs in various sizes, taxidermized animal heads of all types, camping gear, an empty gun rack over the stove, and a camouflaged compound bow and quiver set hanging beneath the gun rack. *Of course* Crossman lived here. Wyatt shouldn't have expected anything else.

Only the large bookshelf awkwardly lodged in the corner looked out of place. Wyatt might have worried that he was trespassing, intruding on some hapless northerner's trashed hunting cabin, if he hadn't shined his light across the weathered spines of the dozens of old reference books and spotted a photo he remembered all too well. It was the same photo he had hanging in his own house, taken nearly a decade before on a remote patrol base in southern Afghanistan. He was in it, clad in a flak jacket and camouflage utilities, his M4 across his chest with its fat M203 hanging off its barrel. There was Siggy, Doc, Bauer, and the rest of the squad. And there, just at the edge of the group, stood Crossman. Wiry and tall, staring stoically from under a tangle of short blond hair.

Instinctually, Wyatt once again unlocked his phone to make a call. The phone simply shone bright with NO SIGNAL. He searched around the cabin to find some source of light. Only a few bare bulbs hung overhead, but none of them lit up when he pulled their swinging chains. Pulling a small handful of tinder from a neat pile beside the stove, he set about lighting a fire. It struck him halfway through the process of blowing the small flames to life that the stove itself was stone cold. With the night air outside already dropping close to freezing some nights back at his home in New Hampshire, the cold steel confirmed that Crossman hadn't stayed in the cabin in a while.

He found a lukewarm case of beer in the icebox and helped himself to one. Just as he popped the cap off, a bright light shone from outside. With a sign of relief, he strode out the door and into the driveway, waving to the headlights as they edged down the long dirt driveway.

As soon as he entered the light, the vehicle came to a squeaking halt. "Crossman?" he called, and when there was no reply, "Doc? That you?"

Shielding his eyes from the headlights, he could make out that it was a truck. The chipped white paint of the hood and hard edges of the cab gave it away as an 80's era Ford — much older than anything Doc would have taken on such a long trek.

The truck idled, motionless.

Wyatt's welcoming smile dissolved. A pit formed in his stomach and his hand clenched tighter around the bottle.

Red backup lights lit up the forest behind the truck, and it let out a *chu-chunk*. With a flurry of dirt and gravel it reversed hard, and the headlights shot backwards through the rows of trees until they finally disappeared completely into the blackness. There was another distant *chu-chunk*. The rumble of the old engine followed the road, fading away against the noises of the night.

This time Wyatt didn't second guess himself as he withdrew the revolver from his truck. He sat in the shadows of the porch, his beer growing flat beside him as he replayed the visage of the old white truck. Of the faceless silhouette inside, watching him. The pistol rested on his lap.

Just in case.

4

Siggy

"AND THEN the dog walks in on the priest and shouts, 'That's *my* job!'"

Doc didn't respond, or so much as crack a smile. He was focused intently on the darkness beyond his high beams.

"Eh, I guess that one's not for everyone," Siggy muttered.

Doc's eyes snapped over for a half-second, though his focused squint didn't break. "I'm sorry, man. I'm just… do you think that last turn was the right one?"

"Probably." Siggy shrugged.

For the past several hours they had been slowly cruising the overgrown country roads, pausing at every rough intersection, and debating just *how* lost they were. Now, after backtracking and restarting a second time, they finally seemed to be on the right track. Maybe.

Another split in the dirt road grew out of the darkness ahead. Doc groaned, and Siggy looked over at him. Dark bags hung under his eyes from the long drive, but his cheeks were still rosy and the slight pudge of his face was crinkled in focus. Doc had always been husky, even in the military. But that was a Navy Corpsman's prerogative; the mother hen of every infantry squad, semi-docile, and often rotund beasts of men who cared for their Marines when they weren't dodging bullets and saving lives. And Doc had been a hell of a Corpsman. Now the mess of golden brown locks that had once sprouted from Doc's head had made their escape, though it seemed that more than a few had simply migrated from the top of his skull down to the taxidermy rabbit that hung from his upper lip. Still, a decade later, Doc somehow maintained the same aura of warmth and gruffness that he always had back in those days.

He glanced back over at Siggy. "What?"

"Nothing, my dude. You aged well. The whole mustachioed Lex Luthor thing serves you."

"Bite me." This time Doc did smile, but only for a moment before asking, "Is this it? The last split before the driveway?"

Siggy nodded with a false confidence. He had no fucking idea. "Yeah, hundred percent. Another like… I don't know, quarter mile after this split and Crossman's house should be on the right."

Doc guided the SUV down the road, slowing to a crawl after only a few hundred feet and staring hopefully through the dark pines. After a few minutes of silence, Doc spoke up. "How you holding up?"

"Not bad. I mean, pretty good for a kidnap victim." He said it with a grin, but it wasn't entirely untrue.

Earlier that morning Siggy had been pushed out the door of the hospital. The mask-clad nurses barely gave him time to shed the mandatory polka dot gown and redress in his own clothes before ushering him through the bustling hallways full of the desperately ill COVID patients. They'd shown him no love during his stay, no doubt exhausted by the fact that they'd needed to care for an overdose in the middle of one of the worst pandemics in modern history. He didn't blame them.

He hadn't had a plan of what to do next as he walked out of those oversized sliding doors and into the blinding sunlight. Luckily, or maybe unluckily, someone else had.

Doc had been waiting for him by the exit. At first Siggy hadn't recognized him, but after a few calls of "*Hey! Siggy!*" the pair had reunited. It was awkward. Siggy was still doped on a handful of medications that had dulled his senses and made his head throb. He'd weakly protested to Doc's insistence that he get into the SUV, but Doc had no trouble wearing him down into compliance.

Then they were on the road. Siggy hadn't even asked where they were going. He knew what was coming and had no intention of sitting through an intervention. It was the sad hopefulness in Doc's already sleep-strained eyes that obliged him to play along for at least a little bit. Besides, it wasn't like he had anywhere else to be.

While they headed toward wherever they were going, the drugs that he'd received in the hospital mixed with the gentle thrum of the highway and ended up easing him into a deep sleep. By the time he awoke, they were at a gas station. Siggy considered leaving then, with Doc otherwise occupied. He figured he could slip away unnoticed and hitch a ride to a bus station and save everyone from the embarrassment of his rejection. But the air was chilly when he opened the car door and, besides the gas station, he saw nothing but an empty back road and trees.

Doc had returned with coffee and a pack of Newports for Siggy. Both were welcomed gifts. They helped to remedy the growing sourness in his gut about being shanghaied in his addled state. Over the next few hours, they'd reminisced casually over where life had taken them. Doc spoke mostly of his job at the ironworks, the online classes he'd recently started, and maintaining his little house. When Siggy had asked about Sally and the kids, he'd just given a curt "good." But otherwise, he seemed to be doing well enough.

Siggy had then recounted a few of his own exploits to fill the time, though he'd left the darker parts out. He'd told Doc of his years of jumping from college to college, burning up his GI Bill while searching for a passion worth pursuing. He talked about his time as a carpenter's assistant, then a mason, then a dockworker. He told about the yearlong sojourn he'd taken to South America and all about the craziness and drugs he got up to there. He left out the crippling anxiety and depression that had led to such a drastic flight from society. He also left out most of the past five years, as the devolving drug abuse and general criminality was a subject he wasn't eager to take on. He never lied, but he also never told the whole truth. A truth that was written in dimpled scars along the inside of his arm.

Up ahead they saw a break in the trees. It looked like another road, though it was hard to tell, as they hadn't seen a telephone pole or electrical wire in hours. Doc hesitated before pulling in. A few hundred yards down the winding driveway, they caught the reflection of glass. As they pulled in, they saw a brand new GMC truck parked next to an old grey one, and beyond those, a cabin.

Doc angled the SUV to park beside the trucks, the headlights bathing the cabin and its porch in bright white. A figure jerked awake from one of the plastic Adirondack chairs. It was Wyatt, and there was a pistol in his hand.

"What the hell…" Doc muttered.

"Maybe he saw a werewolf," Siggy jeered. "You didn't tell me ol' lead-hands was going to be here."

"You didn't ask."

Siggy suppressed his anxiety and climbed out of the vehicle. It didn't matter. "Whoa, whoa! Don't shoot, we give up!" he called out, raising his arms in mock surrender.

Wyatt stood quickly, rubbing sleep from his eyes and shoving the gun into his belt. "Glad to see you two finally made it."

Siggy took all three stairs in one bound, slapping away Wyatt's outstretched hand and wrapping him in a bearhug. Wyatt hugged back. Surprisingly, it felt good, that sudden and strong nostalgia of the old days.

"How the hell are you, brother?" Wyatt asked once they'd pulled away.

"Oh, you know me. Just peachy. How about yourself?"

"Can't complain." Wyatt was smiling, but there was something off about it. A placating awkwardness. It was the look in Wyatt's eyes, Siggy realized. They bore that same sad cloudiness as Doc's. He looked concerned. Pitying, even.

"You got fat." Siggy stabbed a finger in Wyatt's kidney. It wasn't true. Wyatt had the build of a Viking berserker, befitting the man Siggy had once known. But he knew the fastest way under the skin of a gym rat was through the ego, and some part of him wanted to remind his old friend that they were, at least at one time, peers.

"Yeah, yeah. When the beer's good, who am I to refuse?" Wyatt muttered with the same wan smile. "You look good, man. I like the tats."

A light frost formed on the inside wall of Siggy's chest. He knew he didn't look good. He looked strung out, thinner and paler than ever and in desperate need of a bath. The old Wyatt wouldn't have hesitated to enlighten him to that fact, especially in response to an insult. But even after a single exchange, Siggy saw that *this* Wyatt, the hulking academic success who was years removed from his old friend, had changed. He'd transformed, maybe even into someone else entirely. Someone who pitied Siggy.

There was nothing Siggy could stand less than being pitied.

"I try," Siggy said. "You afraid of the dark nowadays?" He nodded to the revolver in Wyatt's belt.

"Uh yeah… Someone drove in earlier. Creepy ass vibes."

"This whole place has creepy ass vibes." Doc strode over, eyeing the cabin beyond them. He and Wyatt greeted each other, and after all the back clapping and pleasantries they made their way into the dark cabin.

"Crossman's not here." Wyatt walked them through the mess. "I'd guess he's been gone a while. Stove was cold, and it looks like a storm must've blown through and taken out some windows. Why do you think he invited us up here if we wasn't going to be around?"

Doc wandered through the weather-ransacked cabin. "I guess he didn't technically invite us up…"

"What?" Wyatt asked.

"Yeah. His email had an auto response set up. It basically said the boys were free to drop in."

The darkness hid Siggy's smirk as Wyatt spun on Doc. "You didn't think that was worth mentioning over the phone?"

Doc shrugged sheepishly. "Where else did we have to go?"

"What's with all this shit on the wall?" Siggy intervened. "Crossman hunting skinwalkers out here?"

"Or, you know, people…" Doc's joke carried a hint of genuine worry.

"Would you be surprised?" Wyatt asked. "Crossman always was…"

"Yeah… a fuckin' weirdo," Siggy finished.

They set about cleaning the mess of papers, piling the few that weren't completely ruined by water on the desk. Doc swept up the broken glass while Siggy and Wyatt searched for a generator around the back of the building. It took a couple pulls, but they got it running. With the stove cranking and the lights finally on, the little cabin actually began to feel homey.

They decided to leave the downed tree leaning on the cabin, but only after checking to make sure that the damage hadn't compromised the integrity of the roof. Both of the others seemed impressed by Siggy's knowledge of carpentry and architecture as he went through the steps of ensuring that they wouldn't be crushed in their sleep. Their skepticism stung a bit. More and more the sour feeling in his gut of being infantilized grew, and again and again he reminded himself why these two had brought him here. Of course they were treating him like a child. He was the charity case of the weekend. The junkie. The fuckup.

Were they wrong?

He managed to cut off his mental self-flagellation before it went too far, distracting himself by offloading the SUV and setting up a couple of the dusty cots that they found tucked in a corner of the cabin. It was past midnight by the time they settled in, and a gentle breeze had begun blowing through the broken window. Some of the papers caught and feathered to the ground, and the folded-over map that hung above the desk flapped loudly.

"Can someone grab those, and fix that damn window," Doc muttered as he hauled in an armload of groceries.

Siggy took care of it, weighing down the papers with a book before pinning a canvas tarp over the broken window. Lastly he straightened the map and re-pinned it to the wall. It was a topographical map and looked to encompass a vast expanse of wilderness. A large red circle in the north-most section was marked "Hyperborea." Beyond that, a handful of smaller, hand-drawn labels dotted the map, as well as the thick marker line that appeared to denote a route.

"You think this is where Crossman is?" Siggy asked, pointing to the red lettering.

"We'll figure it out in the morning," Wyatt assured him. "Doc, you clearly need to get some sleep."

"Yeah, I do," Doc grumbled. He meandered over to one of the cots, but both Siggy and Wyatt shooed him toward the single bed. He made to fight but didn't have the energy. Minutes after collapsing onto the mattress, he was snoring loudly.

The flames danced in the glass-fronted stove and cast the cabin in a warm orange glow. Siggy and Wyatt sat in silence for a time listening to the crackling logs. A few times Wyatt made like he was going to speak. But each time he hesitated, swallowing whatever words he'd been about to offer. Siggy knew what he was trying to get out: the big thing, the big question. The confrontation.

Why?

Was it on purpose?

What the hell is wrong with you?

But the questions never came. Wyatt made a quick trip to piss outside. Siggy heard the truck door shut and the beep as it locked and noted that the revolver was missing from Wyatt's belt when he returned.

Of course, Siggy can't be trusted around a gun. Not in his state.

After a few more mundane exchanges, Wyatt went to bed. Siggy sat still until he heard the rhythmic pulse of Wyatt's sleeping breath. Then, quiet as a mouse, he left the cabin and sat down on the sagging steps outside. He pulled out the pack of cigarettes and lit one. The smoke was harsh, but it felt good, a righteous punishment for his own general shittiness.

Alone now, he tried to engage with the muted sense of appreciation he felt for the two men inside. He knew he'd likely come off as an ass, but he still loved those guys. After all, they *were* there for him. Maybe they hadn't been in the past, but he also never outright asked them to be. What did he expect? Friendship was a two-way street, and it wasn't like he'd put in much effort in recent years. But he was grateful — maybe even a little happy — that they were all together once again.

He decided that it was the *itch* that did that to him. It made him grumpy, a pissant with the temper of a three year old. The first time he'd quit heroin, nearly a year before, he'd turned into an insufferably pathetic wounded animal. But he'd been clean a long time before this recent overdose, so this withdrawal hadn't been as bad. Still, somewhere down in the recesses of his mind the writhing monster of addiction clawed at his reasoning, begging to be indulged. Insisting he give in. Tearing away at his sanity.

He drew again from the cigarette, inhaling the smoke straight into his lungs from the burning ember. His throat burned and he closed his eyes and focused on it.

Tomorrow he'd do better.

ς

Doc

DOC WOKE up shivering. The lumpy mattress beneath him had done a number on his back. As he sat up, he felt the tightness of the muscles along his spine. The glow of dawn seeped through the windows alongside a cold breeze. His stomach grumbled, a mix of hunger and the pained bloat of gas from the handful of fast food meals he'd devoured during the twenty-some-odd hour drive the day before. Wyatt and Siggy still lay asleep in their fold out cots. Both were curled in tight balls in an attempt to fend off the morning chill. The fire in the stove beyond them had died to just the tiniest glow of embers. Doc searched through the various storage compartments around the cabin, finally discovering a handful of musty wool blankets in a chest that lay near the foot of the bed. Like a mother tucking in her children, he carefully laid them over his friends, making sure not to disturb their slumber. Next, he added a hearty handful of kindling to the stove. As the flames began to rekindle, something in his stomach shifted, and his guts began to churn. He knew the feeling all too well and was painfully aware of what was about to come next.

The outside air stung and he almost slipped on the light frost that had formed on the porch steps, but, to his relief, he spotted a small structure only a short ways off through the trees. Making his way in a shambling, excruciatingly careful walk, he reached the outhouse just in time. It was a simple structure. A tall wooden box outfitted inside with a metal tube topped with a porcelain crown. It was better than the burn-shitters he'd used so many times in his youth, although not by much.

A short time later, he returned to the cabin with a sense of relief, although his shiver had returned. The interior of the cabin looked far less menacing in the light of day. Still, it seemed a bit rugged for the modern era — even for Crossman. Doc tried to imagine the wiry stoic meandering about, eating from cans for months on end and speaking only to his own shadow. Of course, that probably wasn't the case. It was just as likely that this was just some hunting cabin that Crossman used as a getaway between deployments — if he was even still in the Marine Corps, that is. Doc had no idea what their former squad leader had been up to over the past few years, but a part of him doubted Crossman would get out anywhere shy of his twenty year mark.

But Crossman *did* get out, Doc found to his surprise. As he aimlessly milled through the various sheafs of paper they'd cleaned from the floor the night before, he came across a telltale form: Crossman's discharge papers, or at least a photocopy of them. He'd been out for over a year.

"What'd you got there?" Siggy's groggy voice made him jump.

Doc turned to find Siggy climbing from his cot. He held out the papers. "Crossman's DD-214. Guess he's out."

"No way, *him*?"

"Yeah, last year."

"He only got in — what? — four years before we did? That would put him getting out at… fifteen, maybe sixteen years. That doesn't sound right."

"Fifteen years, six months." Doc found the number at the bottom of the form.

"Weird."

"Probably got pushed out after the war ended," Wyatt muttered from his rack.

"Yeah." Siggy glanced over the papers. "No room in the garrison Corps for a guy like Crossman."

The morning began as a dreary affair. Wyatt brewed a bitter batch of instant coffee on the stove while Doc scrounged up some Spam and beans from Crossman's stores. The propane stove worked well enough to fry everything up, and while Doc set about making their breakfast, the other two managed to get the fallen tree removed from the side of the cabin.

"What, no toast?" Siggy chided as they all sat down before the stove with full plates and steaming mugs.

Doc shook his head. "Nah, man. I can't do bread no more. I'll be honest, I thought I was going to die this morning from all that junk we ate on the way up here."

Wyatt gave a knowing grunt. "I thought I was the only one. I've got to ask: you guys think it was the food over there? I heard some rumors about how they would poison the shit we ate from the bazaars. Not like arsenic or anything, more like long-term stuff. Antifreeze and motor oil and rat poison. Stuff that would punish us on the back end after we went home."

"Maybe." Siggy shrugged. "I've heard the same shit."

Doc shook his head again, this time in disbelief. "Jesus. You don't think it might have more to do with a decade of aggressive alcohol abuse, energy drinks, tobacco, and just generally treating your body like a punching bag?"

Siggy waved him off. "Fuck off, Doc. Don't make this *our* fault." They all shared a chuckle, then Siggy held up a finger. "Speaking of being delinquent pieces of shit…" He put his unfinished plate aside before crossing the cabin to fuss around in the cabinets. Doc couldn't see what he was up to, but a moment later he returned with three full shot glasses expertly balanced in one hand and a trio of beers in the other. "Can't relive the old days without going all in."

"Where the hell did you get liquor?" Wyatt demanded.

Siggy placed all the shots in a row on the end table. "Came across it last night. Crossman's got a whole stash under the sink."

Wyatt shot Doc a nervous glance, which Doc returned before attempting to mitigate. "Siggy, I… I don't think that's such a great idea."

"Why not?"

"I…" Doc began, but the words were lost on him. He didn't exactly know how to approach the topic. A part of him had been dreading this moment. The Talk, so to speak. He'd seen reality shows on interventions before, but the few lessons he'd gleaned seemed out of place when he tried to apply them now. How could he tell Siggy, another grown man, that what he was doing was inherently self-destructive? How could Siggy not know that the purpose of them being here was to help him clean up his act? Was that even what Siggy wanted?

Doc met his old friend's eyes and saw instantly that not only was Siggy entirely aware of his dilemma, but also that he was enjoying it. His lips were pulled tight in a thin smirk that didn't reach his eyes, which darted between the two men expectantly. He was testing them, seeing what he could get away with.

"Siggy, fuck off. You just OD'd." Wyatt's blunt statement cut the tension. "We're obviously not going to be cool with getting you hammered at *seven in the morning*."

"You fuck off." Siggy's face remained unchanged. "I fucked up, yeah. But I detoxed already, and then you dickheads kidnapped me and here we are. I slipped up with smack, not booze. You can't honestly believe I was going to give up drinking? Have we *met*?"

"I mean, it's a gateway to—" Doc tried.

Siggy cut him off with a cackle. "Fuck off with all that too. Where am I going to get a fix around here? Carrier pigeon? The Squirrel Mafia?

If you think I'm sitting around this stupid cabin all day without a drink, you're nuts." With that, he plucked up one of the three glasses and, before the others could protest, upended it. "There. Now it's out of your hands. Either you boys help me out with these next two, or I'm taking them myself. What's it gonna be?"

Doc swallowed hard but didn't budge, entirely lost on how to respond. Then, with an air of reluctancy, Wyatt rose and took one of the shots before handing the other to Doc.

It took another two rounds of shots before the tension in the cabin began to loosen. Slowly stories of the glory days began to gain momentum. Those long forgotten adventures of their youth came to the forefront and the events of the past decade apart seemed to grow more distant. They laughed and drank to dead friends, chastised and mocked the scumbags and higherups they'd grown to hate, and poked fun at each other's youthful stupidity. By the time the sun hung high above the treetops, the temperature outside had risen to a pleasant seventy degrees. They passed around more and more shots as they sprawled out on the front lawn, singing like drunken kids. Doc felt good. No, he felt *great*. It was suddenly like they'd been transported back in time to when the stakes were high but life was simple and ripe with carefree hedonism.

At a certain point, the conversation inevitably turned back to Crossman.

"Where do you think he's at?" Wyatt asked, wincing off another shot of cheap bourbon.

"Who the hell knows," Siggy drawled. "Maybe he's off in Hyper-boner-area."

"Huh?" Wyatt grunted.

Siggy pointed a lazy finger toward the cabin. "The map on the wall. There's a path drawn out to a place called 'hyperbornoria' or some shit."

"Hyperborea?" Wyatt asked.

"That's it."

"Weird…" Wyatt muttered.

Doc noticed the way Wyatt's brow knitted at the name. "What is it? You've heard of this place?"

"No. I mean, yes, but not really." Wyatt shrugged. "It's an old Greek legend. Kind of like Atlantis, but to the north. I did a unit on it in undergrad. Well, like, a third of a unit."

"So, Crossman's gone off to meet some ancient aliens?" Siggy leaned over and seized the bottle from beside Wyatt. "Sounds like fun."

"I think you figured it out, slick." Wyatt tried to grab the bottle back but missed and immediately gave up.

Doc couldn't shake his odd feeling though. Crossman's absence was growing heavier with the day. "It *is* weird that he's not here. Maybe we should reach out to someone. You think he's got family around here?"

"He ain't got a family." Siggy slugged the bottle and then took his time lighting a cigarette. "Back when he was Sergeant of the Guard, he would come visit me on post from time to time. Dude was quiet, yeah, but up there, in the middle of the night with nothing but time, sometimes he'd talk. One night he told me about coming up in an orphanage. I remember it being weird 'cause I didn't even know those places still existed. Thought it sounded pretty Oliver Twist, you know. I figured orphans all ended up in foster care and shit nowadays. Anyway, I guess that's where he came from. Explained a lot about him really. No family, no girl, shit, no friends that he ever really spoke of. Dude was the definition of a loner. Good Marine though."

Doc lay on the grass watching the velvety clouds pass overhead and tried to think of any personal anecdotes he'd ever heard from Crossman. For all the time they'd spent together, he still couldn't think of a single one.

"From the looks of this place, I'd say he never found a wife," Wyatt said quietly.

"We should ask around about him," Doc decided. "If he was out here alone, something could have happened to him."

Siggy grunted as he stood up and cupped his hands around his mouth. "Crossman!" he shouted at the tree line. "You out there? Crossman!"

The trees were silent.

Siggy sighed drunkenly. "Oh well. Hey, you guys want to see a magic trick?" He held a full beer aloft. "Behold, as I make this… disappear!" He upended the can, chugging its contents. The others awarded him an obligatory applause as he belched and took a deep bow. "Who needs another one?"

By noon the bottle of whiskey was dry, and soon after the last of the beers were gone. The sun clouded over and a light shower of rain began. It wasn't long after that their profane festival of comradery began to wind down. As much as the morning might have felt like they had returned to their late teens and early twenties, the afternoon proved that they were in fact now in their early thirties. The warm rush of alcohol gave way to aching heads and soured guts. Crossman's bitter coffee did nothing but make Doc have to shit again, and again, until he was certain he could find the outhouse blindfolded. They had fed on jerky and more canned goods throughout the day, but as the sun grew lower in the sky, the prospect of needing to cook something felt overwhelming to Doc. Now, with all of them already hitting the hangover stage, Siggy's suggestion to go explore the nearby village for a resupply and a hot meal seemed like the most brilliant idea Doc had ever heard.

6

Wyatt

AFTER A wrong turn they once again found themselves lost on the old country roads. It was by pure luck that they happened upon a convenience store. While Doc got directions to the local restaurant, Wyatt and Siggy busied themselves loading their arms with the essential provisions that the cabin was lacking — namely smokes, several bottles of liquor, and a fresh case of beer.

The rain had waned to a drizzle and it was growing dark by the time they rolled into the muddy parking lot of Matilda's Kitchen and Bar. A few rusted trucks spotted the lot, along with a trio of freshly waxed Harleys. The building had the ramshackle appearance of a repurposed grange hall, and a flickering neon OPEN sign lit the entryway. Inside, the air was musty and carried the telltale stink of stale cigarette butts and depression. Only a handful of other patrons dotted the dining area, sipping their flat beers and shooting darting looks at the newcomers.

Wyatt led them to the bar that stretched along the far wall. Down on the opposite end, three biker types chatted loudly, no doubt the owners of the Harleys outside.

"So, he comes up to me, right? And I'm like, 'you better watch it, you fuckin' ni—" one of the bikers at the end of the bar began to shout, then he caught himself before the next word left his mouth. The old woman behind the bar hissed at them and the biker held up his hands apologetically.

Typical rural America, Wyatt thought ruefully. Out of the corner of his eye, he caught Siggy's thin-eyed glare. He recognized it all too well, and for a second considered herding Doc and Siggy back to the cabin. But he didn't.

The bartender came over and introduced herself as Tilde, the owner. She handed out menus, and Siggy's scowl melted into a soft smile. They ordered three burgers, and the bartender poured them their drinks. She was older, maybe in her late fifties, with an outwardly soft demeanor that did little to mask that frank northern toughness. Wyatt thanked her as she placed his scotch down on the bar, then took a shot in the dark. "Hey, can I ask you something? We've got a buddy that lives up here who we were supposed to meet up with. His name's Crossman, does that ring a bell?"

"Sorry, don't recognize the name." She shrugged.

"Here, maybe you'd recognize his face." Wyatt pulled a photo up on his phone: the same photo from the bookshelf. He zoomed in on Crossman.

"Oh, yeah," she said. "Know him as Ian. Never got his last name. He looks a bit younger there. These days he's all scraggly and what not. He's been coming in pretty regular over the past year or so."

"Do you remember the last time you saw him?"

Tilde nodded. "Yeah. Maybe a couple weeks or so back? Keeps to himself for the most part. Sometimes he'll get on to jabber jaw'n with the old timers, but mostly he's over in the corner with a book. He's…"

"A weirdo?" Siggy chimed in.

She chuckled. "I didn't say it… He likes to talk about weird stuff when he does open up. Legends and what not. Always struck me as a bit like one of them Unabomber types. Are you fellas actually his friends?" She eyed Wyatt. "'Cause you look kinda like a Fed…"

"Nah, not a Fed." Wyatt smiled disarmingly. "Just old war buddies reconnecting."

"You look a bit young to have *old* war buddies."

"You're too kind," Wyatt said. "Did you guys have a storm up here recently?"

"Yeah, we have them all the time."

"I mean a bad one. The type that takes out trees?"

"Last bad one we got was a bit ago. Friday before last, I think? Pretty good fall nor'easter. Took out a few powerlines, winds were strong enough to knock some trees."

One of the bikers called out to her, and she sighed. As she began to turn, she paused, then said, "Last I saw Ian, I remember him being a bit out of sorts. Not that he was the cleanest of fellas, but he looked like he'd been in the woods a while." With that, she left.

"What's with the weather report?" Siggy asked.

"Just getting a timeline on how long he's been gone," Wyatt replied. "You know he wouldn't have left the cabin like that."

"Maybe he's off traveling."

Wyatt shook his head. "I don't know."

"One tragedy at a time, man," Siggy muttered.

Wyatt didn't argue. Their food came out not long after. The burgers were dry and overdone and topped with wilted lettuce and pale tomatoes. Still, it was good to eat something that wasn't beef jerky. While they ate, Siggy struck up a conversation with an old man sitting on the next stool over. The two chuckled as Siggy went on about some obscure story regarding boats. Wyatt couldn't help but grin as Siggy drew a steady stream of laughs from the grizzled old woodsman. It really was his gift, Wyatt thought. Through all their years of friendship, it never ceased to amaze him, the way Siggy could immediately bond so seamlessly with whomever just so happened to inhabit the space next to him.

When they finished the burgers, Wyatt ordered another drink before excusing himself to take a leak. The bathroom was little more than a small closet with a steel trough and a pair of rickety stalls. The sour scent of ammonia permeated the air, and a single flickering fluorescent bulb cast the room in a piercing white glow. He was busy relieving himself into the trough when one of the bikers came drunkenly banging through the door. After half a second's consideration, the man fumbled his way into one of the stalls, and Wyatt heard the unmistakable sound of urine splashing off just about everything but the inside of a toilet bowl. Finished, Wyatt scrubbed his hands in the cracked porcelain sink.

Just as he was about to dry his hands, his eyes caught on a small blur of writing on the wall beside the sink. The painted cinderblocks had clearly been repeatedly scrubbed over the years in an attempt to remove the countless faded curses and racial slurs that decorated the walls, but this one bit had been left undisturbed.

Follow the North Wind.

"Hey, you done?"

Wyatt turned to see the drunken man swaying behind him, a stupid look of annoyance plastered across his face and both hands raised limply as if to say "well?"

The words "don't fucking worry about it" almost slipped out of Wyatt's lips, but he swallowed them, instead nodding cordially and leaving the bathroom.

Back at the bar, Doc was still enraptured by a football game on TV. The old woodsman sat next to Siggy's now empty stool.

"Where'd Siggy go?" Wyatt asked.

Doc glanced over. "He went for a smoke. You want to stick around for a while or head back?"

Wyatt waved him off. "Nah not yet. You can finish the game. It's not like we have much going on back at the cabin."

The biker came stumbling out of the bathroom. He whistled across the bar as he made for the door. The other two stood and followed suit.

Wyatt sipped on his scotch and considered their next move. "How do we deal with him?"

"What's that?" Doc asked, still focused by the TV.

"Siggy. I mean, how long do we keep him up here? What do we say? I get the feeling that he doesn't want to—"

A furious shout echoed in through the door. Wyatt spun on his stool. There was another, then another, and then the gruff shouts gave way to a vicious cacophony of curses and insults. In a heartbeat, Wyatt was moving in long strides. He pushed through the door and found all three of the bikers closing in on their motorcycles, shouting and hollering with fists raised. The dirt parking lot was lit by a single dim floodlight, but otherwise the night was dark and the moon still hid behind the surrounding trees. Beside the motorcycles stood a shadowy silhouette. Even at a distance and in the relative darkness, Wyatt could make out the unmistakable arc of piss splattering onto their chrome tanks.

One of the bikers reached the figure and shoved him hard. The gangly mess of arms and legs spun to the ground, sending a line of piss splashing across his assailant's leg. Siggy's unmistakable cackle drifted through the night.

Fuck.

"You think this is fucking funny?" the biker screeched, delivering a hard kick that cut Siggy's laugh short.

No active decision making occurred in Wyatt's mind — just the electric surge of adrenaline dumping through his body. One minute he was standing at the threshold of the diner, and the next he was in a full sprint, winding up a clenched fist.

The first biker must have heard the skipping step at his back because he turned just in time to catch Wyatt's fist square to the cheekbone. There was a vicious crack as knuckles drove against bone. Wyatt's momentum carried him tumbling over the biker's collapsing form.

Before Wyatt could regain his footing, a meaty hand seized his shirt and a bottle glanced off the side of his head, disorienting him. He shifted his weight low and dipped his chin, angling himself toward the nearest aggressor and throwing a wild uppercut. It connected with something soft in a meaty thump. Then a knee slammed into his thigh, resulting in a seizing pain. Gripping a handful of patched denim, he drove forward like a lineman, and both of them toppled. They hit the ground hard. As Wyatt tried to stand, a vicious toe kick sent an explosion of sharp pain through his ribs. He cinched his arm down against his side and caught the next kick in the bicep. The third glanced off the back of his head as he tried to roll away, but the fourth caught him in the face and the world exploded in stars. Then a fleshy arm looped around his neck, and a voice rasped, "I'm gonna fucking kill you."

There was a reason Wyatt had a wild reputation back in the day. A good reason.

His teeth slid against the biker's sweaty forearm, finding purchase in the fatty flesh. An explosion of sweet blood flooded his palate, and the man behind him shrieked in pain. The arm tightened, but Wyatt didn't let go, ripping his head side to side like an animal until the man lunged away. Wyatt spun and landed a tackle that would have made his high school coaches proud. He rode the tumbling figure to the ground, splashing down hard into a puddle of mud. Then he was on top in full mount. His right fist was a hammer, his left a vice pinning the matted hair down in the brown water as he pummeled down again and again. Each strike landed with a flat *thwack*.

Wyatt had no idea how many times he struck. It could have been twice, it could have been twenty times. The biker managed to get his arms up, curling his body into the fetal position and squealing like a dying pig. Every bit of humanity in him was gone in those moments, just a rabid dog blind with rage.

Still unsatisfied, still caught in the carnal bloodlust, Wyatt locked his offhand thumb outward like a dagger and jammed it hard into the biker's ear canal. There was a yowl of pain. Wyatt felt his nail cutting tender flesh as he drove it deeper with his weight. The biker's face sunk in the mud and the screams dissolved into nothing more than a burst of brown bubbles.

"You'll kill me?" He was growling, though the biker doubtlessly couldn't hear him. "*You'll* kill *me! Huh?*"

Someone grabbed Wyatt from behind. He spun, elbow raised, but Doc's desperate voice brought him crashing back to reality. "Stop! Stop, Wyatt! You're gonna kill him!"

The parking lot was silent besides the buzz of the floodlight above. Wyatt rose to his feet, his vision panning over the aftermath. The largest of the bikers lay in a crumpled pile where he'd first been hit. Another one, sporting a now torn denim vest, huddled against the tire of an old truck, still shielding his face and panting. The third lay gasping for air at Wyatt's feet.

Siggy leaned against one of the bikes, covered in mud and with a thin smile plastered across his face.

"The motherfuckin' sheriff's on his way, assholes!" Tilde's harsh shriek echoed across the lot.

The ride back to the cabin was mostly silent. About halfway there, Siggy chuckled from the backseat. "That right there is the shit I missed."

Wyatt ignored him, mopping the blood from his face with a napkin courtesy of Doc's glovebox stash. He tossed the bloody paper down onto the floor, adding to the crimson-stained pile. All he could think of was what came next. An arrest? They hadn't waited for the sheriff. Hell, they hadn't waited on anything. Luckily he didn't remember giving Tilde their names… But she knew they were here for Crossman, and how long would it take the sheriffs to find the cabin? Would they be arrested that night? Arraigned in some shithole jailhouse in northern Maine alongside meth-heads and moose-fuckers?

Then what? His job— fuck if he'd be able to land anything in the academic world with an assault on his record, pickings were slim enough already. A ten year career down the drain.

Beside him, Doc looked to share his worries. He drove silently, still breathing slowly and glancing nervously in the rear view mirror at least every third second.

Only Siggy was unfazed.

The piece of shit.

No one spoke for the rest of the drive.

There was a small mirror hanging in the corner of the cabin by the kitchenette. Wyatt glared at his own reflection. The right side of his jaw throbbed, and his lip was split. His left eye was blackened and swollen from what he still presumed to be a bottle. A lump had already started to form on the crest of his brow. He took a hardcover book in his hands, one of Crossman's encyclopedias, and flattened the lump with a painful *thwack*.

Doc was outside, likely shitting, or at least pretending to in order to escape the tense silence that had settled over the group. Siggy shuffled around the kitchenette, taking stock of their new booze supply and sipping a cocktail. Wyatt saw the animosity played out on his own features as he watched Siggy through the reflection in the mirror. The little fucker was unmarred except for a shallow cut above one eye. He was doubled over a bit, clearly nursing some bruised ribs from the kicking, but if Wyatt didn't know any better, he'd say Siggy was no worse for wear.

Siggy glanced up, spotting Wyatt's gaze in the mirror, and smiled. "Good to have you back, killer."

Wyatt didn't respond at first, then blurted out furiously, "What the fuck is wrong with you?"

"What?"

"Don't '*what*' me, you son of a bitch. I saw you pissing on their fucking bikes!"

"I had to piss," Siggy said innocently.

"Are you kidding me? We're not kids anymore. We can end up in jail over this shit!"

"Over a barfight?"

"Yes!"

"Oh, come on." Siggy waved him off. "Nobody gives a fuck out here. We're fine, trust me."

"Trust you?" Wyatt spat. "Trust *you*?" He stopped himself.

Siggy let the unsaid words fizzle, but only for a moment. "Don't pretend you didn't like it."

Wyatt ground his teeth.

"Oh, come on!" Siggy said again, sighing and pointing an accusatory finger. "Don't bullshit me. Bullshit your stupid professor friends and your students, but don't bullshit me. And don't bullshit yourself. The whole fancy pants, functioning member of society bullshit is an act, and a shit one at that. Tonight, back there, that's the *real* you. Quit fucking around and let that little dude inside breathe for once."

"Who the fuck are *you* to tell me who I am?"

"I'm the guy that's been watching you walk around here the past twenty four hours wound up tighter than a school shooter. I got tired of it, *so sorry*," he added sarcastically. "I wanted my old friend back, and even just for a minute there, it was good to see him again. You gotta let loose sometimes, you know that right?"

"Let loose?" Wyatt muttered in astonishment, then the dam broke, and he was shouting. "Let *loose*? Oh, yeah, like shooting-fucking-heroin-until-your-heart-stops type letting loose? Like calling people who you barely know anymore and who've grown up past your childish fucking antics to come save your loser ass? Is that *letting loose*? Is that what I need, you fucking junkie? Who the fuck are *you* to diagnose *me*? I don't need your fucking help, of *all* people. Who the fuck do you think you are?"

Siggy handled the berating with a stone face, his eyes never breaking from Wyatt's enflamed gaze. When he was satisfied that it was over, he nodded. "Talk about the pot calling the kettle black."

The words almost sunk through Wyatt's anger-soaked brain, but he rejected them, instead continuing on the offensive. "You know what your problem is, Sigmund? It's not the war, that's a bullshit excuse everyone fucking uses. It's that you're too much of a *coward* to try for anything more than a joke. Empty fucking hedonism at everyone else's expense. That's your life. And my God, what a weak ass pillar to base your existence on. Man, I knew you'd gone to shit, but I guess I'm somehow still surprised by how much of a fucking turd you've turned into." Wyatt finished, catching his breath. Then, in a final, somber tone he added, "fuck you."

Siggy stared back, his expression still unchanged throughout the tirade. "Whelp, at least I'm having a good time."

"You won't be if you don't shut the fuck up."

Siggy snorted again. "*Oh no, beat me up then, big scary Wyatt,*" he mocked. "Trust me. I've had worse." He crossed the room and plopped down on his cot, pushing a pair of earbuds into his ears and setting to work on a phone game as if nothing had happened.

"You bitch," Wyatt muttered, grabbing a bottle of cheap scotch from the counter and storming out.

Doc was sitting on the porch steps. He looked tired, his hands clenched atop his stomach inside of his hoodie pocket. Wyatt silently took the seat next to him and peeled off the paper holding the scotch's cork, then took a long swig.

"That was harsh," Doc said softly after a second.

"Am I wrong?"

Doc scrunched up his face. "I don't think it's about being right or wrong."

Wyatt didn't respond. His blood was boiling, but the cold night air seemed to tame it, and a part of him suddenly felt very foolish. He took another drink, then handed the bottle to Doc, who grimaced as it touched his lips. They sat for a long time, listening to the crickets and the wind through the dying leaves.

Doc spoke first. "Do you remember Rambo Santa?"

"Huh?"

"You know — that fat old AUP commander who always wore all those ridiculous bandoleers?"

"What about him?"

"Do you remember what he'd always say when we asked him why he was fighting on our side?"

"No."

"He'd say, 'the enemy of my friend is my enemy.' We tried to correct him with the right phrase, you know, in the right order, but he just insisted on what he'd said. The Americans had helped him back in the day against the Russians, so when the war came to the Taliban, he joined up with our cause."

"Doc, what's your point?" Wyatt said curtly. He knew Doc was leading somewhere, but he was too caught up stewing in his own anger to particularly care.

"Do you remember when he died?"

Wyatt paused. Doc's face was somber. "Yeah," Wyatt responded. "He took the blast right in front of Siggy. I remember finding all those grenades from his stupid bandoleers. Almost turned himself into a goddamn cluster bomb."

"Yup. I… uh, I remember Siggy asking me about it after." Doc took a deep breath. "He got his bell rung, but he'd seen it happen and he knew I was the one to render aid. I remember later that night in the hooch, he asked me if it was quick. I lied and told him it was. But the truth is, the old man didn't go quick. Not quick enough, at least. He was all torn up, legs split to ribbons and choking on his own lungs from the shrapnel. He was like a fish out of water, gasping at the air without really taking a breath. Probably only lasted a handful of seconds, maybe half a minute, but it felt like a lot longer at the time. It was the only time I really considered mercy killing someone, you know?"

There were no tears, but Doc's voice cracked a bit. Wyatt didn't know what to do. Suddenly the hot air of frustration that had filled him earlier had dissolved. He laid a comforting hand on Doc's shoulder.

"Anyway," Doc went on. "His face there at the end. It's one of those things I could never really get out of my mind. I thought about him a lot after I got out. Barely fucking knew the guy, but there he was, gasping for one last breath that he'd never catch. Sally made me go to therapy after a while, for that, but other things too. I was drinking too much, being an ass, I suppose. When I told the therapist about Rambo Santa, she suggested I try to remember something else about him. What he was like when he was alive, in those few interactions we had. There was really just that one time, with the 'terp and his fucked up phrase, that stuck out to me. I started thinking about that when he'd pop up in my head, thinking about what kind of man he was, how honor had bound him to fighting again. It humanized him. It helped, man. It really did fucking help me."

Doc took a longer slug from the whiskey, and this time he didn't wince. "My point is, and I know this is a roundabout way to get there, but my point is that what he said makes sense to me now. I mean, if the *enemy* of my *enemy* is my *friend* means that friendships are built through mutual hatred, then the *enemy* of my *friend* is my *enemy* stands to be even more true. It's about loyalty. Any son-of-a-bitch who messes with your friend has gotta be your enemy by default. You get me?"

"I guess."

"No, you don't. You jumped into that fight because of Siggy. No hesitation. I didn't even have time to get in there before you'd torn them up. And I know you didn't want that. I know you're past that stuff in life. But you didn't hesitate, and that speaks worlds. As far as I'm concerned, that *proves* that Siggy is still your friend. And honestly, I don't think he has too many friends left. Yeah, sure, he's a scumbag, and I wouldn't blame you for taking off tonight and never talking to him again. But you know, somewhere deep, *deep* down that it's up to us to help him. We're… well, we're pretty much all he's got left."

"He doesn't want help," Wyatt said bitterly.

"Yeah. I know. But he needs it."

Somewhere in the depths of the forest, a deer snorted. It was a noise Wyatt recognized from his childhood. He tried to pinpoint the direction, trying to imagine the angry doe bounding away in frustration. Then he imagined the roads beyond the trees, and his house in New Hampshire, the blonde TA he'd left behind, really anything to avoid confronting the truth in Doc's words. The distractions failed, and instead he thought of Siggy. About the kid that always volunteered to walk point. About the kid who risked NJPs to steal them the good chow from the higherups and always, *always* had your back in a fight, no matter the odds.

Yeah, Siggy was an ass. Yeah, he might have risked ruining Wyatt's career tonight over some stupid shit. But a long time ago, Siggy had also saved his life.

"Okay, Doc. I get it," he mumbled. "You dick."

Doc grinned sadly, then stood and entered the cabin. Wyatt heard some muffled words before Doc reappeared, Siggy in tow with a loose cigarette hanging from his lips.

"You got an extra one of those?" Wyatt asked as Siggy took a seat in one of the plastic porch chairs. Siggy silently passed him one and a lighter. Wyatt returned the lighter, along with the bottle of scotch.

And so it was that the three of them sat there well into the night, silently passing the bottle, smoking harsh menthols, and shivering in the chilly October air.

1

Siggy

HER EYES.

A kaleidoscopic universe contained in a gentle orb of deep ocean blue. They matched his gaze, capturing his face and reflecting it back.

Around the edges, deep red veins began to grow. They bulged and wriggled like worms until they were fat enough to burst. But they didn't explode. Instead, they began to leak, sullying the perfect white canvas with spreading pools of crimson. Then the eyes themselves began to sink back into her head. The blue dried and cracked to a muddled, opaque grey. The cornea withered and pulled tighter and tighter like shrink wrap over heat. Deeper they retreated, the darkness of the mud-stained brow absorbing them more and more until they were finally gone.

Then there were just holes.

Stinking, fetid holes framed by crow-picked lids.

Siggy opened his eyes. His heart throbbed loudly in his ears, pulsing with the overwhelming fog of dread that saturated his veins. The cool wetness of tears stained the bridge of his nose.

He pulled back the blanket and sat up slowly, keeping his back to the other slumbering men. His elbows found his knees, and his hands found his face, and he silently battled the impulse to sob. One deep breath, then two. Three. Four. Finally fifty, then one hundred. He buried his face deeper into his sweaty palms and pictured the cabin around him, orienting his reality. The rough canvas cot beneath him, the hardwood desk sitting nearby, the kitchenette, the scraggly bear head and twin deer skulls mounted beyond. He pictured the rows of outdoor gear hung neatly along the walls and the bookcase nestled near the door, and the two men snoring gently behind him.

He retrieved his phone and rose. It was just past 3:30AM; he'd only slept for an hour. Despite the overwhelming exhaustion he felt, he knew he wouldn't get any more rest — at least not until tomorrow night. Maybe not then, either. That's just how it went sometimes.

It was always in those dark, sleepless hours that the itch was the worst. The incessant compulsion to chase oblivion threatened to bleed through the freshly sutured wound of addiction. He knew the urge was a lie, that the needle would not save him. But he also knew that, given the opportunity, he would relapse right then and there. But there were no pills to take, no syringes to inject or powders to snort away the pain. Not out here. He would find no sweet release to silence the gut wrenching remorse and self-loathing that dominated him in that moment.

With nowhere else to turn, he did the next best thing. He silently padded over to the kitchenette and poured a heavy splash of vodka into one of the solo cups that scattered the counter. With a single long swig, it was gone. He poured another, this time letting the bottle glug away for a longer stretch of time. He took a gulp, but his throat reflexively spasmed, and he had to stifle a cough which quickly turned into a gag. He flexed his face against the burn and tried not to make a noise.

With shaking hands, he withdrew a cigarette from one of the scattered packs and exited to the porch. The acrid smoke worked as a chaser. The best chaser, as far as he was concerned. The bitter aftertaste of

tobacco-tainted saliva soothed him, but within a few puffs he found the
cold forest air nipping at his fingers and bare toes. He allowed himself
another drag, then tossed the butt away and retreated once again into
the warmth of the cabin. The fire in the stove was still alive, although
dwindling. He fed it a fat log, then pulled the blanket over his shoulders
and sat watching the flames lick at the fresh maple.

Why did you do it?

He cringed as he thought back to the bar. To Wyatt's explosion
afterward. To his own juvenile comebacks and actions as a whole.

Why, damnit?

Because he was a junkie.

He hadn't even considered the motorcycles until he was already on the
dumpy diner's porch. He'd seen the denim cuts of their owners inside.
Run of the mill hooligans. A little methed out maybe, but definitely the
type to carry a stash of pills. He felt great shame now, looking back on
it, but at the time he only had a one track mind. The bikes were right
there. With a little more time, he was sure he'd have found something
good stashed away in those saddlebags.

But then they'd come rolling out, and he'd drunkenly tried to cover his
true intentions by taking a piss. Like an idiot. Like a true fucking junkie.

But none of that was true, was it?

He'd seen the bikers gearing up to leave before he went outside. He'd
been drunk, sure, but he wasn't *that* drunk. Hell, he'd only flipped open
one saddlebag before deciding to piss in it. Why was he so desperate
for a fight?

He asked himself again and again like a mantra, but as the words
lost their meaning in his head, he realized that he knew why; he'd done
it because he needed to see if Wyatt was still in there. To see if his old
friend still had at least a dash of the old breed left in him. And Wyatt
had proved that he did still have it, though it was fleeting.

That was what Siggy had wanted, wasn't it?

To see that old savage reemerge! To *prove* once and for all that Siggy
wasn't the only one who hadn't *really* changed. To confirm that he hadn't

totally missed the bus to adulthood somewhere along the way. To validate the inarguable fact that all the glimmer and shine of Wyatt's newfound life was just a façade, an act meant to properly mimic a real reintegration into regular society.

But instead, Siggy had found himself realizing something else. The opposite of what he'd hoped for, in fact. Wyatt might still have a remnant of his past trapped within him, but it had taken Siggy dragging him so far backward into the muck just to expose a sliver of it. There was no cathartic release back to nostalgia. Wyatt wasn't trapped in some bullshit life, lying to himself and everyone else about who he was. It seemed, Siggy realized, that he'd actually moved on. Somehow, Wyatt had grown the fuck up.

How?

How the fuck did he get over it all? How could that son-of-a-bitch take *anything* seriously after what they'd seen? After what they'd done? How do you stand up before an auditorium full of gabbing brats day after day and spit some useless lecture on the history of some dead assholes when you've…

He shook the thoughts from his head.

It's been a decade, you fucking pussy. Get over it.

He rose and poured more vodka. It wasn't as harsh now, and he took it in sips. The dull throb of a headache inched through the front of his skull. He searched for something to distract himself.

Crossman's bookshelf was useless. It was packed tight with a catalogue of reference books, their subjects spanning from outdoorsmanship to history and philosophy. He fingered through them and found that they were mostly academic in nature: various volumes from historians he recognized from his few years spent flunking out of college — Plato, Aristotle, Pliny the Elder…

Too boring. Way too fucking boring.

On the bottom shelf, sandwiched between a copy of *Gilgamesh* and a tome on survival, he found a thick, unmarked binder. He pulled it out and cracked it open on the kitchenette counter.

The binder was filled with loose printer paper. The first page was a rough charcoal scribble that almost looked like a woodland river. The next was much the same, and the one after it. There was one of an old tree and another one of a burnt building.

The lines were rugged and the style chaotic. Siggy reexamined the binder itself, but there were no markings on its plastic cover. He assumed that these must be Crossman's own drawings.

As he flipped through, he saw that there were dozens of scribbled scenes. He recognized a few figures clad in flak jackets. Mud huts and rising black flames. Flat black bodies sprawled along the ground. There was even one that looked almost like the photo that sat atop the bookshelf — the group of them all back in their glory days. But most of the pages depicted the forest.

As he drew closer to the end of the catalogue, the forest began to change. It grew darker. Smudged charcoal depicted night and jagged branches. Every so often, eyes peered out from between the black trunks, until every paper became a copy of the last — jagged branches outlining a single black blot, two stark white eyes bearing down on Siggy from its center. When Siggy reached the final page, the eyes were red. He brushed a finger over them, feeling the material flake away underneath. They were stained in blood.

"Jesus Christ, Crossman..." he breathed out. "You really need a fuckin' girlfriend."

He flipped the drawing over, making to shut the binder, when he saw letters scrawled in charcoal on the back of the page.

It's out there. If you find this, burn the whole forest.

❧

Siggy flipped on the battery powered radio that rested on the kitchenette counter. He kept the volume low, scrolling through the static until an AC/DC song broke through. He clicked on one of the gas stove's burners and placed the saucepan full of baked beans and chopped hotdogs over the flame. Next, he poured three mugs full of boiling water from the kettle and stirred a scoop of instant coffee into each.

"Turn that shit off," Wyatt grumbled from his rack, pulling the thick wool blanket over his head.

Doc didn't stir. Siggy crossed the room with one of the mugs and sat on the bed beside him. He gently shook Doc's leg until the snoring cut off. "It's time to get up."

Doc looked up at him with bleary eyes. "Why?"

"We need to find Crossman."

"What?"

"Get up, I'll fill you in."

Doc sat up slowly, rubbing his eyes before taking the proffered coffee. Siggy considered shaking Wyatt but thought better of it. Instead, he crossed to the radio and cranked the volume up until "Hells Bells" filled the cabin.

Wyatt tossed the blanket aside and stared at him angrily. The left side of his face was a mess: his eye was swollen almost shut and the split in his lip had opened sometime in the night and bled onto his chin. Siggy felt bad, but not *that* bad.

"Reveille, boys. We've got a field op."

"What the fuck are you talking about?" Wyatt was exasperated, burgeoning on furious.

"Seriously, man, what is all this?" Doc had begun to shake off his sleep. Now he regarded the neatly organized pile of gear splayed across the floor. It was all stuff that Siggy had managed to pull from around the cabin. There were two packs, a small tent, the bow from the wall and a whole mess of food, as well as a myriad of smaller accoutrements such as compasses, maps, mess kits, a water purifier, and more — just about everything he figured they'd need for their journey.

"It's gear, Doc. What the hell does it look like?" Siggy responded.

"I can see that it's gear. I'm asking why it's all over the floor."

"You know you've got to stage your shit before a mission. Duh."

Wyatt shook his head. "I'm going back to sleep."

"Crossman's in trouble." Siggy made sure his voice inflected the gravity of his thoughts. He pulled the binder from the counter and tossed it to Doc, who swore loudly as he spilled coffee on himself while attempting to catch it.

Siggy pointed his chin to the binder. "Go ahead and take a look at that, then tell me Crossman hasn't lost his shit."

At this, Wyatt finally stood up. He waited as Doc perused the pages, his brow furrowed. "What is it?" Wyatt asked.

After a quick examination, Doc handed it to Wyatt, who considered the rough drawings in silence.

"Some kind of art project Crossman had going on. If I had to guess, I'd say maybe a dream journal or some kind of art therapy," Siggy offered.

"That's a stretch…" Wyatt shook his head.

"Not really. I've had doctors tell me to do shit just like it." This time Siggy crossed the room to hand Doc another slip of paper, this one thin and crumpled. "Pulled this receipt out of his trash can. You recognize what that's for?"

"Clozapine…" Doc muttered. "Anti-psychotics. This is a prescription for Crossman."

Wyatt clapped the binder shut. "What's your point? Crossman's on some shrink pills?"

"You didn't look at the last page." Siggy pointed to the binder.

Wyatt let out a begrudged sigh and opened it once more, this time skipping to the final page. He spent a moment looking it over, then flipped it and checked the back. "So what?"

"So what?" Siggy scoffed. "You don't get it?" He jabbed a finger at the large map hanging on the wall. "You don't think that dude's out there somewhere in those woods?"

"He's a big boy. I'm sure he's fine," Wyatt said.

"'*Burn the whole forest*'." Siggy accentuated each syllable.

"So he's a little whacked out, who isn't?" Wyatt came back.

"Exactly." Siggy motioned to the gear. "I've already scrounged up most of the gear we'll need—"

"Pump the brakes," Wyatt said. "I don't know what you've been doing all night, but as far as we know the cops are probably already looking for us. What we need to do is pack up and—"

"Oh, come on, Wyatt!" Siggy cut him off. "You just want to leave him out there? You said yourself that he's been gone at least a week—"

This time it was Wyatt's turn to interrupt. "You don't think you're projecting a little here?"

Siggy felt his face sour. "Sure, let's say I am. Let's say old nutjob Crossman is perfectly mentally healthy and stable, and he's just out in the woods farting around. Except of course the binder full of terrifying drawings and a note that suggests we burn the whole fucking forest. We should totally just leave, though. Yeah, you're right."

Wyatt stared blankly back at him, unimpressed.

Doc attempted to mediate. "Okay, let's just calm down. I think… I think Siggy might be right. None of this seems normal — at all really. We should at least look a little deeper and—"

"Are we just going to pretend that last night didn't happen?" Wyatt spat. "That there probably isn't some hillbilly lynching party being organized a few miles away as we speak? Now you want to, what? Go walk around the woods like seven year olds, calling for our supposedly lost friend who we haven't seen in at least half a decade? This is insane. Doc, you're smarter than this."

Doc stood and made to respond, but Siggy waved him down. "No, no, Doc, he's right." He turned square to Wyatt. "You should go."

"No shit," Wyatt said.

Wyatt stomped across the room to yank on his boots. Then he stopped, propping himself on the counter with his back to them and head hanging. Siggy saw his cracked knuckles flexing white as he gripped the cheap particleboard. Wyatt turned to say something, reconsidered, then just shouted "fuck!" and stormed outside.

Siggy waited just long enough for the air to settle before looking to Doc. "You coming with me or taking off?"

Doc hesitated, then gave a curt nod. "Yeah. I'll go with you."

"Good." Siggy clapped him on the back and crossed to the map hanging over the desk. "I've looked over this map. Looks like he's gone pretty far out there, but his route should be relatively easy to follow. From what I can tell, everything north of here is pure wilderness for hundreds of miles, so it looks like a hell of a trek." He pointed to a thin ribbon of blue. "Luckily, the river should be able to get us about halfway. I saw a canoe out back when we first rolled in. As long as it doesn't have a leak in it, we should be able to make good time on the river."

"How long do you think all this will take?" Doc eyed the map warily.

"A day on the water, then maybe a couple days' hike. Depends how out of shape we are."

"And you really think he's out there?"

"Yeah, I really do, Doc. I think he's out there, and I have a bad feeling that he's not holding his shit together so well."

The door slammed open, and Wyatt stormed back into the cabin. In his hands were the revolver, a box of ammo, and a thin hunting knife. A sporty daypack hung over his shoulder and he'd changed into fresh clothes. He tossed the gun, knife, and bullets on the counter, then grabbed a cigarette from one of the loose packs and lit it right there in the cabin.

"So." Siggy nodded to the pack on Wyatt's shoulder. "I take it you're coming with?"

Wyatt stared coldly at him for a moment, then jabbed an accusatory finger at him. "This isn't a get better party for you anymore, okay? Whatever bullshit you've been bringing to the table, it stays here in this cabin. If we go out there, it's to find Crossman. You pull some stupid shit again like last night and I will beat you to a pulp and leave you out in those fucking woods. Do you understand?"

Siggy suppressed the urge to say something snarky. This was too important, and besides, Wyatt was right — it was time for this pity party to end, thank God. Instead, he mustered his most serious face and nodded. Only after Wyatt turned away did he indulge himself by turning to Doc and flashing a sly wink.

Doc didn't smile. His face was dark with worry, almost sick. "Let's try and make this quick, yeah?"

Part Two

Into the Woods

8

Doc

THE RIVER lay only a few hundred feet beyond Crossman's cabin. It was thin but deep, with a heavy northbound current that threw bursts of white froth along its stony banks. Only a few wispy clouds dotted the sky above as the three men tested the buoyancy of the old canoe.

The canoe passed its test, and they set about loading it with their gear. With only enough room left over in the small craft for two, Wyatt returned to the cabin and managed to find a cheap plastic kayak stored near the outhouse. If floated well enough, so it was decided that Doc, the heaviest, and Siggy, the lightest, would man the canoe while Wyatt would take the kayak.

At first Doc found the teetering little vessel to be uncomfortable. He had never been one for the water, the irony of which did not escape him as the only seaman present. However, once his body grew accustomed to the gentle rocking as the current pulled them downriver, he managed to relax.

The morning sun leaked through the foliage to the east, sprinkling down its warm rays. Fall was hitting its peak here, and Doc found himself lost in the arching tunnel of bright oranges, reds, and yellows amid the gentle babble of the river below. Chickadees sang their *fee-bee* whistles from above while a lone pileated woodpecker screeched a warning somewhere to their right. At one point, a small doe snorted at them from the shoreline before darting off between the trees. Even Siggy seemed speechless at the majesty of it all, only once muttering, "okay, Crossman… I get it…"

That said, it wasn't long before Siggy cracked a beer he'd hidden in his pack. Wyatt, a dozen yards ahead in his slick kayak, didn't notice. Not until Siggy yelled at him to slow down some minutes later before hurling the empty can at his head. Wyatt responded with a splash from his oar, and Siggy almost capsized the canoe in a desperate attempt to retaliate. Doc shouted at them to stop, though he couldn't help but grin afterward as they bantered back and forth. It felt oddly surreal. Comfortable in a way that he hadn't experienced in a long time. It was suddenly as if the events of the night before were a distant memory and, bit by bit, the others had begun the transformation into those rough and rowdy men they had been a decade before.

Doc's stomach gurgled, but the thought of squatting in the woods made him recoil. He decided to hold off, that perhaps there would be a campsite or maybe a ranger station along the river ahead.

"You alright?" Siggy asked, looking back over his shoulder.

Doc wiped the discomfort from his face and smiled. "I'm good, just holding one in the chamber."

"Alright, man, we'll pull off."

"No, we can keep going. I'll just wait for a…" Doc started, then drifted off.

"For a what?"

Doc shrugged.

"There's nothing around here, man. You afraid to shit in the woods these days?"

"No, it's fine. We'll pull off," Doc conceded.

It hit him then, as the canoe slipped through the reeds near the bank, just how much *he* had changed. How soft he'd grown. The surprise on

Siggy's face drove it home. The Doc that Siggy had known was a man who dove arm-deep in chest cavities and drank Marines under the table. The man sitting before Siggy now, too modest to shit against a tree, must have been unrecognizable.

As he debarked the canoe and searched for a spot to do his business, he wondered when exactly that change had happened. Slowly, no doubt. Maybe a tiny bit every day for the last handful of years. He hadn't noticed, but he wondered if his wife had. *Ex*-wife now. But nobody knew that yet. Not even his parents. Definitely not these guys.

Not even the kids.

Had Sally watched him slide slowly away from the man she married? Had she held her tongue as he grew softer, plumper, a little more useless every day, year after year, until she finally couldn't take it anymore?

"You good over there?" Siggy called from the river. "Wyatt's pulled up by the bend ahead. He's signaling some shit. I don't know what though."

"I'll just be a minute," Doc responded. He breathed deep through his nose and focused on dismissing the intrusive thoughts.

You are Fred Chapman.
You are a good father.
You were a good husband.
Now, you're being a good friend.

There were slight rapids ahead, just beyond the bend. Wyatt waved them over to the shore just before they saw it, and they ended up carrying the two small crafts down a rough trail along the riverbank before resetting them in the water. Shortly after, they passed a small camping area made up of a rocky plateau bordered by a pair of dull green port-a-potties. A burnt wooden sign was staked into the ground near the launch that read BY RESERVATION ONLY, though Doc doubted anyone actually enforced that rule all the way out here.

"My bad, Doc." Siggy shrugged as they passed the toilets. "I guess it's a good thing you got it out of the way though. I don't think we'll see any more of those where we're going."

The river curved east before turning northward again. Every few miles the angular lines of a cabin or camper would pop up through the trees, and there was even the occasional house. As the morning waned and the farther north they pushed, the scarcer the buildings became, until they disappeared almost entirely.

They stopped around noon to eat a quick lunch and check the map. A split in the river somewhere ahead denoted the next leg of their journey, though they were unsure of the exact distance. Doc lay supine on a flat bit of earth, hoping to stretch the stiffness from his back. It worked, if only for a half hour or so. By midafternoon, though, his back throbbed and his shoulders ached from steering the canoe. When Wyatt signaled ahead for them to pull over to a narrow sandy beach, Doc found himself sighing in relief.

As the canoe nosed into the sand, Wyatt shouted up the steep embankment, "Hey there! You know how far until the split in the river?"

Doc followed Wyatt's gaze and realized there was a surprisingly large house built into the side of the overlooking hill only a couple hundred feet away. A small figure stood in the shade of the porch. A billow of smoke lilted away in the breeze. The figure paused for a moment, then disappeared into the door without a response.

"What a rude Judy," Siggy snorted.

"Whatever." Wyatt stood for a moment, eyeing the house, then made to put the kayak back in the water. "Whoever builds a place like that all the way out here must've done it for privacy. The split should be coming up soon — it's not like we could've missed it."

"Just hold on a minute." Siggy sniffed at the air. Doc smelled it too: the faint skunky stink of marijuana smoke. "Maybe they didn't hear you." With that, Siggy tossed his oar down in the sand and began the trek up the side of the hill.

Wyatt tried to protest, but Siggy ignored him. After a frustrated look to Doc — who just found himself tossing his shoulders in return — the trio was hiking up the hillside toward the building.

The stagnant stink of weed smoke grew heavier as they approached the door. Siggy knocked, but there was no answer. As he raised his hand to knock a second time, the lock clicked, and the door cracked open. The small oval face of a child stared up at them.

"Who are you?" the boy demanded. He was maybe seven or eight, by Doc's best guess, with swarthy features framed by a dirty Ninja Turtles hoodie.

"I'm Siggy. What's your name?"

"I'm not supposed to say."

"Okay, 'Notsupposedtosay.' Are your parents around?"

The child smirked at the cheesy joke, then shook his head. "You're funny."

"Are there any adults home?" Doc chimed in, a sudden concern manifesting.

"There's my sister and Rat. They're upstairs."

"Can you get them for us?"

The boy sighed, then turned and walked away down the hall. The door glided open behind him. All three men looked at each other, unsure of what to do next, until the boy called back, "are you coming?"

The house was dark and spacious. Beyond the initial entryway it turned into an open concept design, featuring a loft built around an oversized stone chimney. Curtains and pinned towels covered the large bay windows that overlooked the river, shrouding the cavernous room in a dull grey hue. In direct contrast to the classiness exhibited in the building's architecture, the house itself was a mess. Empty cans and food wrappers lay scattered across the counters and tables, and the floor shimmered with sticky islands of spilled soda peppered with hardened mud. The air reeked of weed smoke. Doc felt the hair on his neck standing up, and from the sudden shift in the manner in which the other two were carrying themselves, he knew he wasn't the only one who felt that something was off.

"Blue Jay!" the boy shouted up the stairs. There was no answer. The boy shot them an exasperated look. "They're having sex. She's not going to answer."

"Hey, buddy." Doc spoke slowly and calmly. "Where are your parents?"

Suddenly the child's eyes grew thin. "Blue Jay!" he screamed again, this time loud enough that his voice cracked.

"What the fuck do you want?" a girl's voice shouted back from above.

"Someone's here!"

There was a mad scramble on the floor above, then the gawky outline of a shirtless teenage boy appeared at the head of the stairs. He held a baseball bat in one hand while attempting to button his jeans with the other.

"Whoa there, killer! Slow down." Siggy raised his hands high as the teenager stumbled down the stairs brandishing the bat over his head.

"Who the fuck are you?" the teenager demanded. He was pale with a toothpick frame, and a handful of janky tattoos dotted his torso. Doc mimicked Siggy's pose, raising his own hands up in submission. The odd thought occurred to him that this kid seemed eerily familiar, as if they had just found some sort of less evolved Pokémon version of Siggy.

"We're just passing through." Siggy nodded to the child. "Your little friend invited us in."

"He— he what?" the teenager stuttered, then shot a horrified look toward the child. "What the fuck is wrong with you, you little—"

"Don't talk to him like that!" A girl appeared at the top of the stairs wrapped in a blanket. She looked to be the same age as the other teen, if not a bit older, with a heavyset frame and a domineering scowl. She shoved past her emaciated companion and eyed the newcomers. "What do you want?"

"Just wanted to see where on the river we were," Siggy offered innocently.

The girl glared at them. "You're not cops or psychos or anything, right?"

Siggy chuckled. "Do we look like psychos?"

Her eyes danced over the three men before they stopped on Siggy. "Them, no. You… Well, yeah, kind of."

Wyatt laughed aloud at this, and Doc couldn't help but let a burst of air escape his nose.

"Gee, thanks," Siggy muttered.

"Just… just wait down here. I'll be back in a second." She motioned to the darkened living room, then disappeared up the stairs.

Some minutes later, the three men found themselves sitting awkwardly across from the teenager who the little boy had introduced as Rat, awaiting the arrival of the girl. She was clearly the matriarch of this little group. Doc guessed that Rat was somewhere between sixteen and nineteen, though he had no idea where exactly in that spectrum the boy fell. The tattoos that scattered his xylophone ribs looked homemade, and the dark bags under his eyes made Doc suspect that those weren't the only poor life choices the boy had made as of late. Rat maintained a strained silence, glaring in their direction yet never meeting their eyes. The bat lay balanced across his knees.

Nearby, the child was standing and humming a song. At first it sounded familiar, but Doc couldn't place it. "What's that song you're humming?" he asked.

"The 'Power Rangers' song," the boy returned offhand.

"Oh yeah." Doc chuckled. "My oldest loves that show."

"You have a kid?" The boy perked up.

"Yeah, three actually."

"Do you have any toys?" There was a sudden and heartbreaking hopefulness in the boy's voice.

"No, not on me. Sorry, bud."

"Where then?"

"Well, I suppose back home."

"Where's that?"

"Georgia."

"Where's that?"

"Far away, down south."

"Oh." The hopefulness in the boy's voice vanished as quickly as it appeared.

"Think you could tell me your name now, buddy?" Doc asked.

"Mouse."

"Okay, Mouse. What are you doing all the way out here in the woods?"

Rat shot a glare at the small boy, whose face immediately hardened. "Why are *you* here?" Mouse demanded.

"Well, we're looking for a friend of ours."

"Where is he?"

"A ways north of here. In the woods."

Mouse's eyes went wide and he gasped. "You mean he's in Hyper—?"

"Shut up!" Rat spun on the boy with a hiss. Mouse waited until Rat turned back to the men before waving a stubby middle finger at him.

Wyatt spoke up for the first time since entering the house, his words slow and his voice deep. "What was he going to say?"

Rat tensed at the hulking stranger's question, but when Mouse took a breath to talk, he once again uttered a hushed "shut the fuck up, you little shit."

"I told you not to talk to him like that!" the girl called Blue Jay snapped from the top of the stairs. She was dressed now, a loose fitting band t-shirt hanging off of her hefty frame. She joined them and took her place on the arm of the chair beside Rat. A lit cigarette hung from her lips as she tied her hair in a loose bun. "What do you people want?"

"Hyperborea," Wyatt said.

Both of the teenagers froze in place.

"What about it?" she asked slowly.

"Everything."

"Why the fuck are *you* looking for it?" Rat's tone was aggressive, but Doc noticed the boy's hands were shaking in his lap.

"We think a friend of ours is there," Wyatt offered. "We need to find him. We're afraid that he might be unwell."

"One of your kids?" Mouse asked excitedly, his words aimed at Doc.

"No." Doc smiled at the little boy. "More like my big brother."

Mouse laughed. "You have an older brother that's still a kid?"

"What do you—" Doc started.

"Enough." Wyatt raised a hand, cutting him off. Pinched between his fingers was a crisp hundred dollar bill. "The first person to tell me all about Hyperborea gets the money. Who's it going to be?"

The girl was the fastest. She shoved Rat down as she stood, deftly maneuvering around the coffee table to cut off Mouse and seizing the outstretched bill from the air. Wyatt looked on expectantly as she settled back into her seat, her smug smile fading as she realized what she'd agreed to. "Fine. What do you want to know?"

Wyatt nodded patiently. "Let's start with the *what*. Then we can get to the *where*."

"It's just a kid's story—" she started.

"No, it's not! You said it was real!" Mouse snapped.

She sighed. "Yeah. Whatever. Maybe it is, maybe it isn't. It's just a place where people get away to. Like an escape, you know?"

"I don't," Wyatt said flatly.

"Just tell them the story!" Mouse insisted.

Her resulting eye roll displayed a mastery of teenage angst. "Fine." She stubbed out her cigarette directly on the table. "So, way back in the... I don't know, the sixties I guess? Those groovy times where everyone was stoned and fucking everyone, you know? There was this guy— well, two guys, actually. Brothers I think, or maybe they were gay? I don't know. Either way, these two guys go out into the woods and started this community. Like, um... What did they call those things back then?"

"A cult?" Siggy snorted.

"No," she snapped back with a glare.

"A commune," Wyatt suggested.

"Yeah," she agreed. "A commune. Basically, they were both young dudes who grew up orphans, and they had this real bad upbringing, but then they made this awesome commune out in the forest where no one could touch them. They called it Hyperborea. They would like, take people in and stuff. Kids, I mean. Orphans and shit. The idea was simple: freedom. No more bullshit, no more assholes with fake authority. Just people living off the land, the way it should be. But then one day all these greedy logging companies bought up all the land from under them — which is so fucked up, you know? Anyways, these two dudes and their commune, they fought back. Well, they didn't really fight, more like, peaceful? You know, like… like putting sugar in gas tanks type shit. Like they broke stuff, you know what I mean? There's a word for it…"

"Sabotage." Wyatt nodded along.

"Yeah, that. Exactly. Anyways, the logging guys lost their shit and ended up building a dam that really fucked up the woods, turned this whole big part of it into a pond, sunk the commune and all. But the good guys got away. They just restarted way deeper in the woods and kept doing this shit until the loggers eventually gave up. It was this whole thing, but the logging companies kept it on the downlow so people wouldn't, like, join the cause or anything."

"That's all?" Wyatt asked after a moment of silence.

"Well… I mean, kind of. They say that the two brothers made a new spot that was even better. A real awesome place out there where they take in all sorts — depending on who you ask. They say it's real nice, that the dudes who made it ended up getting wicked rich so it's all done up and shit."

"It's like Hogwarts!" Mouse exclaimed.

"And where'd you hear this story?" Wyatt asked. Doc noticed that his eyes were slits, and his tone was less domineering, more coaxing.

"It's just a story—" Blue Jay started.

"Amy, our foster sister!" Mouse cut in, earning a disapproving glare from his sister.

"You're in the system?" Wyatt asked.

All three kids went silent.

"Guys," Wyatt began softly, and Doc quickly realized he was seeing a softer side of his friend. A side he'd never seen. "This isn't real. I'm a teacher, okay? At a college. I teach history mostly, but one of the subjects I dabble in is criminal justice. Stories like these, they're almost always pretend. Just a type of mythology. But when they actually lead somewhere — they're almost always traps. I'm willing to bet you followed a trail here, right?"

Blue Jay looked at her feet but didn't respond.

"I've seen the markings myself, the graffiti, the clues. I bet there are a bunch of them leading up here, yeah?" Wyatt asked.

She looked up and gave a small nod.

"I don't know what's up there, okay? But I know it's not Neverland. It's probably nothing. But if it *is* anything, it's most likely *not* something you want to be a part of. Do you know what human trafficking is?"

"Human trafficking?" Blue Jay scoffed.

"You'd be amazed what people will do…" Wyatt went on slowly. "What they're capable of. Don't go into those woods, okay?"

Blue Jay was the only one who held his eyes, and after a moment her scowl broke and she looked tired, almost teary. "You don't know—"

"I don't. I don't know much, but I know a raw deal when I hear one. Here." Wyatt pulled out his wallet and plucked a handful of bills from it, then scrawled a phone number on a loose napkin and handed the bundle to the girl. "It's enough for hotels and travel expenses, *back* the way you came from. That's a number of a friend of mine. She's a real nice lady, a professor, like me. If you get in contact with her, then she'll help you. She knows a lot of good people who do good things for kids like you. People that won't hurt you, that won't let *anyone* hurt you. I want you to call that number and just tell her my name, it's there on the paper. She'll help you. I promise. Just don't— *don't* go into those woods. Do you understand?"

Blue Jay continued to stare at him but didn't move.

"Do we just…?" Siggy prompted quietly after a moment of heavy silence, nodding slightly toward the door.

"Yeah," Wyatt breathed. "Guys, do we have a deal?"

Blue Jay gave a small nod again. Mouse mimicked her while Rat sat motionless, glaring at the coffee table.

"Okay." Wyatt stood, and the three men made for the exit.

"Wait," the girl called.

"Yeah?"

"Thank you."

"You're welcome." Wyatt gave her a sad smile, then led the two men out the door.

"We aren't really leaving them there, right?" Doc asked as soon as they reached the canoe.

"What else are we going to do?" Wyatt asked, dragging his kayak back into the water.

"Hold on now, are you serious?" Doc felt the volume of his voice rise. "That's a child in there. We can't—"

"What would we do, Doc?" Wyatt came to a halt and looked back. "Call a cop? With what phone? There isn't service for miles in any direction around here. And then what? By the time anyone gets out here those kids will be long gone. You want to kidnap them? Drag them back to civilization, kicking and screaming, a forced abduction by three grown men who the cops are probably already looking for?"

"I don't fucking know," Doc snapped. "But we can't just leave them!"

"They've got five hundred bucks now, and maybe a little hope. Who knows. That's all we can do for now. Okay?"

It wasn't okay. But Doc didn't have an alternative. As Wyatt climbed aboard his kayak and began to drift away along the river, Doc turned to the oddly silent Siggy. "Do you believe this?"

"What's not to believe?" Siggy asked with a shrug. "The world's fucking disgusting."

An hour later they came to the split in the river. They continued north, as the map directed. By late evening they pulled off and stashed the boats among the shrubs on the shore. Too exhausted for conversation, they made camp only a short ways away. They chose to forgo setting up the tent, as the weather was warm and the skies were clear. Doc's sleeping bag was musty, but it served its purpose and he found himself drifting off even before the sun had fully disappeared.

Sometime around midnight, Doc jolted awake. Somewhere in the distance, a muffled gunshot still hung in the air.

"Poachers, far off," Wyatt muttered. He was a statue, seated against a tree beyond the glowing embers. His frame cut against the forest by the moonlight, the bow stretching across his lap.

The image calmed Doc's racing heart. He rolled over and fell into a deep, dreamless sleep.

9

Siggy

THE NEXT morning was hot. The mosquitos had found them in the night, bearing down on their campsite in swarms. Doc was especially irritated. His bald head featured a braille novel of welts. He swore and swatted wildly as they rushed to pack away their gear and made for the boats. The cloud of bloodsuckers only gave up their chase when the canoe hit open water and carried the men away downstream.

An hour of silence on the river passed before Wyatt pulled the kayak up to a rocky opening along the western riverbank. As Doc nosed the canoe into the shore minutes later, Wyatt was already waving them over to a snaggle of overgrown bushes.

Concealed beneath a layer of brambles was another canoe, an exact match to the one Doc and Siggy were using.

"It's Crossman's," Wyatt said as they approached.

Taking a page from Crossman's book, they stowed their own boats in the brush before gearing up. Wyatt took point down the thin path leading into the woods. It wasn't long before the trail dissolved into thick shrubs and acres upon acres of young pines. Wyatt fought through the never-ending wall of brush ahead, only occasionally orienting himself with a compass and checking the map. Siggy didn't question him, not that he even could have with how winded he was. This type of thing had always been Wyatt's bread and butter, after all. It was hard on Siggy. Harder on Doc.

"Let's take a fiver," Siggy called ahead. Doc was panting hard, his face flush while his bald head shimmered in the dappled sunlight. The sweat stains that started at his armpits had now grown, and his clothes were more drenched than they were dry.

"We just took a goddamn break." Wyatt was frustrated, but when he looked past Siggy at Doc, his demeanor softened. "Yeah, alright. We'll take ten. I need to try to orient and shoot another azimuth anyway."

The breaks became more frequent as they pushed on throughout the day. Every so often they would find an old logging road or a game trail that would ease their path, but for the most part they were roughing it through hard terrain. Up one hill, wresting through saplings and brambles, then down a ravine, carefully toeing down loose shale inclines, then up yet another hill, and on and on. By noon they were tired enough that they could have stopped for the day, but after a short meal of canned stew, they decided to push on until at least mid-afternoon.

When the sun finally drifted toward the western horizon, Doc threw in the towel. They made camp in a clearing near the top of a hill, this time setting up the old three-man canvas tent Wyatt had been lugging around in hopes that it might spare them from the mosquitos' fury. They ate, then transferred the rest of their food into one of the packs and hung it in a nearby tree at Wyatt's insistence. Siggy didn't argue; the last thing he wanted was a run-in with a bear. After that, they built a shallow fire pit and reclined around it, basking in the last bits of sunlight.

"So, are we just *not* going to talk about this 'hyper-*boner*-ia' thing, or what?" Siggy asked once they'd settled. The question had been eating at him since the previous day, but their pace kept it on the backburner.

"What about it?" Wyatt asked. He leaned against a rotting log by the fire, nose buried in the map.

"You said it was a legend, right?"

Wyatt lowered the map and regarded the others. "Yeah. Ancient Greek. Kind of Atlantis type shit. The Greeks believed that there were these people far, *far* to the north that lived in the shadow of some great mountain range. These people were perfect and lived a utopic life in this beautiful temperate sanctuary. They lived to be hundreds of years old. There were no wars, no disease, and no work. Their food was the best fruit, and it was so plentiful that it just sprung from the ground. Basically, they just fucked and ate fruit all day."

"Sign me up…" Siggy muttered.

"That's the point," Wyatt went on. "This magical place, they said it existed really far north. So that's what they named it Hyperborea. It's Greek for 'beyond the north wind.' It was a fantasy land. A heaven on Earth. I found some fresh graffiti in the bar bathroom that said, 'follow the north wind.' I should've picked up on it before, but I didn't. My best guess is that it was a marker. Like hobo signs, you know? It all makes sense."

"I'm still lost," Doc said.

"Okay." Wyatt took a moment to reorient. "You heard that girl back there; there's some kind of legend circulating the foster system. A place like that up in these woods, a haven for runaways. This Hyperborea sounds like a trap set up by some sick freak to lure desperate kids up into these woods."

"You think that's why Crossman came out here?" Siggy tossed another stick onto the fire. "Some kind of vigilante shit?"

"I don't know." Wyatt shrugged. "But you said he was an orphan. It would make sense that he'd be protective of kids like that. Hell, maybe he even heard of the story himself when he was a kid. Maybe that's why he moved up here in the first place."

Siggy nodded. "His bookshelf was packed with a bunch of that Greek and Roman shit. What about those drawings though?"

"What about them?"

"I mean…" Siggy paused, not wanting to sound like an idiot. "Whatever was in those drawings, that wasn't some trafficker."

"I don't know. Maybe those really were some form of art therapy, like he had some kind of experience out here when he was a kid, and his mind is covering it up with fantasy. It happens. Or, given the meds, maybe Crossman's just flat out lost it."

"Unless there *is* something out there," Siggy said, lighting a cigarette before glancing nervously around the surrounding forest. "Like a fucking cult or a demon or some shit. I've seen the documentaries, man. This is starting to feel a little too familiar."

"Who knows?" Wyatt shrugged again. "People go missing in these woods all the time. Maybe it's fucking aliens or a serial killer. Or it could be nothing. Hell, maybe we're tying together strings from completely different ropes. Doesn't matter though, does it?"

"Fuck you, 'it doesn't matter.' Don't go bringing up aliens and serial killers and shit then tell me 'it doesn't matter.'" Siggy was only half joking.

"You want to go home?" Wyatt asked seriously. His eyes moved slowly from Siggy to Doc.

Doc took a deep breath. "Crossman's out here. The canoe confirms it. I'm not going back until we find him."

"What about you?" Wyatt asked Siggy.

Siggy snorted. "Fuck you, dude. This was my idea to begin with. Don't act like I'm not all in."

Four hours later, Doc was snoring peacefully inside the tent. Wyatt and Siggy still reclined by the fire, sipping from a flask and smoking cigarettes in the darkness. The sun had long set, and the moon had yet to rise. The crackling fire stood out as an island of light in the surrounding sea of darkness.

"Do you actually think there's something out there?" Siggy asked quietly.

"Yeah. Hopefully Crossman."

"No, dickhead. I mean like in those drawings. You know, something… something evil?"

"No." Wyatt's tone was matter-of-fact.

"So, you just think Crossman's lost his mind?"

"I don't know, Siggy. Maybe. Maybe he just heard a scary story and decided it was real enough to pursue."

"Who the fuck does that though?"

"Someone desperate. Someone who needs there to be something more evil than themselves out there."

"Excuse me?"

Wyatt reclined further against the log. "Come on, man. You know Crossman. You know what he's seen and done, what we all have, and him ten times more than us. You've got to think that there's a point in every man's life where he begins to slow down and reflect. For most guys like us, it's generally just after they get out. You really think it's a coincidence that he came straight to this area right after his EAS?

"What I'm saying is that maybe Crossman *needs* there to be something worse than him out there. Or at least something that's *done* worse. That's the whole point of the devil, isn't it? Trouble is, if the devil doesn't exist, it makes guys like us look a hell of a lot worse."

"Okay, *Professor*," Siggy mocked. "So, you don't believe evil exists? Like, *evil* evil?"

"You mean like in a Biblical sense?"

"I don't know, man. In any fucking sense."

"If we're saying that evil is just one extreme on the spectrum of morality, then yeah, of course it exists. But it's entirely relative. Morality is constantly changing — evolving from generation to generation, shifting from culture to culture. We could look back in time and call every one of our ancestors evil for something or other just because our moral compass doesn't align with theirs. Shit, if there is someone out here preying on kids, that sure looks a lot like evil." Wyatt paused and raised an eyebrow. "But if you're talking about Biblical evil — supernatural shit, anti-God shit, devils and demons and all that. Then no. The concept of evil is just a tool, psychologically speaking. A way for us to make a bigger bad than ourselves."

Siggy sat upright. "You sound pretty goddamn certain there, bud. But I'm inclined to call you full of shit. Evil's real, man. And what's more than that, I think you know it. Sure, I won't argue that morals change. Shit, nowadays they change all the time. But evil… bro, it's something else. Maybe not demons or devils or whatever you wanna call it, but it's there. Always has been. Cavemen knew that shit. All those ancient dudes who would genocide and cannibalize each other all the time knew it. It's not like it just disappeared. It's still here now, lurking in the shadows, maybe even driving us from time to time. You know?"

Wyatt grinned and held out a hand for a cigarette. Siggy lit one and passed it to him.

"Well?" Siggy asked. "Let's hear your next fancy-pants argument."

"Maybe you're right. I don't know."

"Holy shit…" Siggy gave a dramatic gasp. "In all my life, I never imagined I'd hear *those* words come out of *your* mouth!"

Wyatt stuck up a middle finger and they both laughed. After the cigarette, they passed the flask back and forth until it was empty, listening to the squeaks of the bats flapping overhead. At one point, one of them began to hum an old sea shanty. In honesty, Siggy had no idea who started it, but it didn't matter because a minute later they were quietly chanting the crass lines over the dying fire and laughing like idiots.

When they quieted down, out of breath and smiling, Wyatt leaned forward. "We should hit the rack."

"Yeah." Siggy took a stick and jabbed at the last cindering log. Embers chipped away like fossilized scales, and tiny flames erupted along its edges. He almost stood, but something stuck in his chest. He wasn't sure what it was, but it hung there inside of him, eating away. "You *really* don't believe in evil? You don't think anything we did over there was, you know…"

"No." Wyatt scoffed. "Fuck no."

Siggy stared into the dying flames. Just for a hundredth of a second, those blue eyes materialized among the writhing orange. He felt his face flinch.

"You okay?" Wyatt asked.

"Yeah," Siggy said, snapping back to the moment. "Yeah, I'm good. I just…"

Wyatt stared at him for a long moment, then let out a heavy breath and looked down. "Look, man, I'm sorry about the other day. The shit I said."

Siggy waved him off. "No, dude. You were right. What I did was fucked up."

"It was, but I was wrong either way. I don't know. I just… what happened, man? You're a smart guy, one of the smartest I know. Tough, clever, good with chicks… What the fuck happened?"

For just a moment, Siggy considered opening up, pouring the truth out to his oldest friend, tearing a hole in his own ego and owning up to the shitshow that was his life. But he was too sober for that. Shit, there might not even exist a state of inebriation strong enough to unwind that bundle of scum-soaked yarn. Instead, he pulled out the pack of smokes from his pocket, tossed one at Wyatt, then pulled out a thinly rolled joint from between the filtered cigarettes. "You ever consider the idea that Crossman might just be fucking with us? Like, if this is just some big escape room type shit he slapped together to bring us all closer together or some shit?"

Wyatt began to chuckle, but it caught in his throat as Siggy lit up.

"Is that a joint?" Wyatt asked sternly.

"Oh yeah," Siggy got out after a harsh inhale. "Good shit, too. You want some?"

Wyatt's face hardened. "Where did you get it?"

"I've had it, why? This shit's not illegal here, so who cares?"

"Doc picked you up from the hospital and drove you straight to Crossman's. You didn't get out of that hospital with that shit in your pocket. Where did you get it?"

"Fine, fine." Siggy made a face like he'd been caught. "I swiped it off those kids. They had plenty, they won't miss a few jays."

"Are you fucking kidding me?"

"What?"

"And here I was thinking that just for a *second* you might have pulled your shit together," Wyatt spat, his tone a complete one-eighty from moments before. "You didn't think for one second that stealing that shit would ostracize us from those kids? You think you helped their situation at all, becoming one more scumbag adult fucking them over? What are the odds they actually make that phone call now? Huh? What the fuck were you thinking?"

"Five hundred bucks for a few joints is a pretty good deal on their end," Siggy tried to joke.

But Wyatt wasn't having it. "And I bet you pocketed those even before I gave them that money, didn't you? How fucking selfish can you be?"

Siggy rolled his eyes. "Oh, get the fuck off your high horse. If you actually cared so much about those kids, you wouldn't have left them there."

"Fuck you."

"No, man, fuck *you*." And just like that, Siggy was matching Wyatt's anger. "You keep acting like I should be like you, you miserable fuck. Well, you're the history buff, so here's some history: ten billion people fought, screwed, and died so that I could enjoy this life. I'd say it's my ancestral duty to have a good fucking time."

"Is that what you tell yourself?" Wyatt scoffed. "That's a shit way to live. You should know that by now."

"Oh, and you're doing so much better?" Siggy faked a laugh. "'Look at me! I'm Wyatt. I have a 401k and a house, and I'm still a miserable cunt!' Motherfucker, someone smarter than you sold you a dream you never even wanted in the first place. See? The pity goes both ways. Except I don't try to tell you how to live your fucking life."

"I'm not the one who almost killed himself less than a week ago," Wyatt said coldly.

Siggy glared at him. "Like you even actually give a shit."

"Maybe I shouldn't, since you clearly don't."

Siggy suppressed the overwhelming urge to leap across the embers and deliver a kick square into Wyatt's chest. He spat on the ground as he stood. "I never asked for your fucking help."

Wyatt glowered at him silently.

With nowhere else to go, Siggy stormed off into the trees. The forest was dark, but the moon had risen high enough to paint the world in the faintest tones of grey. Siggy walked until the glow of the embers disappeared beyond the black wall of tree trunks. After a short piss, he found a downed log and sat, then pulled another cigarette out and lit it.

"Who the fuck does he think he is?" Siggy mumbled to himself. He clenched his jaw shut and imagined all the ways he could beat the shit out of Wyatt. He pictured waiting a few hours and dragging Wyatt out of the tent in his mummy bag, whaling on him with a branch until Wyatt screamed for mercy. Or maybe running up behind him on the crest of a ravine while they hiked, shoving him hard and watching with glee as the oversized mule tumbled down the rocky embankment, pack and all.

The thought made him smirk. But they were just satisfying fantasies, nothing more. The truth was that Siggy would still die for both of those men back at that campsite, and he knew it. Furthermore, he knew there was at least some modicum of truth to Wyatt's words.

Fuck.

Maybe Wyatt was right. Siggy knew he was a fuckup, and maybe all he was doing was making the world a worse place. It's not like he hadn't considered it before — hell, he'd wholeheartedly believed it from time to time. Was now one of those times?

Either way, Siggy wished now more than ever that the Wyatt from ten years ago would come kick the shit out of the new one. Because that dude back at the fire was a real dick.

Siggy took a puff of the cigarette and sighed, listening to the wind rattle through the leaves. He closed his eyes and imagined a different world. One where *he* was the one giving advice. Where *he* had his shit together... God, that sounded so fucking boring.

Quiet footsteps padding through the pine needles behind him.

Great. Couldn't he get one moment in peace where he wasn't being berated for every decision he'd ever made? Doc's snores still resonated from the campsite, so he knew it was Wyatt without even looking back. "You think you're being sneaky? Huh? What the hell do you want?" Siggy grumbled.

Wyatt didn't respond. He just stood there, silently. Siggy decided to not even acknowledge him, but the foul scent of body odor drifted by in the wind. "And you fucking stink, you know that? At least I know how to use deodorant, you—"

"Did you say something?" Wyatt's gruff voice called from the campsite.

Siggy spun, his eyes darting around the darkness as the hair on the back of his neck bristled.

There was no one there.

He climbed to his feet and his hands formed into fists. Slowly, he rotated in a full circle, searching for movement.

"Siggy?" Wyatt called again.

"Yeah... It's... it's nothing," Siggy called back, seeing nothing but the shadowy outline of trees around him. He swallowed hard, but his mouth was dry.

He strode back to the camp in quick steps, hackles raised and eyes still scanning.

What the fuck did I just smoke?

10

Doc

"MOTHERFUCKER!"

Doc woke with a start. Somewhere outside the tent, Wyatt was shouting furiously. It took Doc half a second to orient before he was scrambling to get out of his sleeping bag and pull on his boots. Siggy had just awakened as well, and they stumbled over each other to escape the crowded canvas enclosure. Wyatt was nowhere to be seen. Doc called for him, and a moment later he emerged from the trees.

"What's wrong?" Doc asked.

Wyatt tossed a stretch of 550 cord at their feet.

Doc recognized it as the same cord they'd used to hang the pack containing their food the night before. "Where's the food?"

"Gone."

"Oh goddamnit," Doc groaned. "Something got to it?"

"No," Wyatt came back flatly. "Not something. Some*one*. It was untied, not chewed."

Doc picked up the cord and, sure enough, both ends were clean. "There's got to be another explanation. We haven't seen another person since—"

"There was someth— I mean, someone last night. Maybe," Siggy said softly.

"Excuse me?" Wyatt demanded.

Siggy looked strange. His cheeks were flush, and he kept his gaze down at his feet. "I don't know, man. I thought I heard…" He shook his head, as if trying to clear a broken Etch A Sketch. When he looked up, he stared at Wyatt. "When I went to piss, there was someone else out in the woods. I thought it was you, but then you yelled to me from the fire, and when I looked again, they were gone."

"And you didn't think this was something you should have fucking shared with us?" Wyatt threw his arms up. "Siggy, what the *fuck*?"

"I don't know, man, I…. I thought maybe it was something in the weed, that I was just being paranoid."

"How much do you want to bet it was those kids?" Wyatt turned to Doc. "Did he tell you, Doc, how he ripped them off?"

"What do you mean?" Doc stared at Siggy, whose regular upbeat confidence was absent.

"I took a few joints when they weren't looking. That's all," Siggy admitted.

"Why would you…?" Doc let the question drift away. He cleared his throat and looked at Wyatt, who was still fuming. "It doesn't matter. Okay? We lost some food, and we need to keep a sharper eye out. But we're all still okay and here, and we've got the rest of our gear—"

"The first aid kit was in the pack with the food," Wyatt said sharply. "The water filter. The fucking iodine tablets. The goddamn bullets. Everything we have left is warming layers, tents, and sleeping bags. How the hell are we 'okay' without food or potable water?"

"Wyatt." Doc stretched a gentle hand toward Wyatt. "You need to take it easy for a minute, okay?"

Wyatt's face froze over in a stony glare. "I'm perfectly easy, Doc." He stalked over to the tent and began tearing it down. "Get your fucking boy in line."

"Doc," Siggy said quietly enough for only the two of them to hear. "He's an asshole, but he's right. I'm sorry."

"Just… just try to remember it's not just you out here, okay? We've got to look out for each other."

Doc had meant the words to be corrective and reassuring, but the look on Siggy's face as he heard them revealed that they might have been the most painful ones yet.

"What now?" Wyatt fumed once their gear was packed. "Whether or not Crossman's actually out here, we won't be able to help him if we're the ones that end up needing rescuing."

"You can do whatever you want, but I'm still pushing on," Siggy stated, and before Wyatt could retaliate he held up the map and pointed to their next checkpoint. Doc stepped forward and read the barely legible writing above the marker: Poulin Guide Service.

"If there's anyone out here with the shit we need, it's a backwoods hunting guide," Siggy continued. "Hell, they might even know Crossman, or at least seen him on his way through. Either way, I'm headed there."

There was a tense silence. Doc genuinely thought that Wyatt might simply turn and start back in the direction they came from. But he only maintained his scowl, pulled on his pack, and began trudging forward.

That day's hike was the worst yet. As the sun climbed higher, the temperature continued to rise. By mid-morning, it felt like Savannah in July — mid-80s and humid as hell. Mosquitos swarmed them relentlessly in the motionless air. The handful of logging roads they'd been lucky enough to traverse the day before were now replaced by dense pine forests. More than once they found themselves wading through stagnant bogs or climbing steep hillsides only to find themselves atop impassable ledges. Doc's stomach grumbled and turned sour with hunger, but they held off on eating the meager rations they had left, which were only a handful of protein bars Wyatt had forgotten he had in his day pack. Despite their parched throats, none of them drank more than a few sips at a time from the Nalgene bottles that contained the remainder of their filtered water.

Dehydration kicked in for Wyatt first, surprisingly. Despite him being in the best shape, his hulking frame demanded far more sustenance than the others. As he slowed, Doc began to consider that maybe their decision to push forward could have been a mistake. But at that point it didn't matter. The guide outpost was only a handful of miles away, and they were now a day and a half from the river. Even if they did turn back, they would face a significant battle in paddling the canoe against the current the whole way back to Crossman's cabin.

Plus, more importantly, Crossman was still out there.

The trio began to swap the two remaining packs among them, each man getting a rotating twenty minute reprieve to air their sweat-soaked backs. As the fatigue began to turn off the finer points of Doc's thought process, he focused on the various rhythms of the march. He hummed Johnny Cash, matching the song's beat to the gentle feeling of his fingers brushing against the knife sheath on his belt. He passed the hours in this trance, panting, humming, groaning as his aching knees were forced to take on yet another hill, then another. However, not once did he complain. Neither did the others.

They finally stopped for a long break early in the afternoon. Wyatt divided the protein bars equally, and they finished what was left of their water. Siggy volunteered to descend the side of a shallow ravine to refill the water bottles in a creek at the bottom. Meanwhile, Doc and Wyatt sat opposite each other on their packs.

"You need to lighten up on him," Doc said quietly once Siggy was out of earshot.

"I know. I know." Wyatt sighed. "The kid's become his own worst enemy. And that's fine when he's on his own, but here? Why can't he just fucking behave?"

"I'm sure a lot of people said the same thing about you back in the day."

Wyatt stood to stretch his legs and back. "You're absolutely right. And I grew up and did something about it."

22

Siggy

THE POULIN Guide Service was located in an overgrown clearing at the center of a narrow valley. Siggy was the first one to spot it. It was late in the day, and as they emerged onto a nearby hilltop, the darkened square of a structure far below caught his eye. He called out to the others triumphantly, pointing to the distant speck and letting out a victorious whoop. They pushed onward, all of them benefiting from a much needed second wind.

When they finally broke into the clearing, their excitement quickly melted. The structure was rugged, built in the same fashion as Crossman's cabin but on a larger scale. There were no vehicles out front, and even at a distance Siggy could see that the dirt road leading away from it was overgrown with saplings. Dull black licks of soot streaked the outer walls, and where there once was a slanted roof was now little more than a broken crater of scattered shingles and charred two-by-fours.

It was clear as they approached that a fire had taken out everything inside. All that was left was a charcoal crusted cave. Years of rain had washed away most of the debris, but the area immediately around the building was still littered with the half burnt remains of what had once been someone's livelihood.

Doc dropped his pack outside the front door and flopped down on it, letting out a drawn out "fuck." Beside him, Wyatt didn't make a peep. He just stared at the blackened relic as if it had insulted him personally.

Siggy let his curiosity overtake his own frustration. He stepped up to the charred archway that had been the front door and gave the logs a hard push. They held strong. The structural integrity of the outer walls seemed moderately intact, and he figured that the place probably went up during a rainstorm. He stepped inside, letting his eyes adjust to the looming darkness, and scanned the building's carcass.

"There ain't shit here. Now what?" Siggy called back to the others.

"Now what? *Now what?* You fucking tell me, Siggy," Wyatt snapped.

Siggy felt a sudden anger bubble up inside of him. "Are you ever going to get off my dick, or do you just live there now?"

"The fuck did you just say?" Wyatt was on his feet, quickly covering the distance between them in long strides before coming to a halt only a few feet from Siggy.

"You heard me, you big dumb bitch," Siggy spat. *Fuck Wyatt.* If he wanted a fight so badly, he could get one.

Both combatants faced off, filthy with dirt and sweat and staring the other down with clenched fists.

Wyatt took a step forward.

"Enough!" Doc shouted loud enough to make them both pause. "Quit playing grab ass and look at this."

Wyatt stopped. Siggy never stopped glaring at him though, instead letting Wyatt break the stare down first.

Doc knelt beside something on the outer wall of the building. Siggy waited until Wyatt was a few steps ahead before following.

The words "Peter 5:8" were carefully carved into the burnt logs, the etched light brown letters standing in stark contrast to their black background. Something hung from a jutting splinter in the wood beneath it. It glinted in the late afternoon sun.

Doc pulled it free, rolling the thin metal dog tags over in his hand. "They're Crossman's."

Wyatt's attention was caught on the lettering. "I'm going to go out on a limb here and guess that neither of you two heathens brought along a Bible."

Siggy shook his head. "Don't need to. 'Be alert and of sober mind. Your enemy the devil prowls around like a roaring lion looking for someone to devour.'"

"What?" Doc and Wyatt said at the same time. They shot him the same shocked expression.

"Peter 5:8." Siggy didn't look up from the carved letters. They were deep and exact. Crossman had taken his time on this. "Old Sister Margaret used to beat that one into my head when I was in school. She never said it, but I swear she believed I was the devil reborn."

"You went to Catholic school?" Doc looked doubtful.

"I never told you that?"

"No," Wyatt muttered. "Makes perfect sense though."

"Fuck you," Siggy came back. Doc took a quick sideways step to place himself between them, but the corners of Wyatt's lips twitched ever so slightly. Siggy couldn't help but match the muted smile.

An hour later, they all sat outside the burnt structure in silence. The air had left their sails, and even Wyatt seemed too exhausted to continue his bullheaded attacks. They needed to rest and recalibrate, plan their next move, but none of them had the energy to talk let alone make a plan, so instead they plopped down where they were and waited. To pass the time, Siggy tossed a pebble at a nearby boulder. He missed and tried again. Wyatt joined in, flinging half-dollar-sized rocks until one clacked off the larger stone. Then the target shifted to an old tree stump, then a smaller boulder farther away. Doc watched them, failing to hide the bewildered expression on his face. Siggy could read his thoughts: Marines... Fucking cavemen, every one of them.

"We'll camp here," Wyatt announced as the sun sank beyond sight. "Then figure out what comes next in the morning."

They agreed, and as Wyatt and Doc set up the tent, Siggy retreated around the back of the building to take a piss. The air was cooling quickly. After he finished, he lit a cigarette and took a seat atop a rotting picnic table to watch the sun set over the field ahead. The orange glow of the clouds blended with the majesty of the fiery treetops. Below the crown of flames, acres of uncultivated grass danced wildly in the breeze to the tune of the crickets and songbirds.

It was a bit more awestriking than Siggy had expected. Chaotic beauty incarnate. He found himself enraptured in the wild rhythms and swirling colors, lost in the beauty of the moment.

He was so enraptured, in fact, that his brain didn't initially register the dark silhouette standing in the opposite tree line.

When his vision finally drifted over it, he felt himself flinch. It looked like a man's figure in the distance. The shadows of the trees did much in concealing the statuesque shape, and for a long moment Siggy wasn't sure if what he was seeing was anything more than an oddly shaped stump or clump of brush. But as he adjusted his focus, he swore he could make out the faded contours of a naked body.

He called softly to the others. "Guys, come tell me I'm not losing it."

"You're fucking losing it," Wyatt shouted sarcastically.

The figure bolted into the woods.

The nerves yanked tight in Siggy's spine until he could feel the tingle in the bottom of his throat. "I know you're not going to believe me," he called. "But regardless, we're gonna need to set up a fire watch tonight."

12

Doc

DOC WAS laying in his bed. The sheets were satin smooth and the comforter held the warmth of the two bodies. The soft skin of his wife's thigh brushed against his fingers, and he felt the rush of heat course through him.

"Sally," he whispered.

She giggled, such a perfect, teasing little noise. One she only made when the time was right, when the outside world melted away and it was just the two of them in their little cocoon. He let his fingers glide gently up her leg, over her hips and along her side as he kissed her neck. Somewhere in another room, one of the kids said something to their sibling. He couldn't tell who it was; it didn't matter. They were supposed to be in bed, sure, but at least they were home. At least they were back.

Her hair smelled like lavender and honey. He closed his eyes, breathing in the scent he'd missed for so long.

But when he opened them she was gone.

He stood. The room wasn't theirs. This one was open, a gentle breeze gliding across his bare chest. The warm sand beneath his feet swallowed his toes. Palm trees swayed all around him. She was ahead, laughing, beckoning him to follow. The shirt she wore was thin. It was one of his, a cheap button-up he'd bought for their honeymoon. The hemline barely covered her hips, and as she walked the breeze revealed that her curves were the only thing hidden underneath.

He felt himself flush as he made to follow her. The sand was deep, and he had to kick his way free with each step. But she was slow, always just ahead. Just out of reach. She made it to the palm trees, and he followed, where the warmth of the sun gave way to a cool shaded forest. She darted among the trees, teasing him. But they weren't palm trees anymore. They were pines. When he looked down, he saw that the sand had turned to mud. Warm, *schlocking* mud. She didn't seem to touch it, though. She glided above it, beckoning him deeper and deeper into the darkness until he could barely make out her shape. He felt something, deep down in the recesses of his soul. A distinct ping of danger that a hunger resonated from the darkness. But then she was there again, just ahead, the top of one ample breast peeking out from the unbuttoned shirt. He pushed faster, harder, intent on his target. This time she didn't flee. Finally, he caught her, and they collapsed to the hard ground, rolling and tumbling amid the crackle of leaves.

13

Wyatt

WYATT WOKE to a dull ache in his gut. It wasn't a typical stomachache or even the hunger pangs he'd begun to grow accustomed to. It was something he couldn't quite place, something he might have guessed was rooted in anxiety or fear. But he didn't have any nightmares that night. Hell, he hadn't had any in days.

He sat up on an elbow. The tent around him was dark, and Siggy's gentle snores nearly drowned out the chirps of the crickets outside. Doc's sleeping bag lay deflated between them. For a second, Wyatt felt a spike of panic. Then he remembered that Doc had drawn the first shift of fire watch and was no doubt sitting bored in the darkness just outside.

A large part of Wyatt didn't believe Siggy's story from that evening. Had the kid actually seen someone? Maybe. But Siggy's track record was pretty iffy at this point. Maybe it had been a hunter or even a poacher clad in black. Or a hiker or a camper or any number of other reasonable explanations. But a naked man? In this environment? Wyatt shuddered at the thought. The creeping sensation of ticks crawling around his exposed crevasses made him reach down and check.

Either way, regardless of the legitimacy of Siggy's claims, it was worth leaving one of them on guard by the fire. Especially after what happened with their food.

Wyatt lay back down and tried to force sleep, but it evaded him. That strange feeling, halfway between anxiety and fear, clung to his mind like a shadow. He checked his watch: quarter to eleven.

"Fuck it," he muttered, stripping away the sleeping bag and pulling on his boots. It was almost his watch anyway. He'd slept fully clothed, not wanting to deal with the annoyance of dressing in the dark. Now he was grateful for the decision.

Outside the night was cool, dark, and damp. As he pushed through the tent flap he saw that the fire had died to embers. A quick glance around told him that Doc was not present.

"Doc!" he called in a hushed tone.

There was no answer.

The burnt structure loomed in the darkness nearby. He clicked on his headlamp and trudged over to it, thinking that maybe Doc was inside, looking for more clues. The shell of a building was empty.

"Doc!" he tried again, only a bit louder.

Still, nothing.

The feeling in his gut grew stronger, validated now by the fleeting images of any number of terrifying possibilities. He retrieved the bow from its position beside the tent, then nocked an arrow. Doc had his revolver — wherever the hell he was.

Don't be overreactive, Wyatt almost whispered aloud to himself. He took a deep breath, listening in the dark. Maybe Doc was taking a shit. Maybe he'd decided to do a lap around the area, check things out. Despite how unlikely both of these scenarios were, the alternatives seemed even crazier.

"Doc!" he finally called out at full volume.

Siggy grumbled in the tent. But there was another noise too, coming from the forest.

"Be quiet," Wyatt hissed through the flap. He waited, ears perked and eyes searching. "Doc!"

The noise came again. A groan, far off in the trees.

"Siggy, on your feet!" Wyatt barked. He didn't wait for a response, charging off in the direction of the noise.

The headlamp's beam bounced with his gait, illuminating the dense underbrush as he crashed through it. "Doc! Doc, where are you?"

The groan came once more, louder, but quickly fell silent.

Wyatt crashed through a copse of young pines and nearly tripped over Doc's prostrate form. He lay there, face-down in the dirt, one of his legs twitching and a quiet murmur slipping from his lips. Something else crashed through the brush nearby. Wyatt pulled the bowstring back and spun to face it, but he was too slow. It was gone in a flurry of shaking ferns and snapping twigs.

"What the hell is going on?" Siggy appeared behind him, panting.

"Something was here." Wyatt lowered the bow.

"Doc." Siggy knelt down beside Doc and gave him a stiff shake.

Doc snapped awake. He fought to his feet, a wide-eyed look of confusion plastered on his face. "What the hell?"

Wyatt kept his eyes locked on the forest. "What the fuck happened, Doc?"

"She was here." Doc spun in a circle, looking desperately in every direction.

"Who?"

Doc shook his head violently then slapped himself. He was breathing heavy, and a stiff erection showed clearly through his pants. "I…" he started, but he let the words fade, staring vacantly out into the darkness.

14

Siggy

"YOU CAN'T tell me this isn't freaking you out." Siggy warmed his hands over the fire. The glow of the sun hung over the trees behind him, casting Wyatt in the shadows of pre-dawn. Neither of them had slept since returning to the camp just a few hours before.

"It's not that crazy," Wyatt said again. "They're big woods, sure. But there's a ton of wildlife out here. Plus, it's bow hunting season up here. If you did see someone—"

"I fucking saw someone."

"Okay, well, it was dusk. People hunt at dusk. And as for Doc, he said it himself that he was sleepwalking."

"And the thing you scared away?"

"Coyote. Maybe a bobcat or even a fisher. Who knows, just some animal coming to check out the ruckus, I'm sure."

"It's too much." Siggy shook his head. "Something weird is going on here. We should've brought a fucking platoon."

"We don't have one." Wyatt stood from his log and circled the fire until he was directly beside Siggy. Behind them, Doc still snored loudly in the tent. "We need food or else we can't push on, no matter how much we might want to find Crossman."

"We can't leave him out here, not with all this shit that's happening to us. Imagine—"

"We're no use to him if *we* end up needing rescuing," Wyatt insisted. He was calm but resolute. "You know that. I know that. Food is our number one priority now."

"You think Uber Eats delivers out here?"

Wyatt eyed the bow. "We need to hunt. Trap, too. Do you know how to make a snare?"

Siggy gave him a sidelong glance. "What do you think?"

Wyatt snorted. "I'll show you."

Wyatt did show him. Together they stripped down a length of 550 cord, exposing the thin white string at its core, and used it to tie a series of slipknots. Next, Wyatt explained the method of setting them and where to do so effectively. By the time they were done, they took their places once more by the fire, ten traps laying nearby, ready to be set.

"I'm going to go set up in the forest with the bow," Wyatt said. "With any luck, a deer might wander by. The wind is going southeast, so I'll find a spot somewhere to the northwest, not too far outside of earshot. I'll take half the snares and set them on the way. You take the other half and set them to the south. Make sure you remember where you set them, okay? These things tend to disappear if you're not paying attention."

Siggy glanced behind him at the tent. "What about Doc?"

"What about him?"

"He seemed a little… I don't know, tripped out last night. You think he's alright?"

Wyatt waved him off. "He's fine. They say not to wake a sleepwalker; he was probably just fucked up from that."

"You've got all the answers, huh?" Siggy didn't mean it to come off as snarky.

"It's easy when the questions are simple." Wyatt nodded to the snares. "*Don't* forget where you put them. The simple fact is that if we can't get some food today, we're going to have to turn back."

It was mid-morning before Doc came crawling out of the tent. Wyatt had been gone for hours already, disappearing into the forest beyond the field. He'd taken the bow and left Siggy with the revolver, just in case some critter came sniffing around.

"Mornin', Doc," Siggy called from inside the burnt building. He'd been digging through the scant remnants of the ruinous blaze for the last hour after setting the snares. So far the only thing of value he'd managed to pull out of the ashes was a soot-stained cast iron pot.

Doc grumbled in response. He sat by the dwindling fire, his back to Siggy. "There any food?"

"Not yet. Wyatt's trying to bag a deer though, so hopefully we'll get a feast."

Doc once again grumbled something he couldn't hear.

"You alright, bud?" Siggy probed.

"Fine."

"You remember what happened last night?"

"Of course I remember," Doc snarled.

Siggy almost left it at that. But Doc was never this way. "Dude, what's going on?"

"What the fuck do you mean, 'what's going on?' I'm fucking hungry."

Siggy stood and wiped the soot from his knees, then strode over to the fire. "Alright, man. No need to bite my head off."

"Then quit asking me dumb fucking questions!" Doc snapped, spinning to face him.

Siggy's reply caught in his throat. Doc's face was pale. His eyes were drawn, and dark bags hung beneath them. "Doc, Jesus Christ, man, are you—"

"Am I what, *Siggy*? Am I *alright*? I already fucking told you—"

"Your face is fucked, dude."

"*Your* face is fucked!" Doc was almost yelling. Then, like a light switch clicking off in his head, the angry glare melted. "Wait, what… what do you mean?"

Siggy took a cautious step forward. Doc suddenly seemed disoriented, staring at him in confusion. "You look sick. Like, *sick* sick. How do you feel?"

"I feel fine," he grumbled, the disorientation suddenly transforming back into irritation. "I feel fine. I just slept like shit. I'm sorry. Okay? I'm sorry." Doc turned to stare at the fire once more.

15

Wyatt

WYATT FOUND a gnarled behemoth sugar maple overlooking a creek. Its lowest branches were thicker than most of the surrounding pine trunks, and Wyatt had no issues climbing a dozen feet up before settling into one of their crooks and surveying his killing grounds. Despite the colorful leaves that still clung to the branches, he managed to carve out a handful of shooting lanes.

The bow he held was a newer model. A compound with a sticker that denoted its seventy pound pull. Siggy had forgotten to grab the trigger when he took it from the cabin, but luckily Wyatt had grown up shooting recurves without one. The attached quiver held six thin carbon fiber arrows, each tipped with a menacing three-sided broadhead. He tried a test shot at a nearby log and found that the sights were still perfectly dialed in.

Nothing moved for nearly an hour after he'd taken his position. As the day drew on and the surrounding creatures slowly forgot his passing, the forest eventually came back to life. Mice rattled the leaves as they burrowed underneath, and fat grey squirrels danced through the surrounding treetops. Birds resumed their end-of-season chirps, and a crow cawed from somewhere to the north. As his presence dissolved into the branches of the old tree, Wyatt found himself oddly at peace.

It had been twenty years since the last time he'd gone hunting.

His father had given him an old 30.06 for his tenth birthday. At the time, Wyatt was ecstatic, bouncing off the walls and begging his father to take him to the rifle range so he could shoot it until his shoulder bruised. That fall, he and the old man had christened the rifle with a trip into the boonies of western Massachusetts. The two of them managed to fill an old deer stand with excited silence for a whole six hours before a doe wandered by.

She was less than a hundred yards out, grazing along the edge of the field they lorded over. Wyatt still remembered with painful accuracy the careful breaths he pulled in as he lined up the crosshairs behind her broadside shoulder, the gentle pressure as he squeezed the trigger, and his surprise when the rifle finally bucked in his hands. He'd felt such pride in that first moment after the shot. He remembered looking over to his father with a bright smile as the old man stared through his binoculars in the direction of the surely dead deer. The shot had been perfect. Wyatt was sure of it.

But when the binoculars dropped, so did young Wyatt's stomach. His father was a kind man, but not one to hide his emotions well. The crestfallen frown told the ten-year-old boy all he needed to know.

According to the old man, somewhere in the half second that existed between the pull of the trigger and the impact of the round, the young deer had bolted, shifting the point of impact nearly a foot backwards along her side. The lead-tipped bullet tore into her stomach an inch behind her ribs, its soft tip mushrooming and exploding a distended glob of entrails out her other side. Wyatt managed to bring the scope back to his eye just in time to catch the reddish pink flare of the organs that trailed from her side as she bounded away across the dusky field.

His father decided that they wouldn't track it, at least not yet. He said that a deer wounded in such a manner needed time to bed down and die of blood loss. If they went out that night, they ran too high of a risk that they would bump her deeper into the woods, extending her misery and potentially losing her trail as she clotted up.

Wyatt didn't sleep at all that night. He tossed and turned in their tent and secretly cried shameful tears just quiet enough to not wake his father sleeping beside him.

They found the doe the next morning. She ran over a mile from where she'd been shot. Wyatt's father had done well in wearing a chipper mask as they followed the sparse blood trail, but that façade broke when they came upon where she'd been dragged down. The coyotes had been at her in the night — not before she'd passed though. The violence was clear in the crater of displaced leaves and torn earth she lay in. It had not been quick, and her mutilated remains told a story of tremendous agony.

His father told him that it was alright. That it happened to the best of hunters. That there was nothing they could do about the past. But for months after that, Wyatt would lay in bed at night and weep, imagining that poor animal's final moments: that big-eyed young doe limping helplessly through the underbrush, a trail of her own innards dragging beside her in the dirt and every cackling yip of her fanged pursuers sending a jolt of primordial terror through her slowly failing heart.

That was the week Wyatt stopped going to church with his mother.

But he went hunting again the next year. And the year after that as well.

Now, his ass was growing numb from the knobby branch he was sitting on. He only left the tree once around noon to stretch his legs after the soreness threatened to overwhelm him. As another hour passed, he found his attention fading and considered how he was going to tell the others that they wouldn't be able to push on to find Crossman.

Had it not been for the snap of a twig below, he might have missed the distinct flash of white through the pines. He took a slow breath, bringing the bow to bear and wrapping his two fingers around the string.

This doe was large. Massive compared to the ones he'd hunted in southern states. He remembered something Crossman had said ages before, about the deer in Maine being "absolute units," as he put it. As the doe nosed its way out of the bushes, Wyatt couldn't help but agree.

She rotated slowly, taking in the entirety of the small clearing. Her coat was a thick beautiful brown. It twitched along her spine, dislodging a handful of deer flies that buzzed over her before they settled once more.

As she took her first cautious step into the open, Wyatt let his breath grow shallow. He focused on his balance, wedging one foot deeper into the crook of the branches and willing the wind not to shift in her direction. Luck was with him, and after a few long seconds she came into range.

He drew slowly, the undernourished muscles in his shoulders burning with the movement. The sights lined up. He dropped the pin just a tad low, as he had been taught, then let out a long breath.

At the snap of the bow she dropped low to the ground — exactly as he had hoped. He watched the bright red-and-white fletching disappear through the center of her ribcage and the blood spurt from her side as she bolted west in mortal panic, crashing haphazardly through the dried leaves and underbrush.

When the sound of her frantic flight faded, silence reclaimed the forest. Wyatt sat completely still, waiting. He'd seen the entry point. The shot was clean, likely tagging both lungs. Still, he didn't want to run the risk of pushing her before she succumbed.

Ten minutes later, he climbed out of the tree and backtracked to the edge of the guide service clearing where they'd made camp. In the distance, he could make out Siggy sitting atop the rotted out picnic table, staring into the distance as a cloud of cigarette smoke lifted away. Wyatt picked up an acorn shell and used it to amplify his whistle until Siggy caught sight of him. He waved for them to join him.

Both Siggy and Doc made the trek across the field, Doc lagging a distance behind. When Siggy finally reached him, Wyatt said, "I only need one of you. Doc should stay back with the gear."

Siggy looked worried. "I don't think so, man. Doc is... Well, something's wrong. I don't think we should split up."

Wyatt began to ask what he meant, but when Doc approached, he realized he didn't need to. Doc was trudging slowly. His skin was pasty and he looked like he hadn't slept in a week.

"You alright, Doc?" he asked.

Doc scowled. "Why do you guys keep asking that? I'm fine. I'm not a child."

"You look sick."

"I'm *fine*."

Wyatt didn't argue. "Let's just get on with it, alright? I tagged a doe a few hundred feet in. She's had time to bleed out, so we'll need to track her down and drag her out. Try to be quiet as we go just in case she's still drawing breath. We all on the same page?"

The others nodded.

"Good. On me."

They made their way back to the creek and Wyatt recovered his arrow. The blood staining the fletching was thin and foamy, a good sign that Wyatt had struck a lung. A clear blood trail made the initial tracking process easy. Wyatt stopped only occasionally, holding up an open hand to signal the others to silence so that he could listen for movement ahead. The forest was quiet.

After a hundred more feet of bloodstained leaves and branches and panicked hoofprints, the deer had made a hard turn north down the slope of an embankment and into a swamp. There, among the canted cedars and mossy logs, the trail dissolved into the watery muck.

"Fuck." Wyatt scanned the shadowy expanse. "We need to form a line and police call. The last thing we want is to wander around and ruin any potential spore. Hopefully she's close, or at least that she came out the other side somewhere and that we can pick the trail back up."

They did as he instructed, forming a line only a few yards from each other and canvasing the marshy stretch like a search party. An hour passed before they'd even made a dent, covering maybe a quarter of the swamp and soaking their boots and pant legs in the process. Doc fell twice, coming up both times filthy and swearing. If it hadn't been for Doc's inflammatory demeanor, Wyatt would have insisted that Doc head back. But his presence seemed like the lesser of two evils.

The sun dropped lower and lower, and Wyatt found himself using the headlamp to try to pick up the distinct red glint of blood. It wasn't until dusk had come in full that he finally got lucky. On the far side of the swamp, a flash of red reflected in his beam. He let out a whistle and pointed. Siggy let out an audible sigh of relief while Doc just grunted.

The trail leading out of the swamp was odd. The doe had zigzagged, bolting first north, then west, then appearing to double back before doubling back once again. This made Wyatt imagine that maybe another predator had happened upon her and given chase, resulting in her serpentine path. He swapped the bow with Siggy, taking back the revolver and securing it on his hip. Just in case.

They found the end of the trail just as full dark had overtaken the forest. Only, there was no deer. A splash of blood and a mad flurry of hoofprints spattered the center of a small wallow. The mud was displaced, the leaves thrashed about above in a whirlwind of violence that brought a sickeningly familiar image to Wyatt's mind.

"Son of a bitch," he muttered, more to himself than the others. "Something else must have gotten to her."

"Wyatt…" Siggy breathed.

Wyatt turned toward him. The headlamp illuminated the ghastly look on his face, then his shaking finger as he pointed upward. Wyatt followed the motion. The light bathed over the deer's limp corpse draped in the branches above.

16

Siggy

IT TOOK both Wyatt and Siggy climbing the thin ash tree to dislodge the doe. She'd tumbled to the ground with a wet thud, and now she lay in the leaves before them. They stood over her, staring in disbelief at the corpse.

Her head flopped backwards toward her spine, grey tongue dangling from her jaws and blank eyes staring vacantly toward the canopy above. She'd been bitten in the neck. The wound was large and oval, and thin tendrils of veins hung from it while dark red patches of dried blood matted her soft coat. One of her hind legs was broken and bore a similar bite mark to the one on her neck.

"What the hell did this?" Doc breathed.

"Cougar," Wyatt said, although his voice shook in a way that betrayed his own disbelief. Then, more confidently, "Cougar. Had to be."

"There are fucking cougars out here?" Siggy asked.

"There aren't supposed to be," Wyatt said. "But sure, people spot them in New England all the time. It probably found her just after the shot. We must have interrupted it before it could eat."

Wyatt bent low, shining his headlamp over the body, then pulled out his knife. "Siggy, hold the front leg up here, alright?"

Siggy did as he was told, and Wyatt lightly slid the sharp blade down the animal's sternum and along its stomach, exposing the white fascial tissue beneath. Siggy waited for the blood to come pouring out, but there was none — even as Wyatt began painstakingly pulling the grey organs from within.

"Why isn't there any blood?" Doc breathed.

Wyatt wiped his forehead with his arm and shrugged. "We need to get it back to camp. Most of this meat should be salvageable." He looked up with an obviously fake smile. "This is a good thing, guys."

Deep down, Siggy highly doubted that.

Together they dragged the deer back along the outskirts of the swamp. The moon had yet to rise, and outside of the yellow beam of Wyatt's headlamp, the forest around them was pure black. Siggy's heart was pounding, and every snapped twig or crunching leaf made him twitch. Some ancient part of him screamed against Wyatt's reassuring words as they plodded along.

Once they finally got the deer back to their camp, Wyatt laid her by the fire and set about the skinning process. He started by making a shallow cut around one of the ankles, then extending the cut up the legs and up to the breastbone. Then he scored away the connective tissue as Siggy held the shedding flesh taut. When he was halfway done skinning the intact hindleg, Wyatt stopped short.

Siggy watched as his friend's face knit in confusion. "What's wrong?"

"It's… nothing. It's nothing. Let it down."

Siggy eased the leg down.

Next, Wyatt circled to the animal's back and cut the skin along the spine. "The backstraps will be a better cut. No need to skin the whole thing." He made another connecting cut along the ribs, then peeled back the strap of hide. Again, he stopped about halfway through.

"You gonna fucking tell us what's wrong?" Siggy insisted.

"Look at the color." Wyatt poked the knife into the exposed meat along the deer's spine. It was a dull grey.

"What's it supposed to look like?"

"Not that. Red. Deep, deep red. Almost purple."

"Is it sick?"

Wyatt almost said something, but he held back. Siggy glanced behind him to Doc, who huddled by the fire, eyes locked onto the carcass.

"I've hunted enough times to know that ain't right," Doc muttered. "It ain't sick either. Something fucking did that to it."

"Yeah, a cougar," Wyatt said again.

"No. Don't bullshit me. Something else. Why isn't there any blood? Huh? Where's the fucking *blood*, Wyatt?" Doc's voice shook with anger, and his eyes were sunken and red.

Wyatt held up his hand. "You need to take a breath and calm down."

"I can feel it. I can feel something wrong. Last night, I felt it—"

"Hey!" Wyatt barked. "Motherfucker, what's wrong with you? You cracking up on us? Get ahold of yourself!"

Doc stared daggers at him in the light of the fire. But his expression gradually softened, and his eyes grew tired. "Yeah. Yeah, okay."

"It was a cougar," Wyatt said with finality. "This is probably just bruising from when it pulled the deer into the tree. You're a hunter, right, Doc? You know how much blood a deer can lose from an arrow. Hell, we saw enough of it on the trail."

Doc stared at his feet and nodded.

Siggy eyed the grey meat. "Are we still going to eat it?"

Wyatt thought for a moment, but eventually shook his head. "No. In case it is diseased, we don't want to add that to our plate."

"Then what do we eat?" Siggy asked.

Wyatt cast the beam of the headlamp toward the woods. "Have you checked your snares?"

They dragged the deer carcass out into the forest as they went to check the snares. Luck was with them. One of the snares had snagged what

Siggy thought was a thin brown rabbit, but according to Wyatt, it was a snowshoe hare. Despite Siggy's initial excitement at the prospect of a hearty meal, he soon found out that the creature's disproportionately large feet made up the majority of its bulk. Wyatt made some quick incisions and pulled the skin off with several hard tugs. After disemboweling it, they took the cast iron pot Siggy had recovered and filled it halfway with water and added the entire remainder of the carcass, bones and all. They chopped up some pine needles, and Siggy managed to find some end-of-season wild chives. With all their ingredients combined, they dumped the tiny bottle of Tabasco that Doc kept on his keychain into the concoction and set it over the fire to boil.

As they sat in the flickering orange glow of the fire, Siggy took in his companions' faces. Doc was distant as he stared through the flames, shivering every so often. Siggy knew the look. It was one he'd seen many times before. Doc wasn't there with them. He was back home, imagining himself wrapped in the warmth of society with a full belly and the love of his family.

Wyatt, on the other hand, ceaselessly fidgeted with the knife in his hands. He spun it casually, as if the blade was just a dull toy, every so often looking as if he might say something. Siggy knew why he didn't, though. Both of them were afraid of pushing Doc further into the hole he'd clearly fallen into.

"Doc, can we talk?" Siggy finally asked.

Doc glanced up innocently. "What's up, man?"

"You just seem… well, out of sorts."

"I know. I'm sorry. I just think it's the hunger. This will help."

Siggy and Wyatt shared a look.

"I think maybe we should turn back," Wyatt said.

"No, no, I'm good, guys, really," Doc insisted.

"We don't have any food, Doc. It's not like this is going to get any easier—"

"You think I'm too fucking weak?" Doc's head snapped up, eyes suddenly slits. "Is that it?"

"No, man. Fuck," Siggy jumped in. "It's like Wyatt said: we're no use to Crossman if we're the ones who need rescuing."

"Then go back," Doc said matter-of-factly. "I'm not fucking leaving. Not without Crossman."

"We don't even know if he's—"

"He's here," Doc said curtly. "He's out here. Trust me."

Siggy didn't know how to respond.

"Something drained that fucking deer," Doc went on. "Something did that. And you two want to just bail on Crossman, leave him out here with that thing."

Wyatt tried to reason with him. "Come on, dude. It was a—"

"A cougar? A *cougar*? Get out of here with that shit. No cougar does that. Stop treating us like we're fucking fourth graders. You might be a smart guy, Wyatt, but we're not fucking idiots."

"What do you think it is then?" Siggy prompted softly.

Doc shook his head. "I don't know. I don't know. Something else. Something bad. Something fucking evil. Can't you *feel* it?"

Neither of them answered. A strained silence settled over the campfire.

Wyatt was the first to speak, stabbing the knife down into the log beside him and standing as if to punctuate his sincerity. "Have you guys ever heard of the lions of Tsavo?"

"No," Siggy said. Doc didn't respond at all.

"Around the turn of the century, the British decided to build this railroad through Kenya. The workers started disappearing shortly after they began. Just gone, vanishing in the night. When they finally started to find the bodies, it was otherworldly: skin all torn up, bodies drained of blood. The meat, though, it was mostly untouched. Whatever was killing them didn't want their flesh. It just wanted their blood."

"Why in the ever living *fuck* are you telling us this?" Siggy cut in.

"Because they figured it out in the end," Wyatt said flatly. "It was a lion. Well, two lions. Two *sick* lions. They had a disease that affected their teeth and gums. It made it impossible for them to take down normal prey that had any kind of hide like zebras or gazelle. Well, humans don't exactly have the toughest skin, and the lions found they could simply lick until they reached blood. Only blood isn't the most nourishing food, so they needed a lot of it. Hundreds of people died. But the people there in the shit were convinced that they were battling against demons and were scared to do anything about it. They never imagined that the lions were just animals, so they never treated the attacks like *animal* attacks. That fucked them in the end."

"So what?"

"So why is it so crazy that a cougar, an animal that *used* to be abundant in these parts and is widely reported here today, might not do something similar?" Wyatt turned to Doc, who hadn't reacted at all. "You know what I'm saying, Doc?"

"Where were the footprints?" Doc asked quietly.

"What?"

"Where were the footprints?" he repeated.

It struck Siggy then that he hadn't seen any cougar prints — or any prints at all — at the kill sight.

"You're a hunter, Doc." Wyatt's tone was placative. "You know tracking is more art than science. We could easily have missed—"

"You really don't *feel* it?" Doc asked, louder now. He looked up from the fire. There was fear in his expression.

"Feel what?" Wyatt responded.

"*It*. The woods, the..." Doc took a deep breath, clearly trying to find his words. "There's something wrong with this place. I can feel it, deep down. It's bad. It's real bad."

"Doc..." Siggy tried to hide the worry in his own voice.

"It's just the woods," Wyatt insisted. "And it's a *big* fucking woods. There's a reason places like this always breed ghost stories. Trust me, boys... trust me: *we* are the scariest things out here."

Neither of the others argued. The stew was boiling hard now, meat sloughing off the hare's bones. Siggy pulled the pot off the fire, and they waited in silence for it to cool. Once it had, they divided it up and gave Doc the largest portion. The meat was tough and gamey, but it hit the spot. Siggy slurped down his portion of the broth while it was still hot, almost choking on a small bone. Afterward, a while passed in uncomfortable silence before Wyatt suggested that they get some sleep while he took first watch. Doc didn't fight it. He crawled into the tent silently, and not a minute later, deep, rhythmic snores emanated from the canvas enclosure.

Once he was sure Doc was asleep, Siggy shifted closer to Wyatt. He lit a cigarette and they passed it back and forth. Siggy was finally on his last pack.

After the cigarette was gone, Wyatt gave Siggy's shoulder a gentle squeeze and said, "You should get some sleep."

Siggy made to stand but paused. "You really think that a cougar did it?"

"Yeah."

"But what—"

Wyatt stopped him with a raised hand. "You don't get it, do you?"

"Get what?"

"It needs to be a cougar."

"But if it isn't—"

"It *needs* to be a cougar."

Siggy gave him a blank stare.

Wyatt's eyes glittered in the firelight. "Do you know what keeps us sane? It's not the *idea* that we understand the world. It's the *fact* that we understand it. We need the things that we believe to be true, to actually *be* true. If they aren't — if we, as men, come to the horrifying conclusion that we have no better grip on reality than a fish or a pig, that's what will break a man's mind. I don't give a fuck what happened to that deer. It could have been a cougar or a bear or a horned up hillbilly running around naked on meth. *It doesn't fucking matter.* What matters is that guy right there" —he pointed to the tent— "and for his sake, we need it to be a cougar. He's cracking. You understand?"

Siggy absorbed the words without response.

Later, as Siggy climbed into the tent, he couldn't help but ask, "Do you still not believe in evil, or is that just another thing that *needs* to not exist?"

Wyatt ignored him, staring instead at the embers as they crinkled like a thousand tiny glass panes spiderwebbing all at once.

17

Doc

DOC KNEW he was dragging ass, and he hated himself for it. Siggy and Wyatt were more often than not far ahead of him. Every now and then they'd cast worried glances over their shoulders and suddenly slow down, but it didn't take long for them to pull away again.

His body felt like it had hit a breaking point. The muscles of his thighs ached and burned constantly, and his arms swung limp at his sides. Every trudging step was a battle. But he pushed onwards, doing his best to ignore the excruciating pounding in his head.

That morning the others had given him the last remnants of the hare meat. He tried to argue, but they wouldn't have it. He was the weakest — he'd *always* been the weakest — so he needed it more than they did. Of course, they didn't *say* that to him. No, it was in their eyes. Splayed out across their pitying expressions. He'd eaten it all and chewed on the bones too. He was so hungry. He was *still* so fucking hungry. The sour gurgle in his abdomen tightened into a knot hours ago. Now, he felt his body eating itself, the void in his stomach consuming even his ability to formulate a clear thought.

That's what you get, you fat shit.

The voice was there. That self-loathing demon perched inside his skull, berating his every insecurity. It wasn't new. It had been there for as long as he could remember. Only now it was loud, amplified louder and louder by every cursed tree in this God-forsaken forest.

You're weak. That's why she left you. That's why she won't even call you.

Siggy passed over a wooded hill ahead, pausing at the top to make sure Doc saw where he was before continuing. After a few stumbling steps, Doc collapsed into a patch of grass at the base of the rocky slope. He lay for a moment before forcing himself to keep going. Even then, he didn't stand. On all fours, he hauled himself up the incline, panting and holding back a defeated sob.

You don't even have a fucking pack on, you fat bitch.

It was true. The others had the packs. Doc just had himself. Even so, he could barely move.

They're going to leave you behind. Just like everyone does.

No. They wouldn't do that—

Where are they then? You're alone now, aren't you? I bet they don't wait. Unlike you, they clearly don't have a hard time shedding useless weight.

"No!" Doc breathed the word with as much force as possible, but it barely came out as a whisper. A loose stone gave way in his hand, and he fell again.

Give up. It's what you're best at. Quit burdening them with your pathetic existence.

"Doc!" Siggy was ahead, coming down the crest of the hill. "You okay, boss?"

Doc nodded. Siggy reached him and hauled him to his feet before he gently forced something into Doc's hand.

An apple.

Siggy was grinning wide. "Come on, man. We found something."

Together they crested the hill, and at its top Doc saw what Siggy was talking about. Ahead, there was a patch of old, gnarled apple trees surrounded by wispy saplings and overgrown grass. In their canopies hung hundreds of delicious red orbs.

For just a moment, the voice was quiet. Doc stumbled to the nearest tree, pulling the plumpest fruit from its branch and burying his teeth in it. The apple was tart and grainy. It might have been the best thing he'd ever tasted.

Eat up, fatass.

He bit again, and again, and again until it was just a core. Then he took another and devoured it, then another until his stomach was bursting and he thought he might vomit. Even then, he filled his cargo pockets. Then he collapsed at the base of the tree and battled against the sobs.

Get it out. Let them see how much of a fucking pussy they brought to tag along with them. To slow them—

"Doc." Wyatt was suddenly beside him, his gentle hand placed on Doc's shoulder. "You got to tell us what's wrong, man."

What's wrong? I'll tell you what's wrong—

"Just shut up!" Doc shouted furiously, causing Wyatt to take a step back. Doc looked at him through the tears. "I'm sorry," he cried. "I'm sorry, I just…" But the words didn't come. They weren't there. The writing was on the wall, they all knew the truth. He was fucking useless.

That's when Siggy plopped down heavily beside him and threw an arm around his shoulder. "It's alright, Doc. It's okay."

It was too much. Doc couldn't stop it this time. His body convulsed with sobs, and Siggy held him closer as he let out a pained groan. His next words cracked as he forced them out. "Sally left me."

The others didn't speak. Siggy just held him, and he felt Wyatt's hand on his other shoulder.

"She's gone. She took the kids two months ago. It's over, she won't even—" A racking sob shook his body and broke his voice again. "She won't even let me talk to them."

"I'm so sorry, Doc," Siggy said softly.

"They were *right*." Doc pulled away. "They were right to go."

"No—" one of the others tried.

Doc cut him off. "They *were*. I was… I wouldn't change. I held them back. I was too much, too… I… I failed them. Just like I'm failing you now. It broke me. I'm fucking useless—"

"That's bullshit." Wyatt's voice had an edge to it. "Fucking bullshit, and you know it. You've done nothing but make us stronger here, you understand?"

Doc looked up at the two men. "No! No, I don't. Because you're just trying to keep me moving. And I don't fucking blame you. But I can't. You need to go. You need to find Crossman and get the hell out of these cursed fucking woods."

Wyatt made to talk, but for once it was Siggy who silenced him with a raised finger. "You know what I think, Doc?"

"Yeah, I *do* know what you think. What you *really* think. You think I'm weak. Fucking useless. And I am."

You are.

"No, Doc, no," Siggy said. "I think you're the only one here who's actually done any good in this world. I think you're the only one of us who's *actually* saved anyone. You saved Mortimer when that IED took his foot off. You saved — shit — *how many* Afghans when they came to our gate for help? How many goddamn medical procedures did you perform out of pocket for those motherfuckers?"

"That was a decade ago—"

"You saved *me*. Last week." Siggy's voice was suddenly gentle but firm. "I'm telling you right now, I would've gone right back to the needle. I'd be dead by now if it wasn't for you. For *this*."

Doc spit on the ground and wiped at the tears that stained his cheeks. "And now, we're all lost countless miles into the wilderness because of my stupid fucking idea."

"We're not lost," Wyatt chirped in. "We've got a map, brother. We know exactly where we are."

Siggy snorted. "See that, Doc? You really gonna let *Wyatt* be the positive one?"

Doc did crack a slight smile at this, though it was fleeting.

Siggy held a hand to Doc's forehead. After a moment, he shot a concerned look to Wyatt. "Okay, I'm calling it. You're burning up, big guy. You need help. Whatever's going on, I say that we don't push it any further."

Another failure. Goodbye, Crossman. Rot in them woods.

"No," Doc muttered. "No. We're not leaving Crossman."

"Crossman might not even be out here."

"He is," Doc insisted, forcing some bit of vigor into his voice. "He is. I can…"

"What?"

"I don't know how to say it. I can *feel* it. There's something… I can feel it in these woods. I can feel that he's here. Don't…" Doc saw the look in both their eyes, like he was losing his mind. And maybe he was. "I know it's insane. I know what I look like right now — how I sound. But he's out here. He needs us."

"And we need *you*," Wyatt said. "So we're going back. We'll re-up, reinforce, and come back out once we know you're safe."

There it is. They're shedding you.

"Fuck you," Doc spat. "You'll have to shoot me and drag my fat ass out of this place before I leave without Crossman."

All three of them went quiet. Doc heard the venom in his voice only after the fact. But it was good. They knew he was serious.

"If that's the case, we need to keep going," Wyatt resigned.

Siggy shot a look at Wyatt, and Doc saw the warning in his expression. Wyatt gave him a knowing look of his own. Then, slowly, Siggy stood. "Okay. Doc, do you need to take a minute?"

"No," Doc responded coldly. Crossman was still out there. He bit down hard on the inside of his cheek, focusing on the pain to center himself. He stood shakily and looked to the forest around them. "I need to piss."

"Okay, man. We'll be here." Siggy patted his back as he ambled away toward the tree line.

There was a spot where the others couldn't see him, a little beyond a thick white birch trunk. Doc made it there just as his legs gave out and he collapsed to the soft dirt. He sobbed silently but hard. There was no piss in him; he was too dehydrated to piss. He just needed to be alone. For a minute. To silence that nasty fucking voice in his head. To beat it into submission with the comforting lies he'd always used in the past.

Fredrick...

"Shut up," he growled, gritting his teeth and violently willing the voice away.

Fredrick...

This time he actually heard it, his name weaving softly through the trees. His eyes shot up to the forest.

He knew the voice. That perfect voice.

Hey...

Deep in the pines, there was a shape. A shadowy silhouette, too dark for the sunny day. It was a stump, maybe an old log. It had to be. There was no way...

Come to me...

She was smiling. Her teeth were perfect in the most imperfect way that always made her too shy to really smile in front of anyone else. The soft slope of her exposed shoulders was covered only by the curly waves of flaxen hair.

"Sally?" he whispered.

She held out a hand through the brush, gently beckoning him. He felt the smile on his own face, and suddenly he felt lighter. Warmth rushed to his limbs, and he was standing, the aches gone.

Come on, baby. Come to me...

Siggy's voice called out from behind him, but he didn't care. She was out there. She was beckoning him closer and clo—

Snap!

The noise was terribly familiar. A horrific, bone shattering clack that sent a shockwave of pain and adrenaline up his spine. He looked down to the source and began to suck in heavy, violent breaths.

The rusty fangs of a bear trap were buried deep in his calf. The lower leg itself was twisted, wrong, no longer in a straight line as it should be. The blood began to flow, staining his filthy pant leg with an ever-growing deep red. He collapsed as a howl of pain filled the air. It took him a second to realize that it was his own scream.

Then Wyatt and Siggy were there. One of them was holding him down, the other wrestling with the trap, fighting to release its excruciating hold. Doc felt himself flailing against it as Wyatt pinned him, screaming in his ear to be still, that it was okay, that they had him.

"She's here," was all Doc managed to get out before the shock set in and the darkness took him. "She's in the woods."

18

Siggy

SIGGY COULDN'T sleep. The light patter of rain against the canvas tent filled his ears. He glanced over at his injured friend, who lay only a couple feet away. Doc's regularly loud snores had been replaced by a staccato of shallow wheezes. He was unconscious, at least. And he was dry and stable. That was more than Siggy could have hoped for that afternoon.

Doc's first scream was one of the most horrifying noises Siggy had ever heard in his life. It started as a deep bellow for just a few seconds before breaking into a high shriek. He swore he could almost *feel* the pain in it from across the apple grove. The bear trap was devastating, to say the least. Its rusted release mechanism had been filed away, so it had taken him at least a couple minutes to pry the bloody jaws far enough apart to withdraw Doc's shattered leg. After that, everything was a flurry. Siggy normally cringed at the phrase, but it was true: the training kicked in. Unfortunately for Doc, Siggy and Wyatt's training was limited to immediate trauma care. Together they'd maintained just enough emergency medical knowledge to stabilize Doc for transport.

But there was no medivac to get him out of here. They were on their own. Despite setting the leg and stopping the bleeding, they had no idea what exactly to do with him next.

And that bear trap hadn't been the only one.

After he'd freed Doc's leg, Siggy almost stumbled straight into another one. Only Wyatt's sharp eye and quick reflexes saved him from a similarly gruesome injury. In total, they discovered seven more traps surrounding the apple grove. A veritable minefield that had them watching their every step as they constructed a stretcher from two large branches and their jackets.

Now the makeshift stretcher leaned against a pine tree outside, only somewhat protected from the drizzling rain.

Wyatt was out there too. Huddled over the fire, no doubt. Keeping watch until it was Siggy's turn to take up that mantle.

Fuck.

Siggy *needed* to sleep. His turn at watch began at 2AM, and the last time he checked, it was nearly midnight.

He rolled onto his back, settling his head on his pack and looking up at the darkness. It was a complete black. The clouds overhead had blotted out the moon even before he'd racked out. Now, entombed in Crossman's musty canvas tent, the lack of light was so absolute that he couldn't even tell if his eyes were shut.

Somewhere deep down, a horrifyingly familiar fear roiled. This was exactly the situation he'd spent his life avoiding. The darkness. Nothing but pure, utter darkness. No distractions, no escape from his own thoughts. Even as a teenager, before it all, he used to sleep with the TV on as a welcomed distraction from himself. As a man, though, the TV wasn't up to the task. For a while, drinking helped. When that stopped working, pills took its spot. But the pills became weak, even the strong ones, and eventually the needle became the final stop on that devolving railroad. The needle always worked — an absolute solution to his excruciating existence.

But there was no needle now. No pills, even, or TV. Nothing but the two thin joints stuffed in his final and nearly empty pack of menthols. And he didn't dare smoke those. Not with everything that had happened — everything that *was* happening. Still… the thought of sweet release played over and over now. The rain pattered overhead, and a gentle insistence slowly morphed into an incessant desire. Then it began to feel like a need.

No. He didn't need that shit. It didn't even exist out here.

Yes, you fucking do.

The sudden compulsion crashed over him like a wave over a stormy beachhead. It overtook him, stronger than he'd felt it in years. He clamped his eyes hard and took slow breaths, battling against it and thinking of the destroyed man lying beside him.

This wasn't the time for his self-indulgent bullshit. Doc needed him. Even Wyatt needed him.

He checked his phone again. The screen blinded him, and the time read 1:26. The battery symbol in the upper right flashed red.

"Fuck it," he muttered, slowly pulling away the sleeping bag so as to not wake Doc. He donned his boots and eased out into the chilly rain.

Wyatt didn't hear him, or at least he didn't budge at Siggy's approach. He sat hunched over, silhouetted against the fire with his back to Siggy and the tent.

"Your relief has arrived, bucko," Siggy said quietly.

Wyatt didn't respond. He didn't move at all.

"Motherfucker, did you fall asleep on watch?" Siggy chortled. Oh, how the tables of responsibility have turned—

The man sitting at the fire wasn't Wyatt.

The sudden realization hit him so hard that his cravings disappeared instantly. The man was large, sure, but he was thicker than Wyatt. Fatter. Long, thin hair wisped away from his balding head.

Siggy's hand darted for his knife, but he'd taken it off his belt to sleep. His hands clenched into tight fists. "Who the fuck are you?"

The stranger's laugh was raspy with drawn out heaves that rolled with his heavy shoulders.

Siggy didn't wait for any further response. He dove, swinging hard. His first strike caught the stranger in the side of the head, dazing him long enough for Siggy to snake a thin arm under his chin and wrench it tight.

"Who the fuck are you?" he screamed though gritted teeth. The stranger writhed in his grip, tossing him side to side with incredible strength. Suddenly he was off the ground as the man struggled to his feet. Siggy, latched to his back like a monkey, could do nothing as the stranger hurled himself backwards. The two of them came crashing down, all of the man's weight driving the air from Siggy's lungs. His arm lost purchase as he gasped for his life. Climbing to his knees, he grappled with his much larger opponent, but a heavy punch drove him back to the earth.

"Siggy!" Wyatt roared.

"He's here! Someone's here!" Siggy tried to shout back, but his breath was still gone. He balled his fists and made to lunge once more.

"What the fuck are you doing?" Wyatt shouted, tossing him aside.

"Get him…" Siggy managed to get out.

"Stop!"

"The… the man…" Siggy waved a finger to the darkness. "He… he was just here…"

Wyatt was just beyond the fire, nursing his throat and glaring at him with furious eyes. "You fucking cunt," he growled. "What the *fuck* is wrong with you?"

Reality came crashing down on Siggy all at once. "There was someone else—"

"You fucking attacked me, psycho shit!"

"No. It wasn't you. I swear it—"

"Give me the gun. *Now!*"

Siggy hadn't even realized he was holding the revolver. He must have taken it off of Wyatt in the struggle, though he had no memory of it.

Suddenly, the cold steel felt heavy in his hand, and he realized that it was aimed directly at Wyatt's chest. He dropped it in the mud.

"I... I didn't..."

Wyatt crossed to him, shoving him backwards before grabbing the pistol. Siggy didn't resist, stumbling away in horror.

Neither of them slept that night. Siggy lay in his sleeping bag playing the events over and over in his mind. It had been real. It had been fucking real.

Wyatt sat outside by the fire, facing the tent with both the pistol and the bow, staring at Siggy through the open flap and nursing his bruised throat.

It *had* to be real.

Part Three
The Darkness

19

Wyatt

THE STORM came with the dawn. It rolled in strong from the west. What had been a gentle breeze in the night grew to heavy gales by morning, slinging the torrential rain like stinging salt pellets. Wyatt held tight to the rear of the stretcher, hoping his grip would hold despite the numbness in his freezing hands. Ahead, Siggy struggled to navigate the windswept brush, both his own hands latched to the stretcher as well. They fought forward, through ankle-deep swamp and creaking timberlands. More than once, a ferocious gust of wind tore away the branches overhead, sending them careening down like spears launched by the Gods themselves.

"We need to turn back!" Siggy screamed.

"No!" Wyatt roared over the thunder. "It's too far back. We need to push on!"

"I mean we need to double back! There's a bog ahead!"

Wyatt looked beyond his companion and realized their dilemma. For as far as he could see in the dense phalanx of cedar, deep pools of water spit back at the pouring rain.

They switched positions and turned back, meaning that it was Wyatt's turn to fight through the brush without the use of his hands. Onward they marched for hours, soaked, shivering, and numb. The muck sucked at their feet, tripping them up and threatening to spill Doc into the filthy water. The bog was wide — horribly, insufferably wide. Every so often Wyatt would think they were nearing the edge, only to realize that they had wandered out onto some long finger extending into the muck, and once again they would have to double back.

By mid-morning, Wyatt was genuinely worried Doc was going to die. By noon, he was sure of it.

Doc was barely breathing when they woke him up that morning. The wound on his leg was gruesome, but it had yet to become infected — at least as far as Wyatt could tell. His forehead was hot despite his trembling blue lips, and he remained confused and incoherent.

It was by pure happenstance that Siggy spotted a void in the center of an outcropping of ancient boulders. The cave was small, just barely deep enough for all of them to fit and start a damp fire. The smoke was so thick that it almost choked them out of the cave, but they managed to fan it away until it caught with the wind at the cave mouth. Still, every few minutes, a gust in the wrong direction would blind them and have them hacking again.

Siggy was quiet. He hadn't said more than a handful of words since the night before. Wyatt's throat was still sore, and he could feel the bruise forming on his windpipe, another addition to the catalogue of injuries he still had from the bar fight. Still, his anger over the attack was drastically overshadowed by a growing concern. Siggy swore that he had seen something — that Wyatt had been someone else.

Siggy was fucking losing it.

"There's another river to the north," Wyatt muttered, huddling close to the flames and pointing to a thin black line on the map. Beside it, a directional arrow pointed east. "If we can get to it and build a makeshift raft, it will bring us closer to the edge of the North Woods. If we stick with it, then maybe we can find a camp along its banks, or even a town."

"How far?" Siggy asked.

"I don't know exactly. Maybe thirty miles. Maybe less."

"Maybe more…" Siggy let out a defeated sigh.

"I know. But what else can we do?"

Siggy cast a worried look at Doc. "That'll take us days. You really think he has that long?"

Wyatt followed his friend's gaze to the silent form between them. They'd put Doc in his sleeping bag, but he was still trembling. Whether it was from the cold or from the fever was anyone's guess.

"No," Wyatt said flatly. "I'll go alone. I'll be faster that way, and I can bring back help."

"That's fucking stupid—"

"You have a better idea?"

Siggy didn't say anything.

Wyatt turned back to the map. "I can find you from the bog; it's big enough that it should be mapped by the forest service."

"And what if you don't come back?"

"Then I'm dead, and it's on you."

Wyatt didn't wait for a response. He made his preparations quickly. He left his pack and took only a Nalgene, a compass, his headlamp, and the bow. He fought to control his shaking fingers as he copied a crude version of the map into a Rite In The Rain notebook. When he was done, he ripped the page free and stored it in a Ziplock bag.

He stood at the mouth of the cave and passed a cigarette back and forth with Siggy as he gave his instructions. "I want you to light a large fire outside once the storm lets up. Keep him warm; try to scrounge up some food but don't venture too far — animals will be able to smell that wound." He unclipped the holster from his belt and handed the revolver to Siggy. "If I don't come back, start moving. Drag him north until you hit the river. I'll leave whatever bread crumb trail I can, but I'm going straight through that bog. If I'm not back by the morning of the third day, assume I'm dead."

"Okay, Gandalf. This is fucking insane. You know that?"

Wyatt forced a chuckle. "Eh, we've seen worse, right?"

Siggy dragged on the cigarette. "No, motherfucker. Not even close."

Wyatt stepped out into the rain and turned back one last time. Siggy stared at him wordlessly. Wyatt gave him a solitary nod and left.

The bog was hardly easier to navigate alone than it had been while hauling Doc. At least now, as the muck sucked at his boots and the water splashed over his knees, he didn't have to worry about spilling his friend into the freezing depths. His watch read 4:30PM when he left the cave. By the time Wyatt emerged from the other side of the bog, its analog face was misty and the seconds hand hung in a puddle of water. *Water resistant, my ass.* Despite the broken timepiece, Wyatt could tell that hours had passed due to how dark it was growing.

He fought on, numb toes squelching in soaked boots as he fought through endless miles of scraggly saplings. Ancient trees groaned in the whipping wind overhead, and more than once he heard the not-so-distant crash of one finally accepting its fate. The dull glow of the sun beyond the rolling black clouds disappeared beyond the edge of the canopy and the forest grew ever darker.

Somewhere along the way, he tripped over a root, sending him sprawling. As he stood, he felt a familiar twinge in his knee. It had taken three surgeries to repair the old war injury, but they worked and he hadn't even thought of it in years. Now it sparked back to life — the deep burning growing from a pinpoint until it encompassed the entirety of the joint. Still, he kept on trudging. Some part of him knew that his body was breaking. The growl of his stomach also stood as a staunch reminder that he had nothing left in the tank. Nothing left to heal himself with. Had he allowed himself to imagine it, he could have envisioned his cells breaking apart his musculature — tearing into the physique he'd worked so hard to attain as his body began to consume itself from the inside out. But he buried those thoughts in the recesses of his mind, allowing only the pathetic image of Doc and Siggy in that smoke-filled cave to dominate his mind's eye.

Full dark came, and he finally found himself falling more often than not. The woods were as thick as any — the type untouched by loggers, where the trees lived long enough to die by their own accord and the carcasses of a thousand fallen behemoths lay crisscrossed among their offspring. His legs ached and cramped. He knew he needed to stop, even if only for a few hours.

When he stumbled across a wide maple with a low hollow, he decided it was as good a place as any to escape the rain and bite of the wind. He burrowed his body into the arching divot in the tree's trunk, trying to ignore the pellets of porcupine shit he sat in. The night was turning cold. Far colder than the previous days, and the rain was now beginning to turn to a slushy mix.

He didn't have the time or resources to make a fire. Or the cover to protect it from the rain. Or even a snowball's chance in hell of finding a bit of wood that wasn't soaked. Instead, he curled inward, fitting as much of himself into the damp hollow as possible, and squeezed his eyes shut. The chattering of his teeth reverberated through his skull like a snare drum as he tried to imagine the warmth of his bed. Hell, even the lumpy cot at Crossman's cabin would do. But every time his mind would catch on some small idea of comfort that might lull him away to sleep, another harsh gust would cut through the trees and blast him back to the present.

Enough time passed that his core temperature began to drop. He felt the wet earth drawing his heat away from him bit by bit. He knew what that meant: it was time to move. He took a deep breath, then another, and clicked on his headlamp and lifted his head from his arms.

The rain had turned to sleet. The headlamp shone through the arcing waves of wet ice as it fell to the earth in sheets, illuminating the wall of ferns beyond.

Blood red eyes reflected back at him.

It was only for a second. They were a dozen feet away and low to the ground, shrouded just beyond a low hanging pine bough. He couldn't make out the body — only the tawny reflection of flesh and the bristle of sparse hair. As its eyes caught the light, it gave an otherworldly hiss that sent a primordial shiver up the back of Wyatt's neck. Then it was gone, bounding away silently through the underbrush.

Wyatt didn't leave the hollow as he had planned. He sat still, bow in hand and arrow nocked and clenched in numb fingers, staring silently out into the shadows. He hadn't seen what he'd seen. It wasn't possible. It was a dream. A nightmare hallucination brought on by Crossman's sick fucking drawings. It must have been.

But it wasn't.

20

Siggy

SIGGY SPENT the previous evening darting around in the rain, gathering wood for the fire. He'd used the folding camp saw they'd taken from Crossman's cabin to cut a number of saplings which now lay in a wet heap by the embers. They were still green under the bark, but they burned better than the soggy refuse that littered the forest floor. He managed to keep the flames up throughout the night, providing a marginal amount of warmth in the small cave. When the temperatures dipped to the point that he lost feeling in his nose and ears, he zipped two sleeping bags together and crawled inside with Doc, then laid the third bag overtop of them as a blanket. Even so, when he awoke in the morning, they were both shivering.

"Thanks for not making a move," he joked as he climbed out into the cold air.

"You're too bony for me," Doc muttered, much to Siggy's surprise.

"Doc, you're back with us?" Siggy asked, chuckling.

"I'm just fucking cold, Sig."

Siggy moved a handful of the thin branches to the embers beside them. They sizzled and poured wet smoke. Outside, the wind still violently shook the forest, but at least the rain seemed to be letting up.

"Where's Wyatt?" Doc asked. His voice was weak, but he seemed to have achieved some level of cognizance.

"He's gone to get us help. How are you holding up?"

"You shouldn't have split up. You should have gone with him."

"Fuck off with that." Siggy waved away the smoke and huddled close to the embers as the sticks began to catch. "How's the leg?"

"Bad. Really, Siggy, you need to go with him. I'll be—"

"No. Besides, he's long gone. You've been out for a hot minute."

Doc groaned and rolled his head back so he could see Siggy. "Is there any food?"

Siggy shook his head.

"If you end up eating me, just avoid my ass. I think I shit myself."

Siggy laughed. "You've been shitting yourself since the car ride up here. Besides, I wouldn't eat you. Meat'd probably be too tough."

"Nah." Doc looked forlornly back to the cave's ceiling. "I'd taste like bacon. I'm sure of it."

Siggy knew they needed food. They'd been fools for not grabbing more apples in their rush to exfil Doc. The mere mention of bacon had Siggy salivating. He thought about laying more snares, but the storm had driven away all the possible game. Even the squirrels that had ceaselessly harassed them over the past few days had disappeared thanks to nature's onslaught. Now more than ever he wished that he had taken the little survival booklet he'd spotted on Crossman's bookshelf. But he forgot to grab it, among other things, and now he had little doubt that playing a guessing game regarding edible plants would result in his or Doc's final demise.

"You need to go," Doc said again. "There's no sense in both of us starving out here."

"You know I'm not going anywhere. When the weather breaks, I'll find us something. Wyatt'll be back in soon with search and rescue and—"

"Siggy, I'm done. I'm burning up and frozen solid at the same time. It's my fault we're out here—"

"Enough, man. Come on. You *know* I'm not leaving. Stop asking."

"You always were a stubborn SOB."

"And you're tougher than you think."

Doc shook his head but didn't say anything else.

The early hours of the morning passed slowly. Eventually the fire grew enough to where the smoke became thin and bearable. Siggy focused what little brainpower he had left trying to recall those stupid survival shows he grew up watching. He remembered something about people eating bark or some type of boiled down pitch. But the memories were foggy. Too foggy to be of value now.

"Why'd you do it?" Doc's voice shook with the cold.

"Huh?"

"What happened to you, man? So many guys…"

Siggy realized that it wasn't just the cold that was making Doc's voice quake. "What do you mean?"

"When you were going to kill yourself…"

"It was just an OD, Doc—"

"Don't lie to me. Not now."

Siggy took a deep breath. There was no good answer. Hell, he wasn't even sure if he had one at all.

"Was it because of us?" Doc asked. "Because we weren't there?"

"No," Siggy insisted. "Fuck no."

"Then why?"

Thunder rumbled in the distance, and Siggy chewed his cheek. "I don't know, man. There's a lot… Do you remember a girl over there, the one with the blue eyes?"

"No."

He hesitated, unsure of what to say. This was not a story he'd ever told before, or ever even imagined telling at all. But now, with Doc's sad eyes boring into him, he found the words seeping out. "She was young, maybe our age. Maybe younger. I remember that for the first few months she was always at the intersection by the bazaar, where all the kids would crowd and beg for pens and candy. She was always covered head to toe just like the rest of the women, but I remember noticing her eyes. She had these striking, sky blue eyes. They reminded me of my mom's eyes.

"I was really infatuated with her. Not in like a creepy way. It was just that her eyes, they got to me. I'd heard the stories of the Russian invasion, how a bunch of the white-looking people we ran into over there were products of the Russian soldiers. I had this thing where I would lay there in my rack when I couldn't sleep and imagine this epic romance that led up to her. Some homesick Russian conscript saving some beautiful Afghan girl, then they'd run off into the desert together, abandoning everything for the sake of each other. It was a nice story. Passed the time, at least. But I knew what the Russians had really been like. I knew that the odds were that the girl was a child of rape. Still, I chose not to believe it."

Doc struggled to shift his body so that he was facing Siggy. "I'm sorry, man. I don't remember her at all."

Siggy gave a sad nod. "You do. You just don't know it yet. Anyway, eventually she disappeared. I didn't think much of it at the time. A while later I was stuck in my rack, sick as fuck from eating some of that bazaar food, and the rest of y'all went on some key leader engagement patrol. It was supposed to be a quick one, not a super high chance of contact, so I didn't feel that bad sitting it out. Then I heard the boom. The radios started going nuts about a suicide bomber."

"Mortimer…" Doc's eyes lit up with recognition.

"Yeah. Mortimer. That's when he lost his leg. Crossman told me later that you saved him."

"Yeah."

Siggy pulled a plastic bag from his pocket and opened it. There were four cigarettes left in the crushed pack. He lit one of them. "That night Gonzales told me the story. He said Mortimer got stupid lucky. He said that a pregnant woman walked right up to him from the side of the road. He said Mortimer didn't even see her until Wyatt had already shot her. That's what gave him the time to dive over that wall, hearing Wyatt's shot. Gonzales gave me all the gritty details; how she dropped to her knees and shrieked; how, when the vest went off, her head just shot upwards like a rocket and came plopping right down in the middle of them. He said it was gruesome, but the wildest part was that her face was untouched. It was so weird that he took a picture of it after you guys got Mortimer on the bird."

"Siggy…"

He hadn't realized that his eyes were wet. "Yeah. It was her. Gonzales was right, too. Her face was untouched. Her eyes were open in the picture. Still that same soft blue, only they were glassy."

"Siggy, I'm sorry—"

"That's not it, Doc. That didn't get me like you'd think. I wasn't there, after all. I didn't see it. I barely even heard it from the hooch. It was what happened after that stuck with me. The next day we went back out to finish the BDA. I went that time, still sick as fuck, but with Mortimer gone we were a man down. When we hit that intersection and set in security, I ended up right by the spot where it happened. That's when I noticed her on the edge of the wadi. There was a rusty piece of rebar sticking up from the dirt, and someone had stuck her head right on it just like a fuckin' lollipop. Before we exfilled, I went up to it — to her. Her eyes were still open. Still that same blue, empty and staring past me at nothing. I wanted to take her down. No one needed to see that shit, not the locals, or the kids, or me. But something stopped me. A hatred, Doc. I remember this deep, sudden fucking hatred for this girl. She'd almost killed my friend. Hell, at that point we didn't even know how bad off Mortimer really was. A few days before he'd been showing off pictures of his newborn back home. Now he was gone somewhere, all fucked up with shrapnel and probably never gonna walk again. I fucking hated her *so much* at that moment that I hawked a fat loogie and spit on her face. I spit on her face and left her to rot.

"Every time we'd patrol to the bazaar after that I'd see her. It didn't faze me at all. Fuck, it felt *good*." His voice broke for a second. He took a drag off the cigarette and gathered himself. "I watched as her eyes dropped back into that empty skull. As her skin shriveled in the sun and birds pecked out her hair. And the stink… but then one day I looked and there was just that rusty stick of rebar. She was gone."

"I do remember the head," Doc said. "Someone had said not to touch it, I don't remember who. Jesus, Siggy, if I had known…"

"Fuck, I might have been the one to say it. I didn't give a fuck. It wasn't until a few years later, after I'd gotten out, that it started to come back. I read this book my mom got me on the Taliban's takeover of Helmand. I read about how they would dope up women and children. Kidnap them from their homes in the night, get them fixed on drugs and then force them to strap on suicide vests while high or desperate for their next hit — when they were so out of it that they didn't know what the fuck was going on. That's when I started to wonder if the glassiness of her eyes was really just from death, or something else. I mean, did she really have a choice? Or did I spit in the face of some poor innocent girl, then leave here out there to rot?" The cigarette had burnt to the filter. He took a final, bitter drag and tossed it into the flames. "That's when I realized I was just as bad as the fucking people who did that to her."

"That's not true."

Siggy wiped his eyes and stood, his knees popping painfully with the motion. "It is what it is, Doc. We need more firewood."

He didn't wait for Doc's response. A halfhearted condolence wouldn't change the truth, and besides, he needed a moment to himself. He left the cave and walked a short way out. The forest floor was wet under his boots. He was already a dozen yards from the cave mouth before he realized he'd forgotten the saw. Fuck it, they needed tinder anyway.

He dropped his eyes to the earth, searching for fallen branches. Instead, he found himself staring at the clear imprint of a human footprint in fresh the mud. It was bare, each of the toes splayed out clearly in the earth.

He felt his heart jump into his throat as he looked around. There were more. Many more. All circling the cave.

24

Wyatt

WHEN WYATT came to, he was freezing. His jacket was gone, and only his soaked t-shirt clung to his chest. He'd experienced cold before, plenty of it. But this was something else. His *bones* were cold. His organs were cold. Every part of him shook violently as his soaked body worked desperately to generate some small bit of heat.

He was so cold that, for at least a minute, he didn't even realize that he was no longer in the woods. Hard steel bars had replaced the tree at his back. The floor beneath him was not mud and moss, but straw and concrete. As his mind finally began to register the world around him, he felt the slightest bit of warmth in the air to his back. He turned, feeling as though his frozen limbs might shatter from even the tiniest movement, and found the heat's source: a fire pit a few yards away. Half-burnt refuse was piled high and billowed with a black cloud that stank of diesel and singed meat. Wyatt snaked his arms through the bars, reaching toward the flames and letting his fingers revel in their warmth.

Then he saw the bones.

There were dozens of them charred and broken and scattered around the fire's perimeter. The alarm bells tolling distantly in his mind finally brought him crashing back to reality. Spinning back, he fully took in his surroundings.

He was in a cramped cage that had barely enough room for him to lie down or stand straight. The air was foul with ammonia and the sour stench of body odor, even despite being outside. There were dozens of other cages around him. In these cages huddled all variety of apes. At least ten chimpanzees mulled aimlessly in their tiny enclosures; an orangutan squatted in a pile of its own filth; a pair of gibbons stared lazily at him; and countless more masses of fur lay half buried in moldy straw. Some of the cages were without coverage, like his, and the animals were soaked and shivering. Others were better kept, notably the cage directly beside his own. It was bigger — the biggest among them, as far as Wyatt could tell. A leaky plywood roof covered the top bars, and a hearty coating of straw covered the concrete floor. In the corner something slept, facing away. Its skin was hairless and mottled brown with filth. Most of its form was concealed by the tawny straw heaped around it. It might have been a man, but the way it curled into its own naked form gave Wyatt the impression of a bald ape of some sort — at least Wyatt hoped it was.

Beyond the cages, surrounding them in a hundred-yard semicircle, was a crudely crafted wall. It was constructed with tree trunks speared toward the sky in the style of an ancient palisade. There was only one gap in the wooden barrier: a chain link gate topped with razor wire. Just beyond the palisade, the trees loomed tall, swallowing the horrifying complex on all sides.

In the center of it all was a camper propped up on cinderblocks. Rusty tools and spare engine parts dotted the muddy yard around it. The camper itself was old. 70's era, by the looks of it, with peeling paint and faded mustard yellow stripes along the upper portion. Just beyond the camper, Wyatt spotted the hard edges of a similarly aged truck.

He recognized the scratched white hood: it was the truck that pulled up to Crossman's cabin the first night he'd arrived.

The camper's door clacked open, and a hunched man walked out. Even from a distance, Wyatt could see from the curve of his back and the shortness of his strides that he was elderly. Still, he walked evenly, carrying a metal clipboard under one arm as he made his way to one of the far cages. A small monkey appeared from beyond the camper. It scampered beside him, pausing expectantly from time to time until he bent and fed it a treat.

Wyatt crawled across the wet concrete of his cage and pressed his face between the bars. The cage that the old man was at had something in it.

No, not something.

Some*one.*

The person locked inside was bone thin and lay completely still until the old man began to speak. Wyatt couldn't make out the words as the old man jotted something on his clipboard, but he could make out the prisoner's pale, skeletal ribcage and the disjointed assortment of tattoos that dotted it.

For half a second, Wyatt's stomach dropped. The person in the cage looked almost like Siggy. But it wasn't. The prisoner was too small, too frail even for Siggy. The mop of greasy hair wasn't quite black enough, and the tattoos a bit too scattered and prison-esque.

It wasn't until the prisoner raised his head that Wyatt recognized the angular face: the teenage boy from the river. The one called Rat.

The old man spoke to the boy for a long time. All Wyatt could make out was the low murmur of their voices. The monkey circled around them, on occasion darting up the old man's back and resting on his shoulders. When he was done, the old man clapped the clipboard shut, drawing a wince from the teen, and made to return to the camper.

"Hey!" Wyatt mustered all of his strength into a shout, rattling the cold bars of his cage. "Hey, asshole! Where the hell am I?"

Some of the slumbering apes woke with a start. The air filled with the disjointed grunts and chirps of their own wretched calls. The old man looked toward Wyatt but only for a second. His gait didn't slow.

"Hey, asshole!" Wyatt tried again.

But the old man was gone, disappearing into the camper with the monkey without so much as another glance.

Wyatt turned his eyes to the teen across the way. The boy was again still, curled into fetal position near the cage's bars and almost comatose, staring blankly into the woods through the chain link gate.

Wyatt fell back, shivering, to the warmth of the fire. The stink of burning diesel drew a cough, and he thought back to the legend that the girl Blue Jay told them about: Hyperborea.

Wyatt had been right all along: it was a trap.

And it was somehow worse than he could have ever imagined.

22

Siggy

IT WAS late in the afternoon. Siggy guessed that it might be around 5PM due to the sun's relative position in the sky, but there was no way of truly knowing since his phone had finally died earlier that morning. Doc's was long dead, likely waterlogged by the feel of it — not that a smartphone in their situation was worth anything more than a timepiece. For the first time in his life, Siggy wished he had a watch.

It had been over twenty-four hours since Wyatt ambled off into the storm. Now they were on a similar route, fighting upward through the hills, Doc dragging on the stretcher behind him. Thankfully the storm had finally passed, though the ground was still treacherously slippery.

They couldn't wait. Not at the cave, at least. Not with some barefoot tormentor circling them in the night.

Doc hadn't fought as he strapped him into the stretcher. Siggy reinforced it with cross-braces cut from green saplings, tied on with what paracord they had left. He consolidated what he could into a single pack and, with Doc dragging behind him, set off west. The bog had to end at some point, and he'd decided to push further along its edge until it did. Then they would go north to the river and be done with this godawful forest.

It was hard going. Much harder solo than it was with two people carrying the stretcher. Siggy only made it a few hundred yards before the burning in his thighs overwhelmed him and he collapsed. As luck would have it, his moment of weakness occurred just beside a haggard crabapple tree that he surely would have overlooked otherwise. He fed Doc first. Then, like a starved dog, he devoured every bitter apple he could find.

The sugar empowered him. Once again he was dragging, hauling Doc's shabby stretcher over logs and through brambles that tore at them both. They reached the end of the bog and shifted northward up what seemed to be a series of never-ending inclines. Dusk came fast, and their pace was slow. Siggy had no idea how far they'd actually made it as they crested a low hill and the orange glow of the sun faded into the mountains to their left.

"Siggy…" Doc breathed.

"Fuck off," Siggy panted. "I'm not leaving you, asshole."

"No…" Doc coughed hard. "Siggy…"

"You shouldn't talk. Save your energy."

"Siggy…"

A fleeting fantasy of letting the stretcher slide back down the hill flitted through his mind. "*What?*"

"A light…"

The words took a second to register. He placed the stretcher down, maybe a bit too roughly based on Doc's resulting grunt, and turned to see what Doc was talking about. Sure enough, a bright yellow dot illuminated a break in the trees only a few hundred yards away. Siggy stared at it from the top of the hill, wondering if he'd finally lost his mind. But Doc saw it too.

A part of him hesitated. The reasoning side of his brain battled to regain control through the fog of exhaustion. The light could be anyone.

It could be their barefooted tormenters. It could be the trap Wyatt warned those kids about. It could be anything, anything *but* good.

But it could be warm… another voice whispered. *Warm and safe…*

His legs were shaking as much as his lips as he shifted his heading and placed the light directly in front of them.

23

Wyatt

THE OLD man left the camper at dusk. Wyatt watched him closely as he crossed the muddy wallow and approached the cage that housed the teen named Rat. He stopped a dozen yards short and pulled a ring of keys from his pocket, picked one off, and handed it to the chittering capuchin beside him. The monkey understood its assignment, clearly having partaken in this exercise more than a few times in the past. It took the key and darted forward to the cage. The tactic was a smart one and no doubt a hard learned lesson; keeping a good standoff distance from the cage in case the captive were to lash out. But Rat didn't so much as look up as the monkey finagled the mechanism. The padlocked dropped to the ground.

"You're free," the old man barked.

Rat twitched, jarred back to reality by the words. He stood, sending the capuchin scuttling back to its master, then eased open the grated door. Once he was outside, he didn't run. Instead, he stumbled like a drunk. His wandering path took him through the open chain link gate to the woods beyond. Wyatt watched as he disappeared into the shadows of the pines.

It was feeding time after that. The old man did his rounds, delivering bowls of slop and rotted vegetables to the occupants of the menagerie two at a time. By the time he finally approached Wyatt's quadrant, it was full dark.

"What the hell is in that?" Wyatt asked as the old man slid a wooden bowl of gruel through a slot near the floor of the cage.

He didn't answer. Even in the darkness Wyatt could make out the old man's deep wrinkles and thin, crooked nose. He was at least seventy, likely older, and moved with measured precision. His hair was scant and wispy, bleach white against his leathery scalp. Though the darkness masked his eyes, Wyatt could feel his gaze.

"You think there aren't people that will come looking for me?" Wyatt needed to elicit some reaction — pull out *some* form of information about where he was.

"They won't find you," the old man stated evenly. His voice was hoarse and tone dry.

"You willing to bet your life on that?"

"Yes." He paused for a second, then departed for the camper.

To Wyatt's surprise, the old man was only in the camper for a short time. He returned with the metal clipboard, the blinding light of a headlamp shining from his forehead and the monkey darting around his feet.

"You know, you were nearly dead when I found you," the old man began, opening the clipboard. "Yet untouched. Very interesting. Do you have a history of mental illness?"

Wyatt was almost too stunned to speak. If it weren't for the immediate circumstances, the old man's tone and calm demeanor made Wyatt feel like he was in a doctor's routine examination. "Who the hell are you?"

"What about a family history of mental illness?" the old man droned on, completely ignoring Wyatt. "Schizophrenia, antisocial personality disorder, Alzheimer's, autism?"

"Eat a dick."

"Over the past few days, have you at any point experienced any extreme highs or lows? Perhaps as a result of an unexplainable event or dream?"

"After you eat a dick, I'm gonna make you eat that monkey."

The old man gave a casual sigh, then clapped the clipboard shut. He angled the cone of light over to the cage next to Wyatt's. The big one.

"Wretch. Wake up, Wretch!"

The huddled mass in the corner twitched.

"Up, Wretch, *up!*" the old man hissed.

The filthy creature slowly stood up. It was a man, or at least it had been once. What pale skin that wasn't covered in dirt and fecal matter almost glowed in the headlamp's beam. His frame was large, like Wyatt's, but his muscles had withered into thin ropes that stretched over jutting bones. The hair on his head was long and tangled in a rat's nest of straw and grime, as was the bush that enveloped his filth-stained penis. He stood hunched, apelike, in the corner of the cage, baring yellow teeth and squinting against the light.

"What the fuck did you do to him?" Wyatt breathed.

"Me? Nothing." The old man opened the clipboard again. "Now, as I was saying, have you had any feelings of—"

"You're a real sick fuck, you know that?"

This time the old man didn't even bother to look up. "I make the same offer to every difficult case: either you play ball and answer the questions honestly, or you go in the cage with Wretch. Do you understand?"

The cold, black eyes of the wild man glinted underneath the mess of matted hair, boring into Wyatt's soul. His gaze was vacant: the eyes of a predator. Wyatt saw no hint of humanity left in them.

"Do you understand?" the old man asked again.

"Yeah."

"Mental illness, yes or no?"

"No."

"And family history?"

"No."

"How about feelings of—"

"No."

"Do you want to end up in there with Wretch? He hasn't eaten in days." The old man looked Wyatt over. "Maybe you could take him, kill him even. But he's a wild one. Plus, how long do you really want to sit there next to a rotting corpse?"

Wyatt managed to break his eyes away from the terrifying creature. "I'll answer your questions, but I want answers too."

"Like what?"

"Is this Hyperborea?"

The old man let out a sharp exhale and shook his head. "No. Hyperborea is a myth. This place is very real. How old are you?"

"Thirty. How many kids have you lured out here with that myth?"

"I've never kept track."

"That's a lie." Wyatt jabbed a finger toward the clipboard. "I bet you keep track of everything."

"Could be. But you're the one in the cage, so you'll have to take the answers I give you. What is your highest level of education?"

"Doctoral candidate." Wyatt's answer caused the old man to pause in his writing. Wyatt went on. "How many people have you killed out here?"

"Me personally? None. What is your current employment status?"

"Employed."

"As what?"

"Monkey food."

The old man waited.

"I'm a professor. History."

"Children?"

"No."

"Spouse?"

"No."

"Were you in the military?"

"No."

"*One* more lie, and you're going to Wretch." The old man pointed his pen to the mud-stained Marine Corps tattoo on Wyatt's forearm. "Did you see combat?"

"Yeah."

"Have you ever been diagnosed with Post-Traumatic Stress?"

"No."

"Have you ever been evaluated for Post-Traumatic Stress?"

"No."

"Why not?"

"I don't believe in it."

"Have you ever felt a strong emotional bond with another human being?"

"What?" Wyatt snorted. "What the fuck kind of questions are these?"

"Just answer them as honestly as you can."

Wyatt shook his head. "No, it's your fucking turn. What's going to happen to me? What happened to that kid?" His thoughts flitted back to the previous night in the tree hollow. "And what in the ever living fuck is out in those woods?"

At this, the old man hesitated. "You saw something?"

"Answer me and I'll answer you."

"Well, I suppose what happens to you depends on your behavior. If you cooperate, you will walk out of here after whatever period of time I deem necessary, just as that boy did. If you don't cooperate, however, you will die. Whether from exposure, starvation, or at the hands of Wretch, I do not know, but you will die. Have I made myself clear?"

"You think you're going to break me? Is that it?"

The old man closed the clipboard for a final time, sliding the pen into its clip and pulling a peanut from a bulging breast pocket full of them. The capuchin scampered up his side, leaving a fresh trail of muddy little footprints on his already filthy jeans and flannel jacket. He handed the peanut to the monkey. It sat there on his shoulders, wrestling with the shell until finally breaking it open to feast on the innards.

"You're an educated man. Do you know what's wrong with him?" The old man nodded to Wretch.

"He's feral. What was he? Your kid? You raise him like one of these apes?"

"No. He was a chiropractor, actually. He and his family came out to these woods on vacation, imagining that they might find some sort of solace in the woods to heal their broken marriage and pry the screens out of the children's hands."

"You're a psychopath."

"Technically, yes. But that's beside the point. Do you know how much time has passed since this man made the foolish mistake of venturing into these woods?"

"I don't know. A decade."

"Less than a year."

"Liar."

"I swear it." The old man stepped a hair closer, still out of reach. "Whatever you witnessed in those woods is an incredible thing, my friend. A one-off. An anomaly. A truly magnificent feat of nature. It took this man's family. It did this to him, through some means which I have spent a great deal of time trying to understand."

"Why are you telling me this?"

"Because there are worse things out here than the cage. You asked if I expected to break you? Well, I don't *care* if I can break you. I know for a fact that *she* will." The old man made to turn, then paused. "One last thing. Did you come out here alone?"

"Yes."

"Why?"

"To finish something my friend started."

"Which is?"

"I didn't know at first, but now it's pretty clear: finding and killing *you*."

The old man chuckled. "Eat your food. You never know when the next meal will be."

Wyatt looked down at the food — if it could be called that. It was a lumpy grey gruel with bits of what looked like meat and oats, but he couldn't positively identify any of the ingredients. Not that he wanted to know what was in the slop regardless.

He ate every last bit.

24

Siggy

AS SIGGY emerged from the trees, he found himself staring at a house. The rustic structure sat nestled among the trees and built into the side of a hill that overlooked a hundred acres of forest below. A detached garage stood nearby, and next to that, there was a large chicken coop that rustled with activity.

He couldn't help but laugh victoriously as he dragged Doc the last few steps out of the darkness and into the floodlight. From somewhere beyond the windows came the flowing tones of classical music. He'd never heard anything more beautiful.

He knocked, politely at first. When there was no answer, he balled his fist and banged harder, sending bits of the peeling paint feathering to the ground. The music cut off, and a shadowy figure passed slowly beyond the window.

"Hello?" Siggy called. "We need help!"

The door cracked open just an inch, and the suspicious face of an old woman peeked out.

"My friend is hurt." Siggy stood aside, motioning to the stretcher behind him. "We need a hospital. Do you have a phone?"

The woman looked him up and down before glancing past him to Doc. Her face melted into a sudden warmth. "Oh, dear. Come in, quickly now." She flung the door open, waving them through. "Get him out of the cold."

Siggy dragged the stretcher through the entrance. The sudden blast of warmth and scents nearly made his head spin. The air was thick with the aromas of honey and roasted meat. A fire crackled nearby in a glass-fronted stove, and the dull glow of the decorative lamps cast the room in a rich orange hue.

If the forest was hell, then surely this was heaven.

The woman guided him to the stove, Doc in tow. Although she moved as if walking was painful, she still possessed a healthy sense of urgency. She was clad in a simple set of pajamas and sported a ponytail of salt-and-pepper hair that nearly reached her waist. As he set Doc's stretcher down before the fire, she asked, "What on earth happened?"

"A bear trap got his leg. He was already sick though, I think."

"Oh my," she gasped, placing a wrinkled hand on Doc's forehead. Her grandmotherly aura reminded Siggy of every Hallmark movie he'd been too lazy to change away from while stoned. "We need to get him warm. Did the trap break skin?"

"Yeah, skin *and* bone."

Doc was pale and shaking violently. Siggy dropped his pack and worked to strip away his friend's wet clothes while the woman ambled back to the kitchen and pulled a hefty first aid kit from one of the cabinets.

"You're okay, Doc. We're out of the woods, buddy. We'll be okay." Siggy muttered as much to himself as to his unconscious friend. His eyes followed the woman, then drifted around the room. The house was laid out in a lofted floorplan, though the oversized kitchen and den that he was now standing in looked to be a more recent addition. The whole first floor was modestly furnished, and the few spots on the walls that weren't covered in packed bookshelves were dotted with old photos and rich oil paintings.

When the old woman returned, she went directly for Doc's crudely wrapped leg. After withdrawing a pair of medical shears from the kit, she gently angled them under the bandage. Siggy almost stopped her right then to ask if she had any actual medical training, but the deftness with which she manipulated the shears as she cut away the t-shirt they'd used to bind and splint Doc's leg told him all he needed to know.

"I'm going to elevate his leg. Slide that footstool under it." She motioned to a nearby ottoman.

Siggy followed her command, wincing at Doc's groan as they elevated his broken calf.

She finished stripping away the makeshift bandage to reveal the jagged wounds left by the trap's teeth. Slimy grey puss oozed from beneath the wet scabs. She didn't seem fazed though as she quickly moved to retrieve a handful of towels and a pot of warm water from the sink, which she then set atop the woodstove. Siggy held Doc while she cleaned the wound. The warmth from the stove seemed to stir Doc back into some modicum of awareness because when she finished the cleaning and dabbed an alcohol-soaked cotton ball on the wound, he let out a sharp whimper. "Stop, Siggy…"

"We can't, buddy. You've got to take it. We're going to get you out of here, but we've got to do this first, okay?" He turned to the old woman, still at work. "Where's your phone?"

She shook her head without looking up. "No phone, dear. Not out here."

"Shit… Okay, then we're going to need you to give us a ride to somewhere that has one. Or a hospital, if there's one close enough."

She took her eyes off of Doc's leg for just long enough to give Siggy a downcast look. "Yes. Of course. Trouble is my husband has the truck, and I believe he's stuck in town due to the washouts. Happens after these big storms pass through. He might not get back here until tomorrow, or even later."

"Fuck…" Siggy muttered. "Sorry."

"Oh, I don't blame you, dear. Your friend will be okay, though, once we get some real bandages on here and get it re-splinted. Is he cognizant?"

Siggy put a hand on Doc's cheek, guiding the half open eyes to meet his own. "Doc, can you understand me?"

Doc gave a weak nod. He was still shivering, but less violently now. "Yeah. He's with us."

"Tell him I'm sorry, but this will hurt."

Siggy did, but the words proved to be of little value to Doc. His whimper turned into a gasp as she pulled the new bandages tight, but his eyes rolled back and he was out again.

They managed to successfully splint the leg using a pair of wooden spoons. Then, at the woman's instruction, Siggy dragged Doc into a first floor bedroom and hauled him onto the bed. They piled blankets on him, and the woman took the remainder of the hot water from the stove and filled a metal water bottle which they stowed under the blankets with him.

"You must get out of those wet clothes," the old woman insisted. Siggy realized that, despite the warmth of the house, he was still shivering. "When was the last time you ate?"

"I don't remember," he answered honestly.

"Oh, my dear... Come with me."

He gave Doc a backward glance and followed her into the kitchen, where she immediately guided him to a chair and handed him a box of crackers and a glass of water. As he devoured the buttery crackers, savoring every salty bite, she set to heating up a pot of stew from the fridge. An unbelievably savory aroma filled the kitchen.

"I really can't thank you enough," he said. "I'm Tom, by the way. But my friends call me Siggy."

"Siggy." She smiled over her shoulder at him. "It's nice to meet you. My name is Cecilia."

"Well, thank you, Cecilia. You saved our lives."

"You poor boys, out in those woods like this. Here." She ladled some of the stew into a wide bowl and handed it to him. He didn't even wait for it to cool, taking a steaming spoonful and singeing his tongue in the process. He didn't care. It was the best thing he'd ever eaten. Between mouthfuls, he told her about Wyatt — how he was presumably still out in those woods searching for help. She assured him that once her husband arrived with the truck and they had taken care of Doc, the wardens would initiate a search.

"Have you ever—" Siggy began, but he held back, unsure of how to phrase his next question.

"What, dear?"

Fuck it, he thought. "There was some weird shit going on out there. Things like… I mean, I don't know where to start."

She considered him. "It is quite a large forest. Strange things are a normal occurrence, I'm afraid. People in town are often going on with their bigfoot or flying saucer stories. Even my husband once saw some strange lights—"

"Not like that," Siggy cut in. "No, I mean, like, naked people running around—"

This time she cut him off with a stifled laugh. "I'm sorry, dear. But nudists, here? Are you sure you're feeling alright?"

Siggy almost said *no*, but instead he shook his head and offered a thin smile. "Sorry. It doesn't matter."

"You need some sleep. A lack of it can make you imagine all sorts of terrible things, I'm sure. Here." She poured another bowl. "Your friend needs to eat as well. Do you think you can wake him?"

"Yeah, I hope so." Siggy smiled at her again and brought both bowls into the bedroom. Doc barely stirred as Siggy tried to shake him awake. Siggy held the stew close to Doc's face, letting the smell of it waft into his nose. "It's dinner time, Doc. Wake up…"

Doc's eyes opened into slits, and he mumbled, "Okay…"

All in all, Doc managed to get down a quarter of the bowl. When he was done, Siggy consumed the rest.

"Where are we?" Doc got out.

"We found a house. *You* found a house. We're good now, man. You'll be in a hospital soon."

"Where's Wyatt?"

"He's gone to get help. After I get you out of here, I'll find him, okay? We're all getting out of this shit together."

"What… what about Crossman?"

This time Siggy didn't answer. He checked Doc's forehead. It was clammy on the surface yet held a deep heat; the fever was still strong.

"Excuse me." Cecilia's voice appeared behind him. She stood in the open doorway, a folded pile of clothes and towels in her arms. "They're my husband's. Maybe a bit big for you, but they're dry."

"Thank you."

"You really ought to get your core temperature up," she went on. "The shower is just here across the way. There's plenty of hot water."

He thanked her again for what felt like the hundredth time. She simply smiled in return.

Siggy peeled off his filthy clothes, and his own stink hit him for the first time. The water was scalding at first, but eventually he melted into the steam and became one with the soothing flow. His arms and face stung with sunburn, and his feet were soggy and blistered, but he barely felt any of it as he scrubbed away the grime and let the euphoria of warmth drown his cold skin.

It was hard to turn the water off and step out into the steamy air. After a couple of failed attempts, he managed to pull himself from the shower's embrace and towel off. The clothes Cecilia had brought were two sizes too big. He pulled on the oversized hoodie and a pair of cotton gym shorts; they were soft and warm and smelled like detergent.

He could hear Cecilia putzing around the kitchen when he left the bathroom. With a quick glance around the open first floor, he realized that she had set their pack, boots, and Doc's soaked clothes in a neat line in front of the woodstove to dry. He felt his eyes tear up with a sudden and profound gratefulness as he made his way back to the bedroom.

As he opened the door, he caught Doc struggling weakly to escape the blankets. Siggy moved to stop him. "What the hell are you doing?"

"I have to go…" Doc wheezed. His eyes were fully open, but he seemed in a daze.

"What?"

"She's out there."

"Who?"

"Sally…"

"Doc, stop. You need to rest. Sally's back in Georgia."

"I saw her."

"I promise you that you didn't."

"I can *feel* her. She's out there."

"Enough." Siggy pulled the blankets down tight, tucking them under his torso so he couldn't move. "You need to stop. She's not out there. You need to rest, Doc. *I* need to rest. We're almost out of here. Just lay back down, okay?"

Doc conceded, though Siggy figured it was more due to physical weakness than a genuine understanding of their situation.

There was a wingback armchair in the corner of the small room beside an antique writing desk and stool. He tried not to make a racket as he lifted the heavy chair and placed it beside the bedstand at an angle where he could monitor Doc. He pulled the wet holster from his jeans before laying them on the radiator, then tucked the revolver behind the lamp on the nightstand, making sure it was concealed from sight. The last thing he wanted was for the old woman to feel endangered by her strange houseguests. When he collapsed into the soft cushions of the chair, it felt like sinking into a cloud. His exhaustion hit him in full, and his eyelids were unbearably heavy.

Just as he was slipping under, a knock sounded at the door.

"Come in."

Cecilia entered, extending a steaming mug toward him. Siggy took the mug and nodded his thanks. Meanwhile, Cecilia withdrew the stool from the desk and sat opposite him, a mug of her own clasped between her knobby fingers.

"We really can't thank you enough," Siggy said quietly enough not to disturb Doc.

Cecilia waved him off and flashed her warm smile. "No need. I suppose it's nice to have visitors all the way out here, even if it is a bit of a surprise." She sipped from her mug, then nodded toward Siggy's. "It's tea. Homegrown," she added proudly. "Chamomile mostly, but some other small things that help me sleep."

Siggy politely brought the mug to his lips, but when the sweet smell of licorice filled his nose, he decided to only fake a sip for the sake of politeness. He hated licorice.

"If you don't mind me asking, what brought you boys all the way out here?"

"We're looking for someone. An old friend of ours. He came up here maybe a week ago, maybe more. No one's heard from him since."

She put a hand to her chest the way old ladies so often do when hearing unfortunate news. "That's terrible. Do you think he's alright?"

"That's what we're trying to find out."

Cecilia looked down and nodded, as if acknowledging the stupidity of her own question. "This friend, is he from around here?"

"Sort of. We were in the military together. He just recently got out and bought a cabin up here."

"Well, I'm sorry that he's missing, and I do hope he is alright," she offered with another sip. "I'm sure it's not easy, having that happen to someone you care about. My late brother was in Vietnam. I'm sure that he would have done the same thing if one of his friends went missing."

"I believe it."

She paused and looked toward the ceiling, as if recalling something. "'Greater love hath no man than this, that a man lay down his life for his brothers.'"

"That's from the Bible, isn't it?"

"It is."

"You're religious?"

She shook her head. "Hardly. I am a scientist. I just enjoy reading. I find that there's much wisdom in ancient things." Her face sank the smallest bit. "Were you all in the war?"

"Yeah."

"What did you do?"

"Infantry."

"Oh my…" She blew out a long breath.

Siggy let the silence fill the room. Despite his profound gratitude, he was growing weary of entertaining the old woman. Besides, this was a topic he didn't particularly enjoy indulging people in. At least not people who hadn't been there themselves.

Cecilia seemed to take note. She hunched in her chair and let her eyes wander across the room, finally bringing them to rest on Siggy. "What is that one?" She pointed to the tattoo halfway up his thigh.

He looked down to the block letters peeking out of the shorts, then pulled the soft fabric to reveal the words "smart gorilla" printed in all caps, upside down, and facing him — a fact that the tattoo artist had found hilariously foolish at the time.

"That's an odd phrase." She eyed it with a smile, tilting her head to read it.

"It's just something my friend Wyatt used to say — that despite whatever achievements might boost our over-inflated egos, all we can ever aspire to be is a clever ape among a tribe of shit-slingers."

Cecilia laughed genuinely.

"Goofy, I know."

"No." She shook her head, still giggling. "That just reminds me of my husband, that's all. Sometimes I think he imagines himself as an ape as well."

They sat for another few minutes, Cecilia asking the mundane questions of an old woman with nothing but time, and Siggy's answers growing shorter and shorter as his eyelids began to sink. Finally, as she finished her tea and departed, she offered Siggy the spot on the sofa in the main room. He politely rejected.

As the door was shutting, Cecilia paused. "I have to ask, what made you pick the infantry?"

Siggy yawned and rubbed his eyes. "I don't know. I guess I wanted to see if it could break me."

"Did it?"

"Not yet." He chuckled.

"Are you sure?"

His eyes snapped to Cecilia. Maybe it was his own paranoia, or maybe it was real, but the warm veneer seemed to disappear for just a fragment of a second.

"I'm sorry. It's not my place. Get some sleep. You've earned it." She disappeared into the hallway, shutting the door gently behind her.

Siggy pulled a blanket over his chest and nestled into the chair, letting Doc's wheezing snores carry him off into a deep slumber.

25

Wyatt

A BOOMING howl echoed through the dark. Far across the compound, one of the chimps rattled the bars of its cage as it bellowed. Beside it, another started. This one yipped and chirped as it spun in tight circles and jumped up and down. In seconds, the midnight air was filled with the cacophony of distraught apes. The pair of gibbons joined in with their frantic whooping, underscoring the symphony with their high crescendo. Wyatt moved close to the bars, staring out across the moonlit compound. The lights were still on in the camper, and the truck remained in its spot. Beyond that, there was nothing else to see.

As suddenly as it had started, the mad discord cut off. The abrupt stillness was absolute, as if someone hit the mute button on the entire forest. Even the crickets were silent.

The hair on the back of Wyatt's neck stood straight up. He realized that all of the shadowy apes were staring in the same direction: toward the chain link gate and the forest beyond. The night was dark, but even still, he could see that there was nothing standing at the threshold of the compound.

The silence stretched for a full minute. Then two. As Wyatt shuffled to secure a new angle on the gate, he realized just how deafeningly loud his own movements were. But none of the apes looked at him. They were focused — entirely entranced with something he couldn't see.

Then he heard it. In the distance to the north, there was laughter. It was a jubilant and low-toned sound. The type of laugh undercut with steady sobs that one might give when reunited with a long lost loved one. A laugh that embodied genuine happiness. It echoed through the trees and poured into Wyatt's head, filling his ears and drawing goosebumps along his arms.

The laughter grew higher, more hysterical, then suddenly cut off and was replaced with a bloodcurdling scream.

The apes began again, more exuberant than before. They shook their cages, swinging from the bars and throwing themselves against the metal as their own shrieks swallowed the distant cry.

Wyatt's stomach tightened and he crawled back toward the fire, his eyes darting around the dark. He had no doubt who was laughing out in those woods: the boy named Rat. He also knew, deep down, that Rat was dead.

This time the apes' energy petered out slowly. Their madness dampened with each passing second, and eventually the only sounds filling the air were the song of the crickets and the barrage of moths throwing themselves against the camper's windows. Even with it all having come to an end, Wyatt knew he wouldn't sleep again. That scream hung in his ears. It was a scream he'd heard before. That scream was the last desperate noise before a man turned into nothing more than meat.

Wyatt needed to escape.

Though the bars of his cage were rusted, they were solid. He'd checked each one of them the minute the old man had left him that evening. The concrete of the floor was chipped and poorly formed, but it bore no visible weaknesses. The padlock on the door was new and sturdy. For all his clever antics, Wyatt didn't have many options. Still, he checked them again. All of them. Every bar, every fixture, every joint in the steel gate and every crack in the concrete. There *had* to be a way out.

As he moved bar to bar, he noticed that the filthy lump in the next cage over had shifted from his normal spot in the corner. Wretch was now sitting in a low crouch, beady eyes glinting in the moonlight as they followed Wyatt's movements.

Wyatt glared back. The man's skin reflected in the moonlight, silhouetting his wiry frame in a matte grey glow. He didn't move. Even to breathe, it seemed. He just stared at Wyatt with those dead animalistic eyes.

"Can you understand me?" Wyatt asked quietly.

Wretch didn't respond. He didn't move at all or display any signs that he even heard Wyatt's words.

"What happened to you?"

Wyatt could have elicited a stronger response from the ticks he'd pulled off his arms. He picked up a pinecone from the concrete floor of his cell and threw it between the bars. It landed at Wretch's feet. In a sudden flurry of jerky movements, Wretch slammed against the bars of his own cage as one arm snaked through and grasped at the air. He growled and spat, a mad snarl smeared across his face.

Wyatt flinched backwards and tried to control the sudden flurry of his own heart. The pure savagery of this creature terrified him — and a creature it was, for there was no man left inside.

He felt something deep down once the initial shock wore off. A recognition of sorts. And then he realized that some aspect of this creature's visage felt like a funhouse mirror. Wyatt saw himself, his own hateful rage amplified and distorted and thrown back at him tenfold.

"I'm sorry. This whole thing, no one deserves this."

Wretch snapped his teeth hard enough to crack them and thrust his bony arm farther.

Wyatt gathered himself and pressed forward against the bars. "We're both going to die here, that's a given. But not before we have our revenge."

The snarl faltered, only for a second.

Wyatt nodded. "I promise."

26

Siggy

THE BLUISH hue of daylight filtered through the window alongside a mourning dove's gentle coo. Siggy curled tighter into himself, forming a snug ball of warmth beneath the blankets, and tried to drift back to sleep. It almost worked, but the grumble of hunger kept him awake.

He sat upright and took in the room around him. Doc was still laid out on the bed exactly as he had left him, sleeping peacefully. After a quick but satisfying stretch, Siggy rose quietly and checked on him. Doc's snores were shallow, but the color had returned to his face. When Siggy felt his forehead, it seemed that the fever may have gone down just a hair.

He padded out into the hallway. The air was filled with the scents of sausage and fried onions and peppers. A quiet jazz number lilted in from the kitchen. He followed the noise and his nose, emerging from the hall to find the old woman hunched over the counter and brewing a batch of pour-over coffee.

Siggy watched Cecilia for a moment, not wanting to surprise her. She had her back to him and was humming along to the tune that was coming from a record player in the corner. She moved slowly, rocking back and forth as she drizzled boiling water from a kettle into the hourglass-shaped receptacle. The scene reminded Siggy of old black-and-white movies for some reason. Perhaps it was the music, but after a moment of watching, Siggy figured it was the cozy atmosphere as a whole.

"Do you take milk and sugar?" Cecilia's soft words jarred Siggy, who thought his presence was inconspicuous.

"Black."

She turned and smiled, then handed him a mug.

He thanked her and smiled back. He tried to take a sip, but the steaming coffee burned his lips.

"Sit, sit." Cecilia ushered him to the table and pulled out a chair. Siggy graciously complied. She crossed to the stove and spooned out a scramble from a cast iron skillet. Siggy dug in as soon as the plate hit the table. It was delectable, though nothing as good as the stew from the night before. Nothing in the world could probably ever compare to that first meal.

"My husband should be back soon with the truck." Cecilia moved slowly across the kitchen, cleaning and tossing out eggshells as she went. "Earl hates getting stuck in town, but I'm afraid it happens pretty often with the weather being how it's been lately. As soon as he gets in, we'll have you two headed to town."

"Thank God," Siggy muttered. Then, in his most sincere voice, "I can't thank you enough for all of this. For saving us."

"No, no. I just happened to be the lighthouse in the storm. I think you were the one who saved your friend."

"I was the one who got him into this."

"Oh, enough of that." Her voice was especially kind this morning. "You said your other friend had gone for help. Do you think he would have managed to get far?"

"Wyatt's as stubborn as they come. If he hasn't, then something's gone horribly wrong."

"Well, these woods *are* big. Earl and I will keep a close eye out, perhaps go for a hike this evening with a whistle. I do hope he's alright."

Siggy finished his plate just as she began hers. He sat there politely as she ate, waiting for his coffee to cool. After a minute of silence, he finally asked a question that had been weighing on him since the night before. "I've got to ask, what brought you all the way out here?"

"It was my work. Earl's too, to some extent."

"What did you do for work?"

"What *did* we do?" she asked with a scoff. "You think an old woman can't be of any use?"

"Oh, no. I'm sorry—"

She cut him off with a laugh. "No, no. I'm teasing. I'm not the type to retire. My husband might wish he could, but we have our hands full with our work. I'm an ecologist. More specifically, I study rare ecosystems."

"Is that what this place is?"

"I believe so, yes." She paused to take a bite of her breakfast. "This is a very old forest. One of the last few bits of grey on the map, untouched by man. There are things here that people don't see unless they pay attention. The few men who have passed through here in the past never paid attention. Loggers and bootleggers. Would-be settlers and even the Natives. None of them lasted long enough here to make a mark."

"Why not?"

She laughed again. "I suppose there's a threshold to the wilderness that man seldom crosses. Wild places don't often stay wild unless they are so wild that they manage to repel mankind. This seems to be one of those places. I'm sure that, eventually, these trees will fall to the paper mills and the hills will be dotted with mini malls. Mankind's proclivity for expansion is unending, after all. Until then, I believe it is our job to record life as it is before the steam rollers."

"There is something different here, isn't there? I…" His voice trailed off, suddenly embarrassed as he thought of his last attempt of questioning the night before.

"What is it?"

"Nothing. I just, it feels stupid to say out loud, but these woods, they're strange. There's something else to them. It's like I can feel it, you know?"

"And what does it feel like?" She placed her fork down and stared at him curiously.

Siggy searched for the words but found himself coming up short. "It's not like it's outwardly ominous. But some things out there, some *feelings*, they almost felt magnified. Urges, you know? Like there was a little voice in my head telling me to do things I know I shouldn't. I sound crazy, I'm sure, but it was almost like the trees were whispering to me. I almost feel like they led me here."

"You're not crazy." She shook her head. "The wilderness opens us up to ourselves. The trouble is that most people don't like what they see in the mirror once the distractions of society are gone. I'm sure many people have felt that way out here for a long time. The French loggers used to call this place '*La Forêt de la Folie*.' Do you know what that means? The Forest of Madness. A terrifying idea, yes, and one that kept them at bay. Before them, the Natives had an even more frightening name for it: Hungry Trees. This is an inhospitable little slice of the world, one that has chewed up and spit out most who enter it, and all who disrespect it. I believe that's what has protected it for so long. And, if I'm being perfectly honest," she added sheepishly. "I wouldn't mind if those stories continued on. It will be a heartbreaking day when civilization finally makes it here."

"Hungry trees, huh?" Siggy pretended that the words didn't faze him, but he doubted he was successful. "What about Hyperborea?"

At this, Cecilia tilted her head, and she regarded him with a wrinkled brow. "The Greek legend?"

"Yeah..." Siggy felt foolish again. "I mean, it's just that we've heard a few people call it that. Something about a commune out here for runaways."

"There's nothing out here for people like that, unfortunately. Just another myth among many. No nudist colonies, either," she said with a wink.

He hurried to change the topic. "Why here? Like, specifically this ecosystem?"

She waited, as if searching for an answer. "It really is easier to experience than to explain. Would you like to see?"

"Sure."

"Finish your coffee, and I'll show you." She smiled, her face creasing and emanating warmth.

Siggy raised the mug to his lips and took a long sip. It was bitter and just the right temperature, and he savored it in his mouth.

Just then, Siggy could hear the distant rumble of an approaching vehicle.

"There's Earl now," Cecilia chirped. "I'm sure he'll be excited to meet you."

An old white Ford rolled down the driveway and parked in front of the house. The man who stepped out was elderly and clad in a pair of mud-stained jeans and a flannel jacket. He stomped his shoes on the mat outside before entering. "Cecilia!" he called as he pushed through the door. "Got another one."

"Earl, dear. We have company," she said quickly.

The old man's eyes darted up to Siggy, who had stood up from his seat and now extended a hand. "Thomas Sigmund. But you can call me Siggy."

Earl glanced from the extended hand to Cecilia with a slight look of disbelief, then shook it. "Earl." His calloused grip was firm for his age.

Siggy gave a polite nod.

"Siggy here was just finishing his coffee," Cecilia explained. "I told him you would take him and his injured friend in the bedroom to the hospital."

"Yeah..." Earl still seemed a bit struck. "What's wrong with the friend?"

"Some damn trapper left a whole bunch of bear traps out by the old orchard. Almost took the poor boy's leg off," Cecilia said. "He seems to be doing better now, though."

Siggy took another long swig of the coffee, nearly draining it, and turned toward the bedroom. "I'll see if he's awake. I might need help getting him—" Slowly he turned back to the old couple. "I never said anything about an orchard."

Cecilia's smile twitched, and Earl took a slow step back. Siggy felt a twinge of panic.

"Why did you say by... by the orchard?" Siggy demanded, his tongue suddenly heavy.

"That's what you told me, dear."

"No. I don't think so. I, uh... I think..." Siggy fought to get the idea out of his mouth. "What the fuck? What... why am I..."

"Strong coffee." Earl chuckled.

There was a sharp clatter at his feet. Siggy's eyes followed the sound down to the tin coffee cup rolling on the hardwood floor, the last of its contents staining the timeworn wood. He tried to reach down to retrieve it, surprised by his own clumsiness, but the shift in weight caused him to stumble forward. He caught himself on the granite-topped island, but he overcorrected and went crashing to the floor.

Cecilia's grandmotherly face stared down at him.

"You... fucking..." Siggy got out.

"You said you wanted to see what made this place so special." Cecilia's words were distant. They echoed in his mind, losing meaning with each iteration. "Go to sleep now. You'll see."

Her face faded away into obscurity.

27

Doc

"CAN YOU hear me?"

Doc opened his eyes. His leg radiated an excruciating ache and his stomach felt sour. For the first time in days his core temperature seemed to have stabilized. The old woman was sitting on a stool beside the bed. Cecilia, Siggy had said her name was. In her hands was a thick metal clipboard.

"Yeah. I can hear you," he replied.

"Good. What is your age?"

"Thirty three." Doc scanned the room for Siggy, but he wasn't there. "Why?"

"You wear a wedding band. Are you married?"

"Where's Siggy?"

"He's off to bring in some firewood from the shed. Are you married?"

"Yeah. I mean, separated, but yeah."

"And do you still feel affection for your wife?"

Something had changed in the old lady's demeanor since the night before, but the throbbing in his head stole his ability to think clearly.

"What?" he asked, confused. "Of course."

"Do you have children?"

"Why?" Doc realized why she was suddenly so unnerving: her voice no longer carried the grandmotherly warmth it had before. Now it was flat. Mechanical.

"Please answer the questions. Do you have a history of mental illness?"

"Get me Siggy." He tried to sound strong.

She ignored his request, probing further. "During your time in the forest, have you experienced at any point a feeling of extreme euphoria or depression? Perhaps resulting from an impulsive desire?"

Doc felt his jaw tighten. "What is this?"

"Just a quick survey before we get you taken care of. As soon as we're done we'll have you on your way."

"Where the hell is Siggy?"

She sighed and lowered the clipboard. "I need you to answer the questions."

"Why?" Doc demanded, stronger now. His blood was pumping, and he tasted pennies on the back of his tongue. When she didn't respond, he mustered all of his strength into a bellow. "Siggy!"

Cecilia made to stand, the stool clattering behind her. Doc's eyes darted to the revolver tucked away on the back of the nightstand. The lamp had concealed it from her, but her eyes followed his. He was fast, even in his weakened state, but not fast enough. She darted forward and managed to slap the pistol onto the floor just as his fingers brushed the wooden grip. He shifted his momentum with a grunt, grabbing at her flowing ponytail and yanking. She let out a pained shriek as he pulled her in.

A man appeared in the doorway. He charged across the room and pried at Doc's fingers. When he failed, he spun and brought a closed fist crashing down on Doc's bandaged leg.

The world erupted in an explosion of pain and stars and screams.

28

Wyatt

AT MIDDAY, the sun was bright, beaming down from a cloudless sky into the compound. Puddles of rainwater still dotted the complex — including the floor of Wyatt's cage — but the few remaining leaves that clung to the trees had finally lost their wet sheen.

Wyatt lay on the concrete with his face and shoulder pressed hard against the bars. At some point during the night, the wind had launched a thin branch against the side of his cage. Now he held it tight, stretching it as far as he could toward the smoldering fire pit and the long white shape of an animal femur that lay near its edge.

The old man had left early that morning in the truck, but Wyatt knew he could be back any time.

From atop a nearby log, the capuchin watched him closely. When it grew bored of watching, it darted forward and playfully grabbed at the branch. Wyatt swatted him away with a frustrated grunt and returned to his efforts to dislodge the bone.

Finally, he managed to wrestle it free. It was a precarious procedure, dragging the femur toward the cell bars as the monkey did its best to thwart him. Again and again, the monkey scurried forward and attempted to seize the loose bone. Again and again, Wyatt whacked it with the branch. Only after a particularly solid strike did it hiss and retreat. But the insistent beast continued to bound in wide circles around the cage, squawking and yipping the whole time, a frustrated little siren awaiting its master's return.

Finally, with the femur within reach, Wyatt managed to pluck it from the mud. It was rough and riddled with teeth marks, and he prayed that it wasn't too brittle for the job to come.

He peeled off his shirt and sopped it in one of the puddles at his feet until it was soaked. Despite the warm sun, the air still had a harsh bite to it, and the breeze brought on an immediate shiver. He took the dripping fabric and wound it around two of the bars at the rear of the cage. Tying off the ends, he then secured the long bone in its folds and began to twist.

He had no idea if his plan would work — hell, he'd come up with the idea based on a Jackie Chan movie he watched as a child. Still, it was his only option.

The bars creaked as he wrenched the bone tighter against the twisted fabric. He turned it again, leaning all of his strength against the lever. Above his head, one of the rusted joints groaned. One more twist, and the bar began to bend. He cranked the bone again.

The femur snapped in his hands, sending him staggering away.

The monkey danced outside, mocking him. He examined the broken femur pieces; one of the two sections was *just* long enough that it might work.

"One more shot," he muttered, wiping his brow. "Come on, you motherfucker…"

This time the bone held, and by the fourth turn, the bar was bent in a crescent that nearly touched the one beside it. He felt a glimmer of hope and tried to squeeze through, but the gap was far too thin.

"One more… One more…" He chanted under his breath, listening closely for the sound of the truck returning. There was nothing. He repeated the procedure, tying the soaked shirt in a loop around the next bar over, then torquing the bone tighter and tighter until the bars met.

The spider monkey yowled, yanking Wyatt's attention back to the gate. He heard the distant roar of an engine.

Fuck.

Wyatt sucked in a deep breath then exhaled hard and jammed himself between the bent bars. His shoulder made it through easily, but the thickness of his chest stopped him short. He pulled back into the cage, sucking in another deep breath before emptying his lungs as completely as he could and launching his upper body through the opening. The bars dug into his skin, but he only managed to get half of his chest through. Across the compound, the truck engine died to an idle and the chain securing the gate rattled free.

With a defeated curse, Wyatt struggled his way back into the cage. Next to the camper, the monkey was hollering and dancing as the white Ford pulled into its parking spot. Wyatt leaned casually against the bent bars, hoping his body would conceal them from the old man's sight.

The old man gingerly climbed out of the truck, carrying his clipboard under his arm. Swatting away the panicked monkey, he cast a cautionary glance around the compound, his eyes coming to rest on Wyatt for only a moment before he disappeared into the camper.

Wyatt waited for the door to clack shut behind the old man. Then, as fast and hard as he could, he spun and threw himself into the gap between the bars. The flaking rust cut into his flesh and he felt the warmth of his own blood running thin lines down his stomach. His sternum popped and a sharp pain shot through his core as one of his ribs shifted out of position. He was almost through. Only a few more inches…

He squeezed his eyes shut and pushed harder, manifesting the image of freedom.

A deafening *ping* just overhead brought him crashing back to reality. Wrenching his neck as far as he could, he managed to look backwards toward the camper.

The old man stood by the door, a scoped hunting rifle tucked tight into his shoulder and aimed directly at Wyatt.

"Fuck you." Wyatt forced the words out along with the last puff of air in his lungs and threw everything he had forward. His upper body slipped free just as another bullet snapped by. For a fraction of a second he dangled there, bent over with his hips still trapped, half in and half out of the cage. The old man shouted a curse and Wyatt heard the distinct *chuck-chuck* of the rifle's bolt recycling. He hauled his legs through and hit the mud hard just as a third bullet slapped the wet wood of the palisade beyond him, then a fourth. But Wyatt was already scuttling away, his bloody chest pressed to the mud as he made for the sliver of cover provided by the raised concrete floor of Wretch's cage.

The air echoed with the whooping chorus of the apes. The compound was their Colosseum, and their calls the savage chants for blood. Wyatt burrowed harder into the earth as another bullet snapped overhead. He knew he was pinned down, half-naked and bleeding in the mud with barely a foot of raised concrete between him and certain death. He couldn't imagine many worse scenarios.

Out of other options, he began to wail in pain. "Enough!" he screamed, his hands scouring the dirt for some form of weapon. "Enough, I'm done! You shot me, you son of a bitch!"

The old man didn't respond. Another bullet clacked off the concrete just over Wyatt's head. He cried out again, this time acting as if the shot had landed, just as his hands closed around the jagged edges of a rock. He lifted it from the muck; it was little more than the size of a soda can.

The capuchin was still prattling on. Wyatt knew that if he put his head up, he was a dead man, but from the relative distance of the monkey's panicked calls as it circled its master, he managed to place the old man's movements. Wyatt was pinned in the thin alley between Wretch's cage and the palisade. His one tactical advantage was that he technically held the high ground. In order for Wyatt's adversary to get a clean angle on him, the old man would have to close within fifty feet of Wretch's cage. They weren't good odds, but they were the odds Wyatt had.

He curled his legs to the side, readying them to spring. He listened as the monkey grew louder and louder, until he could hear its tiny feet splashing through a puddle just beyond the cage. There was a soft thud and the monkey squealed before going silent. Wyatt imagined the old man realizing his one handicap and kicking the monkey away.

But the man was too late; Wyatt knew where he was.

The electric charge of adrenaline coursed through his body and he sprang. Another bullet pinged off Wretch's bars as Wyatt spun around the edge of the cage and into the open, arm cocked back. The old man stood thirty feet off, closer than Wyatt expected, and the rock only winged off the side of his neck. Still, the impact seemed to momentarily stagger him and the rifle's barrel drooped toward the ground.

Wyatt charged. He wasn't fast enough. The rifle's barrel darted back up and the old man shot from the hip. The bullet slammed into Wyatt's side just below his ribs, sending him spinning away from the cage. Somehow he managed to keep his momentum, staggering forward as the old man struggled to chamber the next round. This time Wyatt was faster. He lowered his shoulder and drove his full weight into the man. Together they crashed against the cage. A flurry of peanuts exploded from the old man's bulging chest pocket, and the rifle spun away into the mud.

Wyatt drew back and brought his head slamming forward into the stunned old man's face. He heard the faint click of a knife. Before it even registered, Wyatt felt the thin blade jam into his ribs. He swung a hard forearm down, knocking the pocketknife from the old man's grasp. Still, the old man seemed to have some fight in him. Wyatt drove a knee into him and pummeled his ribcage with a low cross. Finally, he reared his head back one last time. There was an eruption of blood as Wyatt's forehead hammered the crooked nose flat. The old man collapsed to a seat, propped up by the cage behind him.

Wyatt stepped back from the limp form, never letting it out of his sight as he searched for the pocketknife. The blade was at his feet. He picked it up and examined the small lock blade. The tip had broken off, and when Wyatt brushed his fingers against his side, he could feel the chip of steel jutting out of his lowest rib.

The apes continued to hoot and whoop, though the capuchin had gone silent. It scampered about, plucking up the peanuts and wrestling open their shells.

Wyatt held the knife out, blade pointed at his enemy. "I told you…" he panted. "I told you I'd kill you. Now here we are."

The old man coughed blood onto his shirt and rolled his head up to regard Wyatt. His voice was thick and his eyes dazed. "No. No, you won't. You'll never make it out of here alive without me."

"I'll take my chances. Now tell me what the fuck is in those woods."

The old man spat on the ground, and his face twisted into a bloody smirk. "A nightmare. *Your* nightmare. It will be horrible. She'll bleed you. Tear out your soul and feed on your body until there's nothing left…"

"What is it?" Wyatt barked.

"Exactly what you hope it isn't." The old man's face never lost its smile. "I'll make it slow."

"You do what you wish." The old man's gaze drifted upwards to the now leafless trees, and his voice was melancholic. "A lifetime of work…"

The old man must have seen the shadow grow behind him because for just a moment, his eyes bulged out in terror. A broken "No!" he was all he was able to yell before a python of filth-mottled flesh looped through the bars and around his chest. Long fingers dug under his collarbone and he screamed. There was a hard tug, and his shoulder, head, and neck were wrenched sideways through the bars. Another filthy hand gripped a patch of wispy hair as he tried to fight back. Then both hands were on his head in a white-knuckled grip, grimy fingers disappearing into his eye sockets with a burst of thick blood.

Wretch let out a triumphant shriek as he bashed the old man's skull against the bars again and again until it lost its form. The audience of apes howled their applause.

Wyatt watched the whole thing with apathy. When he finally turned away, he found the monkey scuttling around his feet, gorging itself on the spilled peanuts. It only glanced up one time at the sack of flesh that was once its master before it returned to its feast.

As Wyatt's adrenaline ebbed, the pain in his side exploded, dominating all other senses. He forced himself to look down. A torrent of blood flowed down over his right hip and soaked his jeans. The bullet had entered less than an inch below his ribs, far on the right side. He reached around to his back and gently brushed his fingers along the exit wound. It was small — the bullet must have been a full metal jacket. Thank God. Still, the entry wound placed the bullet's passing in the proximity of his kidney, and he knew if the bullet had struck his kidney that he stood no chance; he'd die of blood loss in short order. He pulled the rifle from the mud and slung it over his opposite shoulder, then clamped his hand as hard as he dared over the wound and stumbled down to the trailer.

Up close, the camper was even grimier than he initially thought. Splotches of green mold clung to the corrugated side panels and rats skittered into the dark depths beneath as he approached. He yanked open the screen door, nearly taking it off its creaking hinges, and stepped inside. What met him stood in stark contrast to the rest of the compound.

Hundreds, maybe thousands of neatly stacked folders and binders covered nearly every available surface. They were organized alphabetically. A catalogue, each bearing a series of codes reaching into the thousands. Near the door, atop a pile of folders, was the metal clipboard. Wyatt threw it open and scanned the first page. It was a psychological profile. Under the NAME heading was only the code M1381. A series of checkmarks dotted the various fields, and at the bottom of the page was a neatly scrawled entry:

Description: White male, 30, large build. Hypothermic upon entry. Claims to have had contact with the specimen though no effects reported or visibly present. Possibly another case of neurodivergence. Will begin regiment of psilocybin in PM. Expect results to emulate F472 and M1231.

Wyatt tossed the clipboard aside. Psilocybin? Fuck that. He'd take the bullet wound over a bad trip in this hellish ape house.

He walked farther down the thin alley between the countless stacks of data, his blood trailing on the wood-grained linoleum. In the back corner of the camper was a stubby desk sporting what looked to be a 90s-era computer beside an equally archaic printer. Opposite that was a thin mattress atop a fold-out cot. Wyatt saw a blot of red under the cot and when he nudged it with his foot, he could see that it was a neatly stowed cardboard box with a large red cross printed on its center. He grimaced at the horrible jolt of pain as he bent to retrieve it, then carefully eased himself onto the bed.

Inside the box he found all manner of medical accoutrements. This was beyond a standard first aid kid — it was a trauma kit. He dug through it, tossing sterile bandages and gauze onto the mattress beside him. Near the bottom, he found an olive green packet that he recognized: QuikClot.

He hesitated at the thought. He'd never used the stuff himself, but he'd seen it work during the war, and he knew it had to be surgically removed after it served its purpose. He pulled his hand away from the wound, warm blood pooling in his palm as he did.

With shaking hands, he pulled on a pair of the light blue surgical gloves. As carefully as he could manage, he ripped the green package open. Some of the grainy powder spilled and he instinctively flinched away from it as it sizzled on the blood-stained floor.

After a few deep breaths, he lay back onto the mattress and cinched his eyes shut.

He sucked in one last deep breath, and as fast as he could effectively move, he held the wound open with one hand while he poured a short stream of the brown powder inside.

The first and only sensation he felt was like someone had jammed a red hot poker through his side. He felt the deep ache in his innards even before he felt the burning of his flesh. Someone was screaming, but it couldn't have been him. His mouth and lungs and vocal cords didn't exist.

Not in that moment. The only thing that existed was the excruciating pain as the chemicals seared his torn vessels shut.

When the peak finally passed, he lay there panting and with tears in his eyes. He knew it wasn't over, but he needed a minute. An hour. A fucking year. The mattress was soft and the camper was warm and the pain was almost — *almost* — bearable if he just lay still.

But that wasn't an option.

He tossed the remaining QuikClot onto the computer desk, the gloves along with it, and used a spool of gauze to secure a bandage tightly over both the entry and exit wounds. He felt woozy and his mouth was tacky. The old man had to have water somewhere. When Wyatt stood, his legs wobbled, and he almost fell, catching himself on the desk. There was a cooler nestled between two stacks of binders in the kitchenette portion of the camper. He knocked them over, wrenching the lid of the cooler open to find bottles of water inside. He guzzled the first one without pausing to breathe. Halfway through the second, he felt a wave of nausea and vomited watery bile onto the floor. The heave of his diaphragm brought on a whole new bout of pain. He ground his teeth and bore it, then forced himself to drink slower as he finished the bottle.

Mind clearer than a few minutes before, Wyatt tossed the bottle aside. Siggy and Doc were still out there.

But so was that… whatever it was.

After he shoveled the contents of the trauma kit back into its box and tucked it under his arm, he slung the rifle over his shoulder once more. There was a key rack by the door where his headlamp hung beside the truck keys and the oversized keyring for the cages. He took them all as he stumbled outside and made for the truck.

The capuchin sat on the hood, staring curiously at him.

"Get the fuck out of here," he growled, shooing it away. It scuttled back onto the truck's roof, eyeing the oversized keyring in Wyatt's hand. He looked down at it, then out to the dozens of cages and their pathetic prisoners. His eyes stopped on Wretch, who sat in a squat staring at him.

His jaw moved in rhythmic circles as he chewed and blood streamed down his chin. In his hands was the old man's forearm. There was no way in hell Wyatt was opening that cage — or any of them, for that matter. At least, not while he was still around.

"Here." He tossed the keyring aside, and the monkey scampered to pick it out of the mud. "It's on you now, shithead."

As he circled to the driver's side door, something thumped in the bed. He dropped the box, brought the rifle to bear, and eased the barrel over the truck's side.

Laying amidst a pile of worn rope and old gas cans was a man. He was bound, and there was a thick black canvas bag over his head. Still, Wyatt recognized his scrawny frame and the sleeve of shitty tattoos.

29

Siggy

SIGGY DRIFTED back into consciousness to the sound of gunshots and howling animals. The noise was muffled by the thick hood over his face, and he could feel the burn of the coarse rope that bound his hands and feet as he wrestled against the bonds. Another rope was tied tight between his teeth, and he struggled to draw in shallow breaths through his nose. More gunshots came, then a horrifying shriek before the cacophony of hooting beasts died to a murmur.

Whatever sedative he'd been drugged with was still flowing through his system, filling his head with fog and bogging down his limbs. He struggled to roll over only to find himself pinned between a metal sidewall and a soft bundle of what felt like more ropes. The air in the hood was thick and hot, and he felt the rising panic of claustrophobia. Squeezing his eyes shut, he tried to control it — counting down from one hundred, then starting over, then again more times than he could remember.

A hand seized his ankles and dragged him backwards. He had just enough strength to lash out, kicking his bound feet out against his captor. There was a hard thump and someone shouted in pain.

"Siggy, you fucking asshole!"

Siggy felt his heart hit his throat with joy. The hands grabbed him again, and this time Siggy didn't fight. He was hauled upright and the hood was ripped away. Wyatt stood before him, wheezing and half naked while gripping his bloodstained side.

"Wyatt!" Siggy tried to yell, but the gag transformed his joyous cry into a garbled grunt.

"Hold still," Wyatt commanded, pulling out a folding knife and cutting Siggy free.

Once his hands were unbound, Siggy ripped the gag from his mouth. "Wyatt, Jesus Christ, it's good to see you." He pulled himself from the truck bed and wrapped his friend in a tight hug. Wyatt cringed away, nursing his side. "What happened? Are you okay?"

"I'm fine." Wyatt stepped back. "Where the hell is Doc?"

Siggy tried to come up with a concise recap, but the fog muffled his ability to think. "There's an old woman — Cecilia — she took us in, drugged me, and... I don't know. She has Doc. Her husband was there too—"

Wyatt motioned with a thumb toward a large cage a hundred feet away. "Him?"

At the base of the cage lay a corpse. The head was gone, mutilated into a deflated flesh bag beyond any recognition, but the clothes were the same. Siggy stared at the blood-soaked wild man that was standing over the corpse and licking his fingers. With a shiver, Siggy tore his eyes away from the carnage and looked around at the freakshow of a zoo. Dozens of pathetic eyes stared back at him from the shadows of their own enclosures. "Yeah," Siggy muttered, covering his nose from the stink. "Yeah, him. What the fuck is this?"

"Some kind of sick experiment." Wyatt motioned to the truck. "We need to go. If this woman has Doc, we don't have much time."

Siggy stood still, unable to tear his eyes away from the sick menagerie. "Wyatt, what the—"

"No time," Wyatt snapped, climbing in the cab. Siggy followed suit.

Wyatt hesitated before turning the engine over. "Do you still have a lighter on you?"

Siggy patted his sides. The plastic bag containing the nearly empty pack of smokes and lighter was still in his pocket. "Yeah."

Wyatt held out his hand and waited as Siggy fished it out. Wyatt left the truck and disappeared into the camper, grimacing in pain the whole way. A minute later, he reemerged, a billow of smoke following him out the door.

"Do I even want to know what was in there?" Siggy asked as Wyatt climbed behind the wheel.

"Nothing worth saving." The truck rumbled to life, and Wyatt angled it toward the chain link gate. "Do you know how to get back to where Doc is?"

"No, I was out cold. They drugged me— Wyatt? *Wyatt!*" Siggy grasped the dashboard and flexed against the oncoming impact as Wyatt stomped on the accelerator. The truck ripped through the chain link, tearing the poles from the earth and sending the whole ragged mess tumbling over the truck's roof.

Wyatt kept driving as if nothing happened. "I only see one road. Hopefully it's a straight shot back there. I can't imagine these sick fucks have many visitors — not willing ones, at least."

"Dude, what the fuck is going on here?" Siggy demanded. His heart pounded from the surprise of the impact and the fog had just begun to dissipate.

"There's something out in those woods," Wyatt said. "This old shit was running experiments on it, on the people he was sending to it like bait. I saw that kid Rat. He came out here after all, poor bastard."

"What the hell do you mean *something*?"

"Some kind of animal, I don't know. Maybe it's rabid, got some sort of cross-species disease it passes on to humans. The old man claimed it turned people feral or some shit."

"And you believed him?"

"I… I saw it."

"You're not serious."

Wyatt looked over at him, and Siggy knew he was.

"Okay… okay, so what do we do? There's something out in these woods, a monster or something—"

"It's an animal. I don't know what, but it's no monster."

"*Fine.* An animal, and they're feeding people to it? What about the naked motherfucker in the cage?"

Wyatt shook his head. "I don't know. All I know is that I've got some questions for that bastard's old lady."

"She said she was a scientist. An ecologist studying rare ecosystems."

Wyatt snorted. "I'll say."

"Wyatt, what if she already—"

"Hold on," Wyatt cut him off, nodding off through his window to the passing trees. He brought the truck to a halt. "You see that?"

Siggy leaned over. The left side of the road sloped down a steep wooded embankment, and it only took half a second for Siggy's eyes to catch on what Wyatt was talking about. "Are those packs?"

They both exited the vehicle, Wyatt cautiously holding the rifle at the ready. All down the slope of the embankment were hundreds of discarded backpacks. Some of them were so old that only small bits of faded material peeked out from the mud and brush, but others looked fresh, including, Siggy realized, their own packs, which had tumbled down to the stream that ran along the ravine's bottom.

"It's a dump site." Wyatt scanned the avalanche of trashed gear with the rifle's scope. "Some of this shit looks like it dates back to the seventies— Oh shit…"

"What?"

"There." Wyatt lowered the rifle and pointed. "The green atlas pack. There's a name tape on it. How much do you want to bet that's Crossman's?"

Wyatt began to step forward but Siggy held out a hand. "No, you're hurt. I'll go."

The trek was treacherous. As soon as Siggy stepped down off the road, he realized that the embankment was more gear than earth. His feet sank into the wet material, catching on metal pack frames and bundled tent poles. He waded downward, moving slowly and tripping every few steps. When he finally reached the bottom, he found the pack Wyatt had been referencing. It was large and made up of green canvas strapped to a metal frame. Sure enough, a green MARPAT nametape was sewn to the outside flap: Crossman.

"It's his," Siggy called up to the road.

Wyatt simply nodded. "Anything useful?"

Tucked along the straps on the pack's side was a sheathed K-Bar. Siggy pulled it free and tucked it into his belt, then tossed open the flap and dug into it. On top was a soaked standard issue sleeping bag, a Bivy sack, and a poncho liner. Beneath those were a number of basic camping accessories — a mess kit, first aid kit, a fire-starting kit, all the typical things one might expect. However, stuffed at the very base of the pack was something hard and wide and wrapped in a skivvy shirt. Siggy unraveled the fabric and found himself reading the words FRONT TOWARD ENEMY.

"Goddamn, Crossman…" he muttered. "Wyatt! You're going to like this."

He tossed the pack aside and fought his way back up to the road as he held the claymore mine high above his head.

"Jesus." Wyatt shook his head. "Crossman *was* on a mission. Is there an ignition system?"

"Yeah." Siggy brushed his hand against the olive green clacker and cord he'd stowed in his back pockets.

"Good." Wyatt winced as he helped Siggy over the ledge. Siggy handed him the skivvy shirt, which Wyatt gratefully accepted. He flinched as he donned the too-tight shirt. On the way back to the driver seat, Wyatt stumbled.

"Hold on," Siggy said.

Wyatt paused and looked back at him. "What?"

"You look like shit."

Wyatt let out a deflated chuckle and flipped him the bird.

"No, really." Siggy motioned to the splotch of blood that was already growing through Wyatt's shirt. "Why don't you let me drive?"

For a second Wyatt looked like he might argue, but he didn't.

30

Wyatt

"THAT'S HER," Siggy whispered.

They were tucked behind the thick trunk of an ash tree, laying low atop the bed of wet leaves. The house was down the hill from them, bathed in the afternoon sun. The chickens clucked and fluttered about in their coop and a squirrel rattled the birdfeeder in the dooryard. Wyatt focused his vision through the scope, letting the thin crosshairs fall on the old woman washing dishes beyond the kitchen window.

Wyatt's guess had paid off. The singular road had led them directly back to the house. It continued on beyond the driveway, a singular channel back to civilization. All they had to do was get Doc and load him into the truck, then they would be free.

They'd parked the truck around a bend beyond the trees and maneuvered into their elevated position on foot. The hiking was hard on Wyatt's side, but he'd begun to grow used to the pain.

"Shoot the bitch," Siggy prodded.

"No." Wyatt steadied the crosshairs on her wrinkled face. She was singing. "We need her alive."

"Doc's in there. If she catches wind of us, that makes him a hostage—"

"*Alive*, Siggy," Wyatt repeated, this time with more force.

Siggy scowled and shook his head. "Okay. Fine. Then how do you suggest we fuck this pig?"

Wyatt thought hard. They needed to get her into the open where she wouldn't have a chance to retreat into the depths of the house. If there was one thing Wyatt never wanted to experience, it was clearing rooms with a bolt action rifle. "We need to draw her out. If I can put her down without killing her, then we might be able to get what we need out of her before she bleeds out."

"She's like a hundred years old. A spitball would kill her. What do you think a 30.06 will do?"

"It's a .243. Maybe I can tag her below the knee. Is she armed?"

"She's got your revolver in there somewhere. So, yeah. I would assume so."

"Then we can't take any chances. Go get the truck and pull it up. Duck out of sight and see if we can draw her out. If I miss, ram her."

"And if she just starts blasting?"

"Then I'll go center mass and end the bitch."

"Just don't miss." Siggy gave Wyatt's calf a squeeze as he crawled backward out of sight. He checked the rifle, making sure a round was chambered. He only had five rounds in the magazine, not counting the one in the chamber. If this came down to a firefight — even against an old lady — their odds weren't the best.

Wyatt could hear the truck sputter to life nearby. He waited as it eased down the driveway. In the window, Cecilia looked up and smiled as the truck came into view. Siggy parked it out front, and Wyatt watched her through the scope as she waved.

When no one exited the truck, she leaned forward and peered through the window. Tense seconds ticked by. Just as Wyatt started to worry they'd been found out and began easing his finger onto the trigger, she tossed the dishrag aside and disappeared toward the door.

He let out a breath, steadying the rifle on the roots of the tree before him.

"Earl?" her elderly voice called out as she opened the door. She paused at the threshold, just out of Wyatt's line of fire.

"Come on, you asshole. Come on…"

She took a step forward, examining the truck, then another. "Earl?"

Wyatt waited until she stopped just a few steps short of the truck, her face a mask of confusion. He dropped the crosshairs to just below her knee.

The rifle bucked and he worked the bolt. A high pitched wail echoed through the trees and by the time the crosshairs came back down on her, she was splayed out on the ground.

Wyatt jumped to his feet and staggered down the hill, rifle raised. "Don't fucking move! You hear me?"

She didn't even seem to register him, wailing and clutching at her shin as a red stain enveloped her pant leg.

"Siggy, check her!"

Siggy was out of the truck in a flash. He darted over to her and delivered a swift kick that spun her onto her side. Wyatt closed the last few yards, keeping a standoff distance while Siggy patted her down for weapons. He came up dry. She curled into a ball and went silent.

"Get the rope from the truck bed. Tie her hands, then grab the tourniquet from the box in the cab."

Siggy complied wordlessly, binding the stunned woman's hands before propping her against the house and cinching the thin black tourniquet on her upper thigh. She didn't fight at all, instead letting her body go limp and staring in horror at the rifle that bore down on her.

As soon as he was done, Siggy charged into the house, shouting, "Doc!"

Wyatt glared at the old woman. White bone shone through the torn wound in her shin, eerily reminiscent of Doc's own injury. How fitting.

"He's not here!" Siggy called from the depths of the house.

"Where is he?" Wyatt demanded.

Cecilia moaned. Her voice shook and her eyes were pinned shut. "Why… why are you doing this to me?"

Wyatt pulled the trigger, and she flinched as the wood siding next to her face exploded in a burst of splinters. "Where is he?" he shouted.

"I don't know who you're talking about," she groaned.

"Did you kill him?"

"No. Please, I need a hospital…"

"You know damn well that's not happening," Wyatt spat.

The pool of blood in the gravel beneath her leg had grown just a bit, but the tourniquet appeared to have done its job. She would live — for now.

"I don't have the patience for games, lady. I swear on my life that the next bullet is going through your teeth."

She stopped moaning. Slowly, she raised her head and regarded him. Her jaw clenched, and the pathetic expression melted into a flat, furious glare. Wyatt watched as the well-worn mask fell away, revealing the monster beneath.

Siggy came charging back to the front door, his eyes darting from Wyatt to the old woman. "What the fuck did you do with him, you bitch?"

The corner of her wrinkled lips lifted into a smirk.

Wyatt felt his blood boil. "Siggy, get me that gas can."

"Wyatt…" Siggy protested.

"*Do it!*"

Siggy wavered for just a second, then crossed to the bed of the truck and withdrew the red plastic container. It sloshed as he pulled it over the side.

"Pour it on her feet."

"No, Wyatt, come on, man."

"Do you want to see Doc again or not?" Wyatt hissed.

Cecilia cut in, her voice harsh. "Oh, *enough*. Your friend is gone. In the forest. With *her*. You'll never get him back."

"What the hell do you mean 'her'?" Wyatt asked.

"Don't pretend you don't already know. Earl told me you'd seen her out there." She paused, eyeing him up and down. "He also said you were unaffected."

Wyatt lowered the rifle. He took a deep breath, smothering the smoldering rage and instead speaking calmly. "Tell me what it is and maybe, *maybe* I'll let you live."

She scoffed. "That's the question, isn't it? The question we might have been able to find the answer to if you hadn't come in here, guns blazing like an idiot."

"There is no 'we' anymore — your old man is dead."

She didn't so much as flinch. "And his research?"

"Burned to the ground. Just like you will be if I don't start getting answers."

She gave a dry chuckle. "Oh goodness, you men with your threats. You want answers? They're out there. Go find them yourself."

Wyatt grabbed the gas can from Siggy's hand before he could react.

"Fine!" she snapped, wincing as Wyatt took a step toward her. "Such irony. You know, the first settlers through this area burned their women at the stake by the droves. Foolish dullards, every one of them. You might have fit in among their ranks."

"Test me," Wyatt threatened with another step.

"They blamed their misgivings on witchcraft," she went on quickly. "The dark thoughts plying at their weaknesses and driving them to madness. Driving them to walk off into the forest, only to return in the dark of night as bloodthirsty demons. Can you imagine the terror those people felt? Watching their friends and family disappear, one after the other, only to return naked and ferocious? When they finally grasped their reality, they dubbed the creature a 'she-witch.' They believed only a woman could break a man in such a way."

"Don't bullshit me with your ghost stories. Whatever it is that's out there is an animal, nothing more."

"Oh, you're absolutely right. She is an animal. Or, at least, something akin to one. Something our modern sciences have never experienced before. Something strong and ancient and indescribably terrifying."

Wyatt let the gas can down, and the wound in his side throbbed through the muscles of his back. "You're no fucking scientist."

"Fifty years of dedicated research might beg to differ. You think reality is limited by your books and institutions? We love to assume that everything must fit into all those little laws that we've come up with to govern our finite realities. You might call all of this unscientific, but you've seen her. You've seen what she does to people. She's as real as we are. Science isn't limited by your meager fears, dear boy."

Wyatt leaned in closer. "I'm going to burn this place along with everything you've worked for. This is your last chance to tell me what you know. If you don't, I'll make sure you're inside when it goes up."

She sighed. "I'll tell you what I know, if only to preserve some bit of the knowledge you're so hell bent on destroying. Perhaps then you'll reconsider your foolish tantrum." She adjusted herself against the side of the house, fidgeting with the tourniqueted leg that had no doubt grown numb. "At first we thought it was pheromones. Her proximity seems to imbed some sort of deep-seated need in her victims to subject themselves to her. We imagined that it might engage their hormonal response, as if she could flood their systems with endorphins and infuse them with a sort of addictive substance. But our samples have ruled that out. Fascinatingly, her control over her subjects seems to exist beyond the sphere of neurochemistry."

"What control?"

Cecilia laughed. "Her thralls. You haven't seen them skulking in the night? Did Earl not introduce you to his own wretched pet he pulled from her grasp?"

"You're telling me she doesn't eat them?"

"No. Well, not in the way you'd think. You see, she's not a carnivore, not in the traditional sense. You've heard of the *desmodus rotundus*, yes? The common vampire bat? Up until now, we believed that they were the only mammal alive today that are entirely hematophagous."

"The fuck is she talking about, Wyatt?" Siggy asked.

Wyatt answered him without looking back. "It means they only feed on blood."

"Correct," Cecilia said with a nod, almost as if she was praising a student. "Whatever her organs are, they don't seem designed to break down tissue. She subsists solely on the nutrients drawn from blood. This allows her to keep her victims alive for quite some time, tapping from them when she wishes. That's not the interesting part, though. Not at all. The interesting part is how she lures them in and forces them to stay."

"You mean the people you served up to her?" Wyatt spat back. "The campers and hikers and hunters, the fucking runaway children?"

"An unfortunate necessity to further our understanding." She nodded.

"I'm getting tired of this. You know what I think? I think you're insane, a pair of serial killers out here with some sick petting zoo animal lurking in the brush."

"However you want to see it is up to you."

Siggy cleared his throat. Wyatt glanced over to him. His face was drawn and body tense. "We don't have time for this."

"You're right," Wyatt agreed and regarded the old woman. "Cecilia's your name, right? Well, Cecilia, it's been fun, but—"

"Wait!" She threw her hand out for him to pause, and her voice cracked with a sudden desperation. "What if humans weren't the highest ring on the food chain? What says that there couldn't be something else, something that surpassed us at some point, preyed on us from beyond our sight? Fifty-six-million years ago, primates mysteriously vanished from this continent. The people who govern the world of academia might claim that they were killed by disease or ravaged by predators, but the truth is that we *do not know*. Who's to say that primates didn't survive? Who's to say that they didn't thrive, develop over those millions of years into something else — something capable of manipulating and feeding upon their ancient human cousins? Something barely related, convergent evolution that raced beyond our own rung on the evolutionary ladder? Why do you think we're here? Whatever *she* is, whatever *it* is, is worth more than all of our lives combined. This is perhaps the greatest scientific discovery of the last thousand years. Kill me if you feel the need, but don't destroy the research like some simpleminded fools!"

"Then tell us what happened to Doc," Siggy growled.

"He's gone. Earl dropped him off at one of her feeding grounds before he took you to the menagerie. I don't know which one, but he'll be dead before you could ever find him."

"You said she kept them alive," Wyatt said.

"Normally, yes. While his mind was doubtlessly fragile enough for her to dominate, I doubt she'd even bother with that leg of his. He'll likely just be a meal." She glanced over at Siggy. "You, though. She'll keep you."

Siggy's face drained of color. "What the fuck does that mean?"

"That feeling you described to me this morning? About the forest and its draw? I've spent decades hearing that same story over and over and over again. It always ends the same way."

"Fuck that. Fuck you," Siggy replied.

"Even if you manage to tear yourself away, hop in that truck and run back to the world and pretend that none of this ever happened, you'll be back. They always come back. You know it now, deep down, and you can lie to me and you can lie to your friend here, but it's the simple truth."

Siggy began to stutter something out, but Wyatt cut in. "None of this is real, Siggy. She's a nut. They kept humans in cages and tortured animals. They're fucking lunatics."

She made to lunge forward, a knobby hand grasping for Wyatt. He took an unnecessary step back and brought the rifle to bear. "Don't do it," she begged, her frail frame slouched over against the side of the house. "Don't be a fool. You're smarter than this, than them. Don't waste a lifetime of work in the name of petty vengeance…"

"We're gonna do more than that," Wyatt muttered. "Siggy, go inside, tear the place apart, see what you can dig up."

Siggy walked slowly to the door but hesitated at the threshold and gave her one last look. "Once I leave, I'm never coming back here." Then he was gone, and Wyatt heard him tearing through the house, ripping open doors and cabinets.

Wyatt knelt on one knee, easing the pressure off of his wounded side and coming to eye level with her. "If what you're saying is true, then why didn't it affect you or your husband?"

"It's simple. My husband and I both enjoy the same neurodivergent affliction. Neither of us ever had to suffer from empathy. That seems to be the root of her draw, of her control: humankind's incredible emotional frailty."

"You're a sociopath."

"Yes."

Wyatt swallowed hard. "And why hasn't it affected me?"

Her brow knitted in confusion, then a sad smile grew, the wrinkles of her face spiderwebbing away from her pearly teeth. "Oh, I think you know the answer to that, my dear."

He shook his head. It wasn't true. She was just trying to get in his head, to get in one last jab before the bell rang and the fight ended.

He stood and leveled the rifle. "This is your last chance. Where did the old man take Doc?"

She took a deep breath and closed her eyes. "I've said all I have to say."

"Then I guess we're done here."

"I suppose we are. Please, don't be a fool. Please save the resear—"

Wyatt pulled the trigger and her brains splattered against the house.

3l

Siggy

SIGGY WAS in the midst of ransacking the bedroom when he heard the shot. He stopped rifling through the dresser and waited until he heard Wyatt's heavy footsteps in the kitchen. "I'm in here," he called out.

Wyatt entered the room, his face sullen.

"She didn't break?" Siggy asked, though he already knew the answer.

"No," Wyatt muttered. "You manage to find anything useful?"

Siggy reached down to unclip the revolver that now hung at his side. "This was in one of the kitchen drawers. Here, take it."

"No, hold onto it." Wyatt nodded to the rifle hanging from his shoulder. "We should both be armed. Anything else?"

"No, not yet." Siggy pulled out the final drawer from the dresser and emptied it on the ground. Nothing but a bundle of worn clothes tumbled out onto the floor. "There's nothing down here. Let's check upstairs."

The lofted second story was built into a singular large room. The doors were locked, but together the two men managed to force one of them. As the wood surrounding the lock splintered and the door swung open, Siggy found himself stumbling into a haunting laboratory.

The lights were soft yellow, giving the cherry-walled room a warm glow. A long desk stretched along the entire back wall of the room. Hanging over it were dozens of anatomical charts depicting all manner of species, namely bats, apes, and humans. On the desk itself, nestled between stacks upon stacks of data sheets, were dozens of pieces of scientific equipment. There were two microscopes and a centrifuge, but most of the rest Siggy didn't recognize. Hanging in the middle of it all were two doctoral degrees, one from Harvard that bore the name Cecilia Rhodes and one from MIT with Earl Forester.

"They really were scientists," Siggy scoffed.

"Having a degree doesn't make you shit, Siggy." Wyatt was focused on the full shelves all around them. Countless jars were stacked in precise order, each labeled with Cecilia's swooping handwriting. Some were full of liquid, others full of pills or shriveled plant samples. Most, however, bore the clear yellow-greenish tint of formaldehyde and contained all variances of organs: an ape's hand, a number of bats ranging from the fetal stage to adulthood, brains of all sizes, and even a human penis.

Siggy's eyes caught on one particular jar. It was at least half-a-gallon in size and filled nearly to the brim with tiny white pills. The label read "oxycodone."

"Look at this," Wyatt called from across the room.

Siggy tore his eyes away from the jar, hoping Wyatt hadn't noticed.

Wyatt stood over a chest freezer. Siggy looked over his shoulder. Inside, between stacks of TV dinners, was a chimpanzee head wrapped in Saran wrap. White ice crystals had formed beneath the thin plastic layer, giving the animal a terrifyingly yeti-like appearance.

"Sick fucks…"

Wyatt dropped the lid. "They were, without a doubt. But there is something out there, and if we have any shot at finding Doc, we need to know what they knew."

Siggy put a hand on Wyatt's shoulder. "What did you see out there, really?"

Wyatt sighed. "I don't know. It moved like an animal, low to the ground and on all fours. It had red eyes, and it had hair, but it wasn't completely coated. I really only caught a glimpse."

"Red eyes?"

"Yeah, but that could have been the reflection of the headlamp," Wyatt tried to reason.

"You had the red beam on?"

"No…"

Siggy got the sudden impression that Wyatt's confidence in his own words was hanging on by a frayed thread.

Wyatt began to finger through the neat rows of binders until he found one he was looking for, then tossed it to Siggy. "See if you can find an entry for F472."

Siggy caught the binder and cracked it open. There was no index but the page headers were in order. He found the entry while Wyatt rifled through another binder.

"It's a lot of gibberish, checked boxes and shit," Siggy said.

"Flip through it. Is there anything on psilocybin?"

"Psilocybin? You mean 'shrooms?"

"It's a hunch."

Siggy leafed through the pages until he stopped on a scrawled entry. "'Subject's displayed traits co-align with typical symptoms of narcissistic personality disorder. Despite subject's age, 13—' Jesus Christ, Wyatt, they were doing this to kids?"

"Finish it."

"'Despite subject's age, 13, moderate to heavy doses of psilocybin seem to have little effect on her compulsions regarding the creature. Recommend termination.' Dude, what the *fuck*?"

"'M1231,'" Wyatt read aloud from the binder he held. "'Subject reminiscent of F472. NPD tendencies displayed, however after intense psychological scrutiny, it appears that the subject's neurodivergences more likely a result of childhood trauma. Even so, heavy dosing of psilocybin resulted in similar effects as F472. Administration of minimal amounts of lysergic acid diethylamide also had little effect on subject, however a larger dose resulted in subject's auto-cannibalism and subsequent death.'"

"Auto-cannibalism?" Siggy asked.

"It's exactly what you think it is, Siggy."

Siggy felt his stomach sour. "What the fuck are we doing here, man? We need to find Doc."

"I know." Wyatt slammed the binder down and collapsed into an office chair. He dropped his head to his hands. "I know, Siggy, I fucking know…"

Siggy didn't say anything else. For once, Wyatt didn't have the answers. In the past, Siggy might have imagined that moment as a triumph. But now, it weighed on him like a lead sinker in his gut.

When Wyatt finally spoke, his words came out slowly. "You heard what she said. How this thing draws in its victims like an angler fish. How it uses their own minds against them, their emotions?"

"Yeah…"

"What the woman said, about you *feeling* it… is it true?"

"No." It was true, Siggy had felt something in the woods before, but now it was gone. "Not anymore, at least. Whatever she drugged me with, it got me all numbed up man. I can barely fucking think straight."

Wyatt lifted his head. The bruises from the bar fight had yellowed, and the filth and grime and blood accentuated his wild features. Had his hair been a bit longer, Siggy might have mistaken him for a feral human himself. He looked tiredly over at the rows of jars.

"What?" Siggy didn't like his silence.

"I'm sorry, Sig. This isn't going to be fun."

"What, goddamnit?"

Wyatt stood and crossed to one of the shelves. He rifled through the jars sitting there until he found the one he was looking for and pulled it down.

"You've got to be kidding me." Siggy took a step back. "No way…"

Wyatt shook his head. "Come on. We don't have much time."

The trees were breathing.

Siggy wiped his nose. His teeth were chattering and the chills that rolled over his skin had his whole body quivering. He took in deep breaths, focusing on what control he still held over his body. His legs felt heavy and every step was a struggle.

"Are you good?" Wyatt's voice echoed through his head. It sounded tinny and far off.

"Yeah," he got out weakly without looking back.

The sun was melting beyond the mountains to his left. He'd kept it there for what felt like hours, trudging slowly north as the psychedelic mushrooms' effects had intensified. But the sun had been setting the whole time, stuck in place, halfway buried in the black peaks and transforming the fall treetops into a thousand-mile-long bonfire of rich oranges and yellows and reds. A fire that burned cold all around him, sucking the warmth from his core.

Why wouldn't it end? Why did the sun stop?

Was this it? Was this the last sunset, the ancient star stuck there in permanent half-death, helplessly awaiting its inevitable drowning in the forever darkness? Was the sun, like him, ambling slowly into the absolute nothingness of death?

"The sun will rise tomorrow. The sun will rise tomorrow." Siggy breathed the chant, hoping that the man trailing behind him couldn't hear.

The sun might. But you won't.

In a place so evil it could swallow the sun, what chance did he stand?

His legs kept going, his mind caught in the loop of his own impending death as he stumbled onward, head down and breath labored.

A searing pain tore through his hand. He recoiled and almost fell. He looked down as the beads of blood began to seep from the torn skin.

His eyes darted to his attacker — a dense thicket of wiry brambles. How had he not seen them?

Because it was dark.

The sun was gone, only a faded glow on the horizon. It was finally dead. Dead like Doc. Dead like he would soon be...

"Why'd you stop?"

This time Wyatt's voice startled him. He spun and looked at his old friend but found himself staring at a bruised stranger. The right side of the hulking warrior's torso was stained dark with blood. His clothes were ragged and stiff with dirt and sweat and salt, and his face a beaten filthy mess. He stood tall between the trees, the rifle tiny in his grime-stained hands. He was too big for this world. A dying hero whose sad story no one would ever hear.

"Do you feel it yet?"

Siggy felt a great many things. Nausea soured his guts and the cold sank into his flesh, into his bones. His eyes were wet, and the pulsing forest around him resonated with a weight that threatened to grind his broken mind into a fine powder at any second. But through all of that, he knew what Wyatt was asking, and he shook his head.

Wyatt nodded to Siggy's pocket, to the crinkled plastic bag that held more of the shriveled mushrooms alongside his final cigarette. "Do you need to take more?" Wyatt asked.

"No." Siggy felt his voice crack. He'd meant to say, "fuck no," but the words were too harsh for his glass teeth. They were already clicking together so violently, threatening to shatter at any moment. "I'm sorry."

"Try," Wyatt pushed, his dark eyes matching the night around him. "Focus on Doc. Focus on the forest, on anything *good*."

There was no good. This was a carnival of pain and he was strapped in tight on a broken Tilt-a-Whirl, spinning helplessly as the crowds jeered and taunted far below. His stomach turned as the image manifested in his mind. His nausea entwined with a sudden dizziness and he was on all fours. A frothy bout of vomit erupted from his mouth and burned his nose. Wyatt came closer, but Siggy crawled away through the wetness and the leaves, too ashamed to be comforted.

All he wanted right then was to be safe again. To be snuggled on the soft corduroy couch of his childhood, nestled under a pile of blankets while his mother stroked his hair and sang him to sleep. He wanted it so badly that he could almost hear her voice... his mother's sweet voice.

And somewhere out to the west, toward the very last bit of light in the sky, he did hear his mother's voice. The song was faint and distant, but he'd heard that lullaby a thousand times. It was *his* lullaby.

"Do you hear that?" Siggy asked.

"Hear what?"

"Her?"

"No. Where's it coming from?" Wyatt readied the rifle.

Siggy flinched. The vision of this man-at-arms brandishing a weapon at the soft-spoken Melinda Sigmund made him want to curl into a ball and disappear. But he knew that his mother wasn't out there. He knew what was calling him deeper into those woods. "It's this way..."

32

Doc

THE SUN peeped out from behind the rolling white clouds. They were fluffy and white — "Bob Ross-ian," as Sally liked to say. Doc lay back, letting his body relax and sink deeper into the soft caress of the freshly mown grass beneath him. His children bounced on the trampoline nearby, laughing and shouting and spraying each other with the new Super Soakers he'd brought home that morning. He could hear his youngest, Jeb, squeal with delight as he doused Reagan with an especially accurate shot.

The yard was a vibrant green and the privacy fence surrounding it a perfect, brand new white. The summer sun kissed his bare arms, and he smiled wide. Life was good, and the air was filled with the sweet scent of barbeque that drifted out of the smoker's chimney.

No, life wasn't good. It was perfect.

The sliding door scraped open. Sally crossed the patio, her flats tapping the old bricks in the perfect rhythm of her steps that he knew by heart. She paused, shouting out to the children to be careful. He could hear the suppressed giggle that came after. She'd sworn never to become a fussy mother, but she was a wonderful actor for the sake of her babies.

He turned his head ever so slightly, trying to see her through the glare of the sun. Her shape was clear and alluring even through the flowing sundress he loved so much. She set down a sweating jug of sweet tea on the table then turned to him. He smiled, and her perfect smile reflected back. Slowly, she came down to all fours, crawling toward him with a playful snarl. His eyes drifted down to her breasts — he couldn't help himself. They peeked out of the low cut dress, swinging with her lion-like gait as she moved toward him. He caught her gaze; she wasn't blushing. She knew exactly what she was doing.

When she finally reached him, her playful smile turned devilish, the type of smile that could easily lead to a fourth child. He felt her breath on his face. It was sweet and hot as she draped herself over his chest.

"I love you." Her words were barely a whisper as she nibbled his ear lobe.

"I love you too," he breathed back, wrapping an arm around her waist and pulling her tight.

Her lips, so soft and perfect, grazed his jawline. Gently, they worked their way down to his neck. He felt a slight pressure as she kissed him there, then the sharp jolt as she playfully nipped him.

He didn't mind.

33

Wyatt

WYATT KEPT close behind Siggy. The forest around them was dark, lit only by the pale glow of the full moon overhead. They'd been walking for hours, Siggy leading them deeper and deeper into the depths of the wilderness. Wyatt didn't question their path, only making sure to keep the appropriate standoff so as not to distract his old friend from finding their destination — wherever that may be.

Even in just the moonlight, he could tell that Siggy wasn't doing well. The thin man's breath was labored and mixed with the occasional whimper or groan. His gait was hesitant, and his head flicked around nervously at the passing shadows. Wyatt couldn't imagine the terror that the mushrooms must have induced, and even if he could, he didn't want to.

It wasn't like he was doing much better, Wyatt admitted to himself. The pain had come back with a fury. The wound in his side emanated a dull throb that resonated outward all the way to his shoulder and hip. Sharp jabs punctuated every heavy footfall, and he found himself trudging along bent over in a futile attempt to relieve pressure from the bullet wound. It didn't work, and only made it difficult to hold the rifle at the ready.

His thumb brushed the safety, memorizing the textured piece of steel for the thousandth time in an hour. He had three rounds left, and Siggy had only the five rounds of .38 loaded into the short revolver. It was better than nothing but not by much. Of course, the small daypack on his back — one he'd liberated from the old woman's house — held a more effective weapon system. He only hoped that should the time come to use it, the claymore mine would actually go off.

Siggy stopped ahead. "It's getting louder," he mumbled quietly.

Wyatt didn't respond. He wasn't even sure if Siggy remembered that he was there. He took the pause to slug some water and peel away the portions of his pant leg that had started to stiffen with blood. It was still tacky and made his fingers smell like iron and violence.

Hematophagous. That's what the woman had called it. He wondered now if it could smell him coming, a walking smorgasbord stumbling right to the dinner table of his own accord.

Siggy was moving again, this time quicker. Whatever beacon he was following in the silence of the night must have become clearer, more precise, because now they were nearly jogging through the wilting ferns and low hanging pine branches.

"It's close," Siggy mumbled again and again.

They erupted from the brush at the top of a lightly sloping ravine. Wyatt padded up beside Siggy, taking in the crater-like wallow below. Even in the darkness, the bleached white glimmer of hundreds of bones shone out against the mud.

"This is it..." Siggy breathed. He held himself close, like a child in the cold.

"I don't—" Wyatt began, but his heart jumped at a shadow of movement in his periphery. He turned to it and raised the rifle halfway, squinting against the darkness. Something was hunched low near the opposite berm. Its movement was slow and fluid as it swayed in place in a hypnotic rhythm.

Wyatt winced at the pressure in his side as he chicken-winged the rifle and clicked on his headlamp.

It all happened in a split second. The beam of white light cut through the night, illuminating the quivering mass of discolored flesh and sparse, pig-like hair. It was hunched over on four gangly legs, enraptured with the body splayed out in the mud beneath it.

Doc's body.

Siggy shouted something that Wyatt didn't register. The entirety of his focus was on the creature. The rifle was up, and the patchy yellow flesh was bright in the crosshairs as the creature reared back and emitted a raspy shriek. Its eyes reflected back in the light — cat-like slivers of deep crimson.

The rifle bucked against his shoulder, the deafening boom shattering the silence of the night. As the scope came back down, his target had already disappeared. "Where is it?" he shouted at Siggy as he worked the bolt.

"There!" Siggy fired the revolver, the burst of yellow flames flashing in the darkness.

A bullet clacked off stone, and Wyatt followed the shot with his eyes. He just barely saw the dark shape snake itself into a crevasse in the rock face at the end of the ravine.

Beside him, Siggy was shaking violently. "Keep eyes on that cave!" Wyatt shouted as he navigated the bone-riddled muck and made for the unmoving form of their friend.

Doc was unresponsive. His eyes were half open and his lips moved weakly in an attempt to speak, but the direct light of the headlamp drew no reaction. His flesh was ghastly pale and his throat bore a thin wound surrounded by a sea of purple bruising. Wyatt immediately began to apply pressure to the laceration only to find that it wasn't bleeding.

"Did you see it?" Siggy's voice shook behind him. "Did you fucking see it?"

"Yeah," Wyatt called back as Siggy approached. "Yeah, I saw it."

"I… It's not natural." Panic was rising in Siggy's voice.

Wyatt flashed the light toward the crevasse, highlighting the thin trail of blood that wound through the mud. "It's natural enough to bleed."

34

Siggy

SIGGY KNEW he wasn't in control. He knew he couldn't have seen what he'd seen. It had to have been the psychedelics. She was dead, long dead. He huffed in deep breaths. His vision was a tunnel, locked onto Doc's flitting eyelids and quivering lips as they melded together like a living Van Gogh. "We need to go…"

"No." Wyatt was resolute. He'd hovered over Doc for only a moment. Now he pulled off his pack and dug through its contents. "We have to end it."

Siggy's mind replayed the image of the girl's contorted snarl in the split second before the shot. It *was* her. "We have Doc. We need to get him out of here. Just leave it, all of this shit — just leave it!"

Wyatt withdrew the claymore without a backwards glance. His hands worked quickly, pulling out the carefully packaged blasting cap and inserting it into the device. "Just keep eyes on that cave. If you see anything — *anything* — you fucking smoke it."

"Wyatt, it's evil, pure evil—"

"It's an *animal*, damnit! Yes, we have to leave, but if we don't face it now, it will come after us and pick us off one by one. This is it. Do you understand?"

"No. You're *wrong*—"

"And you're tripping fucking balls!" Wyatt snapped. He uncoiled a length of cord and attached it to the last portion of the claymore's ignition system, an olive drab clacker that just barely fit in the palm of his hand.

"Wyatt, it wasn't an animal." Siggy felt the panic in his own voice and knew there was nothing he could say that would make Wyatt believe him. "It was *her*."

Wyatt stopped only for a moment, glancing over with a bruised eyebrow raised.

Siggy tried to express the truth in his voice. "The eyes, they were blue. They were hers—"

"Its eyes were *red*, Siggy."

"No!" Siggy insisted, his own confusion catching him off guard. Had they been? Another image was buried beneath the girl's face, something wrinkled and ape-like. Then it was gone. "No... I just saw them. They were her eyes—"

"Whose?" Wyatt demanded with exasperation.

"The girl from the bazaar, with Mortimer..."

"The s-vest?"

"You remember her?"

Wyatt shook his head. "I stuck her head on a fuckin' pike for what she did. Yeah, I remember her."

Siggy's mind came to a screeching halt. Wyatt knelt before him in the darkness, fiddling with the deadly explosive's wires. Even in the swirling shadows of the headlamp, the swollen pulp of his beaten features stood out. They pulsed and contorted into a broken mask. Though the light itself blinded Siggy to his old friend's eyes, he could feel their shark-like flatness.

Driven. Emotionless. Soulless.

Suddenly, Siggy was more terrified of the man kneeling before him than anything else in the forest. The revolver that hung from his belt was heavy, and the hair on the back of his neck stood high.

"I'm going in there after it," Wyatt said. "If I don't come back or if you hear this thing go off, shoot anything that comes crawling out of that hole." He stood, shoving the rifle into Siggy's chest. "Give me the pistol."

Siggy realized that his hand was already on the revolver's handle. When Wyatt looked down and saw, he stopped dead in his tracks.

"What is it?" Wyatt asked slowly.

"It's in my head," Siggy whispered. "It wants me to kill you. I can feel it pushing."

"Siggy…" Wyatt's voice was calm, but his figure was tense.

"No, listen." Siggy felt sick saying the words, but he knew they were true. "It has to be me. You can't leave me here with Doc. Not like this. I might… it might get me to *do* something. I don't know, but I'm weak right now, and I feel like it knows."

"More the reason for you to stay here while I—"

"It *wants* me down there; it won't fight me if I go."

"You're tripping—"

"And you're shot." Siggy cut him off again. "And more than that, it's afraid of you, Wyatt. It won't let you get close. But me…"

Wyatt stared at him for a long moment, but eventually he pulled the headlamp off. His face was suddenly visible in the moonlight. He looked frayed. A beaten dog after too long a fight. "Here," he muttered, holding out the rifle, the claymore, and its trigger mechanism. Siggy took it all, tucking it under his arm and affixing the headlamp's strap around his head.

"Go with the red light," Wyatt went on, darting back into the pack and pulling out Crossman's K-Bar. He shoved the leather sheath through Siggy's belt as Siggy clicked the lamp over to an eerie red glow. He grabbed a bundle of 550 cord from the pack, unraveled it, and tied an end around Siggy's waist. Siggy stood still as he did, like a child being dressed by his mother.

"We don't know how deep that hole is, but if I had to guess, it's a den of some sort, so it might go on for a while." When Wyatt finished tying the cord, they stood eye to eye. "This is only a hundred feet of cord. I'll be on the other end. If you reach the end of it, come back and we'll figure out some other way. Do you understand?"

Siggy nodded.

"That's only got five shots, well, four now." Wyatt motioned to the revolver. "Use it sparingly. That thing in there is already leaking a fair amount of blood. Hopefully you'll just roll in and find a corpse."

Once again, Siggy nodded. He heard the words and knew their meaning, but it all felt too surreal to actually be happening. "If I don't come back—"

"If you don't come back, then we're all dead. I can't drag him out of here alone, not in this condition," Wyatt said sternly. "So you come back. You fucking come back."

"I will."

Wyatt slapped him hard on the shoulder, and Siggy winced. His skin felt like thin ice, ready to shatter under the lightest pressure. To his surprise, Wyatt grabbed him and pulled him in for a hug. When he stepped back, he looked Siggy over with a grin that held a mixture of pride and grief. "Look at you, a regular tunnel rat. You picked the wrong war, kid."

Siggy couldn't muster a smile. "Really, man. Whatever happens, make sure Doc gets back to his kids."

"*We* will," Wyatt said with a confidence that Siggy didn't believe.

Siggy turned to the jagged crack in the stones and the darkness that swirled in his vision beyond. The opening was thin, just barely wide enough for him to squeeze through, and in the dull red glow of the headlamp, it gave the vicious impression of an axe wound. He raised the revolver and started forward, then paused and turned back one last time.

"I fuckin' love you guys." He felt his voice crack.

Wyatt chuckled in the red glow. "Clearly."

Siggy felt his own lips curl upward just the slightest bit as he turned away and made for the darkness of the cave.

The air in the cave was warmer than the outside. Beyond the thin opening, it widened out into a jagged tunnel. He took a deep breath, his nose filling with the ripe scent of earth and rotting leaves, then leveled the pistol in front of him.

One step.

Two steps.

His heart pounded in his ears, and his whole body vibrated with tensed energy. The red glow of the headlamp dissolved into the endless dark ahead.

Seventeen.

Eighteen.

The air was still. Horribly still, and when he dared a glance down at the ground, he saw that it was worn smooth. Dried mud and bits of debris smeared the stone surface alongside the trickling trail of blood.

Eighty-one.

Eighty-two.

The paracord at his waist pulled tight. He stopped, listening to the ringing in his ears play out above the absolute silence. The darkness of the tunnel wound on ahead forever.

"We have to end it," he breathed Wyatt's words. They were terribly true.

He could go back, but then what? They were here. *He* was here.

Slowly, Siggy holstered the revolver and withdrew the claymore from under his arm. He slid it under his waistband, using his belt to secure its contoured frame against his hollow stomach. Looking down, he couldn't help but let out an ironic snort at the words that peeked out from above his crotch: front toward enemy. He took a deep breath, withdrew the K-Bar, and cut himself free from the paracord that trailed behind him.

35

Wyatt

A COLD fall breeze swept down through the gully, drawing a shiver. It had been some time since Siggy left. Maybe an hour, maybe several. Wyatt couldn't tell. His thoughts were scattered and his vision waning in the dark. He knew the lightheadedness he felt was from blood loss. The bandage wrapped tight to his side was soaked through and warm, and he swore he could feel the congealed mass of QuikClot breaking loose. He sat with his back to the stony outcropping, his eyes glued to the crevasse to his immediate left. The rifle lay balanced on his knees, angled to catch anything that came wandering out.

Doc groaned and began to twitch in his comatose state. Wyatt muttered a soft reassurance, but he knew it was no use. *If* they managed to kill this thing, and *if* they managed to drag Doc out of there, there was still a high chance that the damage done was irreversible. That Doc was experiencing his final, terrible night.

Wyatt thought back to the hooch they'd all shared in Afghanistan. To their squad, and more specifically to Doc and his tidy rack in the corner. He'd always ended up on the receiving end of their pranks, always the butt of their jokes. But he'd taken it with a hearty smile. Doc was soft despite the austerity of their world, and he grounded them to the simple principles of being a good man. He'd been the one to console Costello when his wife cheated on him, and he was the one who gently talked Johnson down after a panic attack following Mortimer's injury. He'd coddled and scolded and cared for the broken teenagers without ever asking for anything in return. Doc was the best of them. He always had been.

He didn't deserve this.

An owl hooted in the distance, drawing Wyatt out of his daze. He realized that he'd only been half awake and that the pool of blood in the dirt beside him had grown substantially. He scanned the crest of the gently sloping ravine. Nothing moved in the silvery moonlight.

"It's alright, Doc…" he breathed, more to himself than to the still figure beside him.

Despite the bleeding, the burning, the aching, despite every bit of pain Wyatt was in, something else was eating at him from the inside — the accusation that had slipped through the old woman's wrinkled lips. Was he really a sociopath? Was that what his existence really boiled down to? An unfeeling machine of destruction? In his youth, his propensity for toughness had always been a boon. But over the last decade, he found something was… off. Whether it was his quick and painless relationships, or simply a funny feeling in his own mind, his uncanny ability to shirk empathy had always seemed to be just beyond the cusp of self-analysis.

He *did* have feelings, after all, so it couldn't be true… could it? He hadn't tortured cats or anything like that in his childhood, shown none of the psychotic patterns that unfeeling sickos seemed to always exhibit. He'd been a happy child. A good kid, a loving teen although a bit combative. When had it all gone awry?

His thoughts drifted to Siggy, to the years after the war, then to the war itself. He'd had feelings then, hadn't he? Empathy, compassion, hell,

DOUGLASS HOOVER

the whole gambit. Maybe he'd been able to turn them off when needed. That was another boon. That on/off switch that had carried him through it all — kept him from being a fuckup or a drunk or some depressive asshole. But when was the last time that switch had been turned to *on*? When was the last time he'd allowed himself to actually engage with the horrors of his past? When was the last time he'd willfully embraced the joy or the hurt of his life? Of *anything*, really?

A pit formed in his stomach as he began to realize that the switch itself might have become stuck somewhere far back in those days, caught in that off position long enough to rust into place, leaving him only the shell of a human. Could he even turn it back on, or had he sabotaged his own life in order to run away from the pain?

An intrusive thought manifested: should both Siggy and Doc die out here, and if he were to somehow make it, would he recover just fine? Would he be able to shove the experience of the last week into a steel box and bury it deep enough in the cold oceans of his heart that even he would never be able to access it again?

No. He wouldn't do that. If there *was* a tomorrow, he wouldn't make the same mistakes.

He laid a gentle hand on Doc's shoulder, the motion causing his side to erupt in agony. He stifled a yelp and looked down. The skin of his hand was pale, and the pool of blood beneath him had grown even larger. Suddenly none of it seemed to matter.

Wyatt knew he wasn't going to make it out of these woods.

Dulce et decorum est, he thought with a rueful smile. It was a lie. The oldest lie ever told. There was no sweetness in dying for one's country.

But this wasn't so bad, dying for his friends. Maybe this is what it had always been leading up to. Maybe his fate had been written in stone from the start and making it back from the war was just some fluke that the universe was finally correcting.

He felt himself slipping under again, the waves of fatigue carrying him gently away from the shores of reality.

Somewhere in the surrounding forest, a twig snapped.

36

Siggy

THE TUNNEL pulsed around him like a dull red artery leading straight into the heart of hell.

Siggy pressed forward, crawling under the low hanging stone ceiling before squeezing through yet another thin gap in the stone. Finally, he reached a section where he could once again stand and stretch some of the ache from his legs.

He'd lost count of his steps long ago. Several times already he'd passed by interconnecting caverns and tunnels, and even in his drug-addled state he knew he was delving deeper and deeper into an unending maze that he'd likely never find his way back out of. Only the thin trail of increasingly sparse blood droplets guided his path through the stone labyrinth.

His mind reeled with a thousand terrible thoughts. He focused away from the darkest ones, drawing instead from the memories of his childhood neighbor, the grizzly Mr. Auger. He was a veteran of the Vietnam War, and as a child Siggy had always been enraptured by his tales of valor and violence. Something Wyatt had said earlier brought him back to that tiny old man. Mr. Auger was a tunnel rat, hunting the Viet Cong in their own underground networks with nothing more than a pistol and a knife. Siggy had always found it fascinating as a boy, but now he looked back on the anguish in the old man's eyes with a stark realization. Those stories weren't of heroism and honor, they were stories of horror. A horror that Siggy now felt deep in his bones. But Mr. Auger made it back... Maybe he could too...

Non Gratum Anus Rodentum.

That was the old man's tattoo. The motto of the tunnel rats, he'd told Siggy: *not worth a rat's ass.*

Despite his attempts at hope, that was exactly how Siggy felt now. Weak. Inhumanely weak against this terrifying world and the monsters that called it home.

You are weak.

The voice was strong. It whispered to him from the oscillating walls, vibrating his skull with its ferocious intensity.

"Fuck you," he hissed back.

Weak. A guppy in a shark tank. Outmatched, simply floundering toward death.

The words ate at him, taunting him and driving him ever closer towards submission. But they weren't all so cruel. There was another voice, soft and sweet. Terrifyingly sweet, hemmed with that little hint of a Michigan accent that sung him to sleep as a little boy. Her words played over the darkness, promising him warmth and comfort if he just gave in.

Why fight? Baby boy, why not rest in the warm? Aren't you tired? Oh, my dear Thomas... it can all be over if you just close your eyes, lay down...

It was so hard to ignore. She was right. What use was he? Why not do what he did best? Give in, lay down, and take some small solace and respite in his last moments.

He forced himself to manifest the images of the dismembered chunks of human anatomy hanging in yellowed jars. The pathetic helplessness of the animals bound to their cages, and the horrible wild man licking the old man's blood from his shit-stained fingers. He pictured Doc and the girl with the blue eyes hanging over him, feeding…

He was resolute. Someone would die today — some*thing*. The soft voice was the greatest liar; there would be no happy endings tonight.

Why not just end it yourself then? On your own terms?

No.

That's what you wanted, isn't it? It's what brought you here in the first place. It's why you cut the cord, right? Why not? Why not just end it once and for all? Why suffer the fate of cattle? You can't win. You'll lose in time. It's inevitable. Why subject yourself to that? You've seen what you will become. Why not just finish it here and now, like a man? Or are you too much of a coward?

Siggy realized he'd stopped walking. His head swirled like a hurricane in a glass bottle, the voices hissing and scratching at the inside of his skull, begging to be released with the pull of a trigger.

Slowly he knelt, letting his hands rest fully on the worn stone floor. It was cool under his fingertips, and the fine dust clung to his skin like flour from a baker's table. He shut his eyes, focusing entirely on the here and now, on the warmth of the air and the slow rhythm of his breath. The voices chanted louder and louder, attacking him viciously from all angles. He muffled them out one at a time, suffocating them with the genuine sensations of touch and feel and smell and taste.

Kill yourself, you weak piece of shit!

"Maybe I will," he said out loud, voice dripping with malice. "But I'm gonna bring you with me."

Silence came rushing into his ears, and he was alone.

It was in that sudden silence that he heard the noises emanating from the darkness ahead. Unlike the voices in his head, this sound rebounded off the stone itself. This sound was a murmur. The distant vibrations of breathing and panting and groaning all blended together. Over it all, someone was sobbing.

Then he caught a whiff of the smell. It was a stench he knew too well — the stench of rot and feces and death.

He rose, pistol in his right hand and clacker held tight in his left, and once again began forward. The murmur grew as he pushed on, as did the stench. The red light of the headlamp revealed a curve in the tunnel ahead, and when he reached it, he found himself peeking into the pitch black maw of a much larger cavern. The cries were clearer up ahead, the noise close enough that the individual parts of the whole began to break away into distinct grunts and cries and sobs in an anguished symphony of pain.

With shaking hands, Siggy yanked the claymore free. He knelt, unfolding the spindly legs and placing it at his feet. Whatever this cavern was, no matter how large, the mouth of the tunnel he stood in now was a choke point. Maybe his last choke point, judging from the echoes thrown back at him. He unwound the cord, keeping the clacker close to his chest. If anything made it by him, they wouldn't make it far...

Keep it on you. Keep it on you and press the clacker. Let it tear you in half. You've seen what that's like. Maybe your dear friend will mount your head on a spike where it belongs.

"Shut up!" Siggy growled. At the sound of his words, the murmur cut off again, replaced only by the wheezing of dozens of raspy breaths. His heart jumped into his throat.

It was now or never.

He stepped over the mine, trailing the cord, and walked into the darkness.

The fetid stench hit him full in the face. He gagged and his eyes watered. The floor was slick with liquid. It wasn't water, nor was it blood. It was something else, gristly and thick. Scattered bones glowed in the dull red light at his feet. He kept to the wall, feeling his way along the edge of the cavern and searching the small area of dull light for movement. Something twitched nearby.

The red light wasn't enough. His opportunity for a true ambush had already passed. *Fuck it.* He held the pistol in front of him as he reached up and switched the headlamp over to its blinding white bulb.

The cavern was expansive and shallow. The sleek stone floor was coated with a thin sheen of rotting fat and slowly dissolving flesh. Bodies of all species and in all stages of decomposition littered the ground, torn and eaten upon. Mounds of rotting filth threw dark shadows in the white light, broken limbs and hooves jutting out of them. Torn flesh hung from them like desecrated flags.

Beyond all the dead and rot, a handful of thin, corpselike figures lay scattered about the ground. They hissed and recoiled at the light, shielding their eyes or feebly rolling away with agonizing groans.

Siggy realized immediately that this was a tomb. A crypt full of the living dead. A fucking slaughterhouse of half fed upon cattle.

He jerked the pistol in a wide arc, sweeping the illuminated cavern for the beast. It wasn't there. There was a beehive of tunnels and caverns dotted high up on the stone walls, far out of reach. She was gone, no doubt crawling away to disappear deeper into the labyrinth.

One of the emaciated humans by his feet curled tighter into a ball. Siggy jumped at the movement, bathing the naked figure in light. Beneath the matted blonde hair stained dark with a filth, he recognized the cowering face.

"Crossman?" he said, unbelieving his eyes, then louder, "Crossman!"

Crossman let out a wheezing yelp as he struggled to worm away from the light. His toothpick arms glided over the volatile mush, searching for a handhold, but he wasn't strong enough to carry himself away.

Siggy bent closer, a sudden hollowness expanding in his chest. When he tried to speak, he realized that he was crying. "Come on, man. Get up. Please… We need to get out of here."

Crossman hissed when Siggy took a step closer. A look of feral terror twisted Crossman's emaciated features, and Siggy immediately knew the truth. Crossman was gone. The creature in front of him was just a shell.

"Please…"

Crossman snarled, baring a mouthful of broken and rotting teeth. Dried blood coated his matted beard, and as Siggy fully took in the image of what was once his friend, he realized what he'd interrupted — the small body that Crossman huddled over, greedily protecting, feeding upon. Siggy recognized the oversized Ninja Turtle sweatshirt that hung tattered from the broken little corpse.

Siggy felt the kick of the revolver before he'd even registered his own actions. The gunshot rang through the cavern like an unholy church bell as his old friend's head snapped backwards. His ears rang as he watched a single line of blood dribble down the crook of Crossman's nose and into the mangy beard.

The other feral creatures began to howl. Their morose wails overlapped with the high pitched ringing that filled Siggy's ears. One of the thralls, less feeble than the rest, darted toward him in a scuttling crawl. Siggy leveled the revolver and fired. The pale figure hitched in its stride, and he fired again. Some voice of reason in the back of his mind demanded that he conserve the ammo, but he ignored it. In that moment, he was numb. Terribly, hopelessly numb. Nothing mattered. They were all dead anyway.

Then there was another noise. A violent, deafening shriek that echoed from the unexplored corridors above. Siggy spun, the cone of white light darting from darkened crevasse to darkened crevasse, searching for the evil bitch that brought all of this to bear.

Just out of the corner of his eye, he caught a shadow bursting forth from the darkness. It bore down on him before he could even turn, and the impact sent him sprawling. The revolver flipped away into the darkness.

She was on him, writhing like a furious panther. Flailing limbs battered him and clawed digits dug into his flesh. A searing pain erupted from his shoulder as jagged teeth clamped down.

He didn't know why he said what he said. Maybe it was out of instinct, maybe it was some final, scalding joke to leave the world with. But as his fingers closed around the clacker attached to his belt loop, he managed to growl the words through clenched teeth: "Allahu Akbar, you cunt."

There was a blinding flash, and the darkness swallowed him whole.

31

Wyatt

WYATT BRACED the rifle against his shoulder. His eyes darted across the black wall of trees. Something was out there. More than one of them, stealthily picking their way through the forest. He couldn't see them, but he could hear them moving and breathing in the night, and he could feel their dead eyes glued to him.

Her thralls. Wretch's unfortunate companions drawn home by their wounded master.

Something to his right slopped in the mud. They were getting closer, emboldened by his stillness. His heart pounded and what little adrenaline he had left began to seep into his veins, leaving a coppery taste on the back of his tongue.

Another shadow darted between the trees only a few dozen feet ahead. Wyatt moved slowly as he leveled the rifle and peered through the scope. As he hovered anxiously over Doc's unconscious form, he would have given anything to have the headlamp back in that moment. But it was with Siggy down in whatever hellish catacomb this creature inhabited.

From between the trunks of two glowing white birches, a figure melted from the dark. A man's silhouette was cast against the silver moonlight, a tangled crown of wild hair framing his hunched head.

Wyatt eased the shadow into the center of the scope. It was too dark for him to make out the crosshairs, but his target was close enough. He squeezed the trigger. The muzzle flash illuminated the graveyard of bones immediately before him, and the figure toppled.

All at once the forest exploded in a deafening cacophony of wild shrieks. Wyatt bolted to his feet, working the rifle's action as another shadow exploded from the darkness to his left. He fired again, and it crumpled, sliding to a halt at his feet in its final gasping death throes. Another appeared, a woman from the sound of her vicious screams, and this time Wyatt only managed to wing her, sending her stumbling to the side.

The rifle clicked empty.

Wyatt spun the gun in his hands, brandishing it by the barrel like a Native American war club. The thralls poured out of the darkness, flooding into the ravine and filling the air with their whooping cries.

Wyatt roared back as he charged headfirst into the fray.

38

Siggy

SIGGY COULDN'T tell if his eyes were open; the darkness was all-encapsulating. The headlamp was gone, his forehead slick with blood and sweat and his own caked, greasy hair. The world was a kaleidoscope of pain. His eardrums rang over the dull throb of his own racing heart, and his head split with a sharp, pounding ache.

Something writhed underneath him. He pulled away, his pulverized joints creaking and swollen. A searching hand latched onto his shoulder. He felt along his side, searching for the gun. It was gone, the empty leather holster tacky with blood. His hand fell on something hard — the K-Bar on his belt. His fingers trembled weakly as he grasped the handle and yanked the blade free, then stabbed it down into the soft mass beneath him. A gargled cry of pain sounded in his deafened ears. He stabbed once more, this time twisting the blade until the cry faded away. He rolled away and tried to stand, but his legs wobbled and he collapsed back into the mattress of stinking gore.

He lay there listening to the viscera that dripped from the cavern's exploded ceiling. Nothing moved for a long time.

Then, finally, something else shifted close by. He listened as it dragged itself along the slimy floor, wheezing in its raspy, inhuman breaths that grew heavier and more distant with each passing second. Siggy had no idea how he knew, but it was the creature. It was still alive. *She* was still alive.

He forced himself onto all fours. There was no voice in his mind. No thoughts of reason or desire or fear, nothing but the hot burning fire that had driven him down into this demonic realm to begin with.

His organs felt fragmented, ruptured, and smashed to a bruised pile of roadkill as he forced one hand in front of the other, dragging himself over the rotting piles and dislodged boulders. It hissed at him as he closed the dark distance between them. He searched through the muck, following her path, until he found a slimy limb with life still in it. She yowled and tried to slither away when he grabbed her.

He launched himself forward, swinging the hungry blade in an arc. It bit deep into her flesh. He used the sunken blade as an anchor, pulling himself forward more, batting away her weak attempts at defense as a primal rage filled him. He wasn't a wounded animal in the dark, backed into a corner with no escape. Not like she was. *He* was the fucking predator. *He* was the apex. *He* was death incarnate and this thing was *his* fucking dinner. He screamed, stabbing, thrashing, slashing at the pulsating mass until only the wet *schlop* of the blade and his own feral cries filled his ears.

Then all was still.

He collapsed into a bloody heap, weeping and panting in the stink of death. It was over. Dead and butchered. Yet, he slowly realized, there was no relief in it. No cathartic release in the victory — just the darkness slowly closing in around him.

He suddenly and desperately needed light just to breathe. He crawled forward, fingers dinging through the pools of bile and innards and corpses, searching for the headlamp. He couldn't find it, but his hand closed around something else — the stippled wood grip of the revolver. He pulled it close and felt his way to the cavern's edge where he sat back against the wall. He had no idea how many bullets he'd fired. He clicked open the cylinder and dropped the shells into his hand. Each one came out empty, all but the last one. The single bullet felt heavy in his palm. He rolled it around in his fingers, then slid it back into the cylinder and held the pistol close. Besides his own wheezing breath, there was no noise at all. The darkness was a vacuum. He listened for a long time, barely breathing. There was nothing. Nothing at all. He was alone.

And he was alive. Somehow, by some cruel twist of fate, he was alive.

Now he needed to escape. To return to the others. To get away from this rotting den, to be anywhere but here. This time when he forced himself to his feet, his legs held, though just barely. He stumbled through the blackness, blindly feeling along the stone walls and tripping over the crumpled bodies and bones and loose rocks. He hadn't been far from the entry tunnel when the claymore went off. There had to be a gap there somewhere. But as he searched the rough stone walls, his hands came across the pile of loose stones.

The tunnel had collapsed.

The image of Wyatt and Doc flooded his mind. Both of them laid out in the elements and mortally wounded. He holstered the revolver and grabbed one of the stones, hauling it from the top of the heaping pile and casting it aside. It splashed down in the muck. Then he grabbed the next and yanked it free. Something in his elbow popped, and he fell back in agony as the searing pain shot up his arm.

He was broken in every conceivable way. A sudden and terrible realization dawned on him: he was inhabiting his own tomb.

But his friends were out there, and they needed him.

They needed him.

He grasped blindly for the stones again, but when he wrenched at their weight, the pain in his elbow became overwhelming. He staggered back and slid down against the wall, eyes flooded with tears.

It was hopeless. He didn't have the energy to go on. There was nothing left in the tank, not even fumes. Even if he did somehow manage to burrow through the impenetrable mass of stone — even if he *was* somehow capable of escaping, what truly waited for him on the other side? The sinking feeling in his gut told him the truth, and it was a truth he rejected with vehemence: Doc and Wyatt were already half past dead, trapped to wheeze out their final desperate breaths in this hellish wilderness. Hell, they might already be dead. Siggy had no idea. All he truly knew at that moment was that the dark was endless and it was getting cold.

He could have sat there for an hour, or it could have been a minute. Siggy had no way of telling in that hellish void. Time had lost all its meaning amongst the hot stinking black.

The pistol felt heavy in his hand as he rotated the last bullet into the chamber.

39

Wyatt

WYATT STIRRED. As he cracked his swollen eyes, he saw the wallow before him bathed in the blue light of pre-dawn. He was leaning heavily against a moss-coated tree stump at the edge of the ravine, his body cast from lead. At his feet was the rifle, snapped in two pieces at the stock. Mud-stained corpses were strewn in the earth around him, emaciated and naked. He tried to draw in a deep breath, but the stabbing pain that filled his torso cut it short. In the distance, over the treetops that stretched out below the little hill, a single fat pillar of smoke rose from the forest. Beyond that, the first yellow glint of dawn peeked over the horizon.

He winced as a hand grasped his shoulder.

"You still with us, dickhead?"

He slowly craned his stiff neck. Siggy knelt beside him.

"Yeah..."

"You look like shit."

"Nah, I feel great," Wyatt snorted.

Siggy cracked a sorrowful smile. He was almost unrecognizable, covered head to toe in blood and filth. A sickening stench wafted off of him, making Wyatt recoil. "You shit yourself?"

"At least once," Siggy joked.

Wyatt couldn't muster another snort. It hurt too much. "How's Doc?"

Siggy glanced down at the dark figure by the cave entrance. "He's breathing."

Wyatt nodded. The motion drew a hoarse cough, and he could taste blood. "Is it over?"

Siggy dropped to a seat beside him and reclined against the stump, bringing them shoulder to shoulder. "Yeah. It's over."

Again, Wyatt nodded. Speaking was too painful. Everything was too painful.

Siggy dug around in his pocket and pulled out the crumpled plastic bag that held the mushrooms and his cigarette pack. He dug his fingers into the flattened cardboard square and withdrew a broken cigarette. "It's our last one," he muttered, lighting it. The tobacco sizzled as he took a long drag, then extended it to Wyatt.

Wyatt reached for it.

"You missing something there, bud?" Siggy asked.

"Huh?" Wyatt looked down. The middle finger of his right hand was missing at the second knuckle, replaced with a muddied scab of a stump. The faded memory of the *crunch* as one of the savages bit it off echoed in the back of Wyatt's mind, and he grinned. "I guess I am."

Siggy chuckled and held the cigarette to Wyatt's lips. The smoke was harsh and drew another cough, sending another spasm of pain throughout his ribcage. He shook his head when Siggy offered it again, then laid back against the tree stump, watching the sun rise over the sea of fall foliage. The pillar of smoke steadily grew thicker.

"It's the camper. I think it's spreading," Siggy said.

"Good," Wyatt muttered, resting his eyes.

"Hey." Siggy shook him.

Wyatt looked over tiredly. He could see the tears growing in Siggy's eyes.

"Come on," Siggy insisted, climbing to his feet. "We need to get going."

Wyatt meant to nod, but his chin barely left his chest. He let his eyes drift shut once more. "Yeah. I know. Just… just a little bit longer…"

Epilogue

LARRY CARTER pulled his golf cart into the shade of a towering willow. The air was muggy and still, and he had to dab the sweat from his wrinkled brow before reclining into the worn cushions. Waves of heat rose from the thin asphalt path that cut between the headstones. This *had* to be the hottest August he'd seen in West Virginia in all of his 67 years. Then again, he remembered thinking that every year.

He glanced around the empty cemetery, making sure he was alone. Satisfied, he pulled a pair of cheap foam headphones over his ears and clicked play on his walkman. The CD skipped at first, but after a moment the gentle tunes of the Beach Boys filled his ears. With the calloused fingers of a groundskeeper, he dug into the little vehicle's ashtray and pulled out a thin joint. Normally he'd wait until after closing hours to begin his evening ritual, but the heat wave had kept the cemetery delightfully empty that day. The only visitors he'd seen had been a trio of young, rowdy-looking fellas up on the hill.

The smoke was sweet and citrusy, a strain of sativa his daughter's new boyfriend grew out near Alderson. *Good shit*, he thought, tapping his foot along to the music. The kid who grew it was a bit of an ass, not really the type of man Larry approved of for his daughter dating. But what could he do? She was damn near forty now, and at least this one seemed to get along with her kids.

He checked his watch: quarter to closing. Stubbing the joint out, he took a long sip of his lemonade and pressed the accelerator. The beat up electric cart whirred to life. He angled it between the headstones and up the hillside.

The three young men were silhouetted against the afternoon sun, laughing and passing around what looked like a bottle of something good. Larry pulled to a halt nearby and dropped his earphones down around his neck. "Hey, fellas! It's about closing time. Gotta ask y'all to finish up!"

The tallest one waved. He bent and, together with his scrawny friend, hauled the third up to his feet from where he sat beside a gravestone. Together they ambled away, moving slow so the one with the cane could keep up.

Larry waited patiently until they'd disappeared through the wrought iron gate. Then he accelerated the cart up the winding path to the gravesite they'd been visiting. He'd found that it was always the drinkers that left behind the most trash, and the last thing he wanted to spend the next morning doing was chasing around food wrappers or grocery bags in the wind.

But the gravesite was clean. Always a bit curious of the happenings in his little realm, Larry glanced over the stone they'd been visiting. The serif lettering chiseled across the reflective granite read Michael Bauer.

There was a jolt of sadness as he realized whose grave this was. He'd helped place it years ago, for a Marine who'd died overseas. Had he realized before, maybe he would have let those boys stay a bit longer, even past closing.

As his eyes drifted upwards they caught on something balanced atop the stone. His knees creaked as he climbed out of the golf cart and approached.

It was a bullet.

He picked it up, rolling the tarnished brass between his fingers. The lettering *38 Special* was stamped at its base.

Normally, Larry Carter would never have left live munitions laying out in the open. After all, there were children that came to visit on occasion, and a good portion of his job was to ensure that the cemetery was a safe space. But, for whatever reason that was lost even to him at that moment, he balanced the bullet back in its spot atop the headstone and went on with his evening routine.

A Note from the Author to Veterans

When I first got into writing back in 2016, my goal was to create a novel that I could use as a vehicle for disseminating the following note. Several books and many years have come and gone since then, but despite the passage of time, it's clear that the same issue that inspired this note initially plagues the veteran community still. I'm including the note once more in this novel because I believe it is still relevant and important. It's the whole reason I ever sat down to write in the first place, and a good part of the reason I have continued.

—Douglass Hoover, April 2023

I felt compelled to add this note at the end of this novel in the hopes that it might reach a veteran struggling to keep it together after rejoining the civilian world.

I served in 1st Battalion 9th Marines from 2008 to 2012. During that time, I was incredibly lucky to be part of an irreplaceable family of young men. We went to hell and back with nothing but each other. We fought together, ate together, shit together, we did everything together, and despite our petty differences, there was absolutely nothing in the world that could have torn us apart... at least until our EAS dates came along.

Four men whom I considered closer than brothers have taken their lives since then. Four wonderful, strong, iron-hearted men with everything to live for took that last step over the ledge and made that irreversible decision.

I can't tell you why they did it. Maybe a part of me knows. I'm sure many veterans reading this understand it on some level even if you can't find the words to express it. All I know is that the world is a much darker place for us without them.

I offer this humble plea hoping that should any of you reading this ever find yourself staring down into that dark abyss, you simply remember and consider it. I beg you to think of us. Your brothers. The men who stood beside you through any and everything. I beg that you consider us before you take that final step. Whatever you suffer from, whether the world around you has become muted and soulless, or terrifyingly sharp and painful, I want you to know that you are not alone. To do that irrevocable thing is to steal all that is good in you away from the people that love you. And there is still good in you. I promise. There is also still good in the world. It can be a sonofabitch to find, I know, but it exists. You owe it to us to keep on pushing, searching, clawing your way forward until you can't push any further, and then keep going.

And if you find yourself helpless, alone, or entirely destroyed, I demand that you reach out to us. Asking for help is never a sign of weakness. Contact those grimy bastards that you stood beside in formation and huddled together with for warmth in a foxhole. Let them know something is wrong, take a drive to see them, get yourself in touch with them in some way beyond a casual text or DM, because they feel it too, and to lose you would break their hearts.

We need each other. We really do. To take yourself away from us is unforgivable.

Please remember this.

Acknowledgements

First off, I need to thank my incredible wife, best friend, and editor, Patience. She is the sole reason any of my work has ever seen the light of day, and if there is any credit to be taken for any of it, she deserves it more than me.

A massive thanks goes to Suzanne Piecuch for her incredible proofreading skills. Also, I need to thank those close friends who provided valuable insight as beta readers: William Bolyard, Nate Gladdin, Josh Ben, and Pete Difilippo.

Lastly, I want to thank you, the reader. Small time authors like myself face an increasingly difficult series of hurdles these days. Thank you not only for picking up this book, but also for seeing it through to the end. I hope that you enjoyed it.

OTHER WORKS BY

THE HOMESTEAD

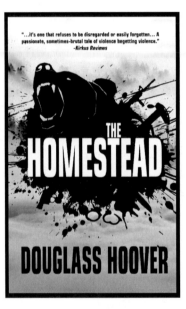

"...it's one that refuses to be disregarded or easily forgotten... A passionate, sometimes-brutal tale of violence begetting violence."
-*Kirkus Reviews*

THE HOMESTEAD

DOUGLASS HOOVER

Centered deep in the Alaskan bush, the Homestead offers a primal refuge for young men and women disenchanted by the modern era. Only accessible via helicopter or a series of rugged, treacherous trails, this Thoreauvian utopia stands as a testament to humanity's ability to thrive in its natural state.

But when a bear attack kicks off an increasingly violent chain of events, the secrets of the Homestead's founder, Augustin Stark, risk being brought into the light. As he grapples to keep the family he's created together, a malevolent outside force joins the fray. One that threatens to destroy not only the community, but the people themselves.

Praise for The Homestead

"This is a thriller with a capital T. Intrigue, action, adventure and mystery all combine to make this an unforgettable novel in every respect. Superbly written with a breath-taking pace, the story sprints into action from the very beginning… An excellent and exciting read."
—Readers' Favorite

"It's one that refuses to be disregarded or easily forgotten, particularly given its jaw-dropping ending. A passionate, sometimes-brutal tale of violence begetting violence."
—Kirkus Reviews

"Hoover pulls no punches—there is blood, language, and violence comparable to reality, and that is a big part of what makes this book so damned good… If you appreciate verisimilitude in what you read or watch on film… this is a book for you. I loved it."
—Lex Allen, Author

"High-quality, highly violent fiction… The Homestead is a book about survival, about love for your brothers, about sacrificing for the people you care about. But, it is also a cautionary tale of the vainglorious nature of violence… I rate this stirring piece of soul-searching a solid four spades and recommend that any of you looking to get lost while also finding something out about yourself scoop this thing up and give it a go."
—OAF Nation

DOUGLASS HOOVER

THE ACCURSED HUNTSMAN

Haunted by the hunting accident that took both his leg and the life of his best friend, wilderness guide Jack Steward exists on the wooded fringes of society. When an infamously foolhardy millionaire offers Jack the means to reconcile his past wrongs in exchange for participating in a remote archaeological dig along the coast of Nova Scotia, Jack straps on his worn prosthetic and ventures forth into a world of mystery, deceit, and horror. Little does Jack know that the mismatched gang of killers, junkies, has-beens, and frauds he is about to join will uncover an artifact that will shake the very foundation of history, and maybe even grant him the ability to defeat the demons of his past. However, the expedition also unearths a horrific truth – the artifact wasn't the only thing hiding deep under the Nova Scotian cliffs...

Praise for The Accursed Huntsman

"You can feel the skies darkening as you read, swelling with moisture and violence, ready to unleash on those foolish enough to be caught in the open. I rate this book a sturdy four spades and I highly recommend that you pick this up and let it consume you this fall."

–*Caleb Taylor, OAF Nation*

"Reminiscent of campfire stories, urban myths, and a Stephen King horror story, this chilling tale is the stuff from which nightmares stem. The dynamic plot and spine-chilling storyline kept me on the edge of my seat until the story reached its harrowing conclusion."

–*Readers' Favorite*

"A rip-roaring adventure through the bloodstained underbrush of the human psyche. I simply couldn't put it down."

–*Joseph Donnelly*

About the Author

Douglass Hoover is the author of *The North Woods*, *The Accursed Huntsman*, and *The Homestead*. He is a Marine Corps infantry combat veteran and holds an MFA from Emerson College. His days are spent writing, hunting, and blacksmithing on his small farm in rural Maine with his wife, Patience, and their three mutts, Bug, Furiosa, and Skootcha Nunchuck Monsterface.

Follow their adventures on Instagram
@StripedDogForge,
@DouglassHooverAuthor, or at
www.strippeddogforge.com

Made in United States
North Haven, CT
13 July 2024

54745060R10162